Lora Leigh's Boun...

"SCORCHING HOT."
—*RT Book Reviews*

"TITILLATING."
—*Publishers Weekly*

"SIZZLING HOT."
—*Fresh Fiction*

"INTENSE AND BLAZING HOT."
—*RRTErotic*

**"WONDERFULLY DELICIOUS...TRULY
DECADENT."**
—*Romance Junkies*

**"FILLED WITH ACTION, ADVENTURE,
AND...SIZZLING HOT SENSUALITY."**
—*Fallen Angels Reviews*

LORA LEIGH

dangerous
pleasure

CLOSE COVER BEFORE STRIKING

St. Martin's Paperbacks

This is a work of fiction. All of the characters, organizations, and events portrayed in this novel are either products of the author's imagination or are used fictitiously.

DANGEROUS PLEASURE

Copyright © 2011 by Lora Leigh.

All rights reserved.

For information address St. Martin's Press, 175 Fifth Avenue, New York, NY 10010.

ISBN: 978-1-250-13621-3

Printed in the United States of America

Our books may be purchased in bulk for promotional, educational, or business use. Please contact your local bookseller or the Macmillan Corporate and Premium Sales Department at 1-800-221-7945, ext. 5442, or by e-mail at MacmillanSpecialMarkets@macmillan.com.

St. Martin's Press tradepaper edition / July 2011
St. Martin's Paperbacks edition / September 2017

St. Martin's Paperbacks are published by St. Martin's Press, 175 Fifth Avenue, New York, NY 10010.

10 9 8 7 6 5 4 3 2 1

author's note

Many liberties have been taken in the creation of this book where Saudi Arabia, and Abram's life there, is concerned.

I hope you can forgive those differences and enjoy the story despite them.

We often wish for so much more.
We look around the lives we live and we question,
What might have been . . .

prologue

She should be embarrassed. At the very least, she should be completely outraged, so totally ashamed of herself that she couldn't look away, and fleeing in fear of her endangered virginity.

She shouldn't be standing there, eyes wide, her senses so dazed she couldn't force herself to move, as she watched her half-brother's half-brother in the act of what appeared to be a very complicated sex position.

A ménage.

She knew what it was called. She knew what it involved. But, Paige had to admit, she hadn't expected to see the object of her own fantasies involved with one.

She recognized the third, a cousin to the Mustafa family, Tariq. But her entire attention was focused on Abram Mustafa as he lay back on the bed, the woman he was fucking stretched out on top of him, her thighs straddling his hips, her head thrown back to rest against the shoulder of the other male behind her.

The dual penetration was obviously incredibly pleasurable for her. She was moaning, crying out.

Paige dared to allow her gaze to slip down once again, where she could glimpse the glistening, thick erections of the two men penetrating their lover. She swallowed tightly, her heart racing, her senses overloading with the sight, the sounds, the sheer implications of what she was seeing.

The total eroticism of the act drove the breath from her body, and she was still attempting to catch it, even as she fought to find the strength to look away.

She couldn't.

And she couldn't decide which she wanted to see more, Abram's face, twisted into a grimace of sublime pleasure, or the sight of his cock, glistening and slick with his lover's arousal as he pushed the heavy length home with hard, fierce thrusts.

Paige's pussy clenched, her thighs tightened. She wanted to moan herself at the sensations suddenly building in her body. She could feel her own juices building between her thighs, easing from her spasming vagina. Her breasts were swollen, her nipples hard and aching, her flesh sensitized as her buttocks tightened at the sight of the engorged cock working itself into the woman's rear.

She'd never thought of allowing a man to take her there. She'd heard about threesomes. There were rumors of a certain sect of men in Alexandria and its neighbor, Squire Point, who shared their lovers, their wives—and she'd even heard rumors that her half-brother, Khalid, who she thought of as her brother, was involved with this sect. But, she had never really believed it, until now.

No, Abram wasn't her brother, and the man sharing the lover he was possessing wasn't her brother. But, she had also heard that Khalid and Abram had often shared their women after the death of Abram's first wife, Lessa.

Had Abram and Khalid shared Lessa? No one seemed to know for certain. Now, Paige believed that they had.

Abram shared his lovers.

And he did it so well.

As she watched, his fingers curved around the woman's breast, lifting it as his head ducked to the hardened, straining tip of her nipple.

He brushed aside a heavy swath of long, rich blond hair with his nose before his tongue reached out, curled around the hard tip, then covered it with his mouth.

"Oh, God. Abram. Yes, fuck me. Fuck me harder." The woman reached back, one hand clamping to the hip of the male behind her as she cried out for more.

Abram's cheeks hollowed as he sucked at her nipple, his hands gripped her hips, his hips moved harder, faster, thrusting inside her with hard, even strokes as he began to do just as the girl asked. To fuck her harder, to fuck her deeper.

And she could have imagined much more to say, to cry out, if she were the one sandwiched between the two men.

If she were with Abram. If she was the one causing that look of intense and utter pleasure.

Paige would do anything. She would give whatever he asked to see that look on his face for her.

Biting her lip, she had to fight to hold back a moan as she heard the broken male groan that left his lips as he pulled back from the woman's breast.

Pulling her head to him, he whispered something in her ear, something that had her crying out his name, her body tightening, a wild cry leaving her lips as she seemed to tense to a point that Paige wondered if she would break.

Her head jerked back as the two men thrust inside her harder, faster. She knew the second they began finding their release.

Or at least, the second Abram found his.

His head tipped back against the pillow, lips tightening, his face contorting into lines of pleasure and pain as he arched tighter into her.

Paige almost orgasmed herself. In the years she had been discovering her own body, she'd never known anything as erotic, as sensual as seeing Abram, imagining he was touching her, filling her with his pleasure.

Her thighs clenched, her fingers balled into fists, and she bit off the need to cry out in feminine fury that she wasn't the one taking the pleasure Abram was giving.

And if she didn't get the hell out of there, there would be no way to hide her presence.

She was stepping back, her knees trembling, when his head suddenly turned, his black eyes opening.

As though he knew, or somehow sensed her presence, his gaze zeroed in on her. As she slipped out of the bedroom she saw them narrow as his expression turned sensual once again.

A purely primal, feminine part of her psyche raised its head, previously hidden, unaware, that part of her was suddenly certain that look had been for her, and for her alone.

Rushing into her bedroom Paige closed the door, her

hand pressing into the panel as she drew in several hard, deep breaths.

"Abram." She closed her eyes, his name slipping past her lips in what she recognized was a moment of pure sensual agony.

She was going to have to change her panties. She could feel her juices soaking the thin silk she wore beneath her jeans. Her clit was swollen, demanding attention and the clench of her thighs did nothing to help the pulsing ache centered there.

Paige was tempted to use the toy she had been given by one of her best friends.

It would ease, perhaps, the sensual pain flooding her, but she had been saving that last veil of innocence.

For Abram.

Her hands slipped beneath her white silk oversized blouse to find the hard tips of her nipples beneath the thin lace of her bra.

The touch of her own fingers had a gasp passing her lips. The pleasure was incredible, but still she knew, not as intense as the pleasure Abram would give her.

She cupped the mound and let her thumb stroke against the sensitive tip.

She was aching. So desperate for his touch.

She closed her eyes as a moan whispered past her lips.

Within seconds she had her jeans off and her panties sliding over her legs. She lay back on the bed she kept at Abram's apartment. Her fingernails raked through the silken curls between her thighs as she spread her legs further and fought to pretend it was Abram. To pretend that it had been her laying in that bed with him and Tariq, that it was her body accepting such pleasure.

He wouldn't touch her gently. She had a feeling he wouldn't touch her lightly. Each touch would be firm, determined, dominant. It would border on erotic pain, and agonizing pleasure.

He would control her body.

Her fingers returned to her breast, nails rasping her nipples before gripping it and pumping it erotically. Her head thrashed against the bed.

It wasn't enough.

She needed more.

Parting the folds of her pussy she ran her fingers over her heavily juiced slit, moved upwards, circled her clit and ran a trail of pleasure around the bundle of nerves.

And still, it wasn't enough.

Desperate, muffled breathy cries were stopped in her throat, the sounds almost silent as she caressed her flesh, sliding downward, circling the entrance and dipping shallowly inside.

And once again, it wasn't enough.

The need was growing worse with each visit Abram made to Virginia, and now, she would never be able to forget the sight of him sharing his lover, or the pleasure that had contorted her face, as well as his.

She wanted it.

She wanted the extreme eroticism she had witnessed between Abram, his lover, and his cousin. She wanted Abram until she felt as though she were burning up inside. Perspiration dotted her body, it felt as though flames were licking over her flesh. Her pussy clenched, her juices spilling to her fingers as she pressed two together, uncaring of the veil of her virginity as she tucked them against the snug entrance.

Wood cracked against wood hard enough to cause her to pull her fingers free of her body and to jerk her upright in shock.

Eyes wide she stared across the room at the vision of pure male outrage, black eyes burning, his hair sensually tousled and laying around his face and shoulders like coarse midnight.

He moved across the room, stalking, predatory, the loose white pants he wore laying low on his hips, his cock jutting beneath it, thick and long, as he moved to the bed.

Paige stared back at him, her breathing harsh, the need so spike sharp now that fingers of hunger struck at her pussy with daggerlike intensity.

Abram's jaw clenched as he stopped at the side of the bed.

His fingers tightened, released, tightened again.

"Lie back." His voice was like an animal's growl.

"Go to hell," she tried to snap, but her voice weakened, the anger, pain, and desperation mixing to create a sound between a plea and a hoarse, broken demand.

"I return there soon enough," he shot back, his voice sharp. "For this moment though, I will touch paradise no matter the curse to my soul for the trespass."

And before she could move, protest, or whimper an objection he gripped her legs, pulled her down along the bed and within a breath, he was stretching his long, powerful frame between her legs

There was no time to argue, to protest, or to push him away. There was no will to reject whatever touch, whatever pleasure he would give her.

His arms looped around her legs, pulling her thighs

apart as his head lowered and his lips buried in her pussy.

"Abram." Shocked, uncertain, the hard, burning waves of arousal began to pour over her and pleasure struck with fiery bursts through her system.

"Fuck, yes," he whispered against the sensitive folds.

"Oh God, yes. Lick me!" The words were torn from her lips. "Abram. Abram please, make me come. Just make me come."

His lips surrounded her clit, sucking it into the liquid heat of his mouth with a firm, almost hard pressure that had her entire sensory system overloading.

Her knees bent, lifting, her heels digging into the mattress as waves of burning sensation began to tear through her. It was a pleasure that bordered pain, pouring through her body with a strength and a speed that she had no hope of defending her heart against.

Abram didn't ease her into it. He wasn't gentle and seductive. He wasn't teasing and tender. It was almost angry, an uncontrolled hunger that imprinted itself on the act with an eroticism that had her fighting for breath. His tongue flicking at the tiny bud, his mouth sucking it, wet heat and shocking, sharp pleasure tearing through the ultrasensitive bud until the rapture of it ripped through her with an explosion of such ecstatic pleasure Paige was certain somehow, she was lost. A part of her was no longer hers alone. A part of her now belonged to Abram, and that wouldn't be a good thing, because that part of her would now never be content with another man's touch.

As she drifted back to earth her lashes opened slowly, warily as she felt him drag himself from the bed.

He was still hard, his cock straining against the cloth of his pants, the tip damp, the flared crest clearly outlined.

His expression was enflamed, with anger or lust, she wasn't entirely certain.

"Stay away from me." He came down, his hands going on each side of her shoulders as his face came within inches of her, the pure fury lighting his gaze, unmistakable now.

Paige flinched, her breath catching.

"Abram," she whispered his name. "I didn't mean . . ."

"Stay the fuck away from me," he snarled. "I don't care that you didn't mean to. I don't care that you burn with the same fucking hunger that's ripping my guts to shreds, stay the fuck away from me, Paige. If you care for your brother, if you have so much as a moment's drop of affection for me, then I beg of you, never tempt me to this length again."

There was such fury, such rage in his face that Paige could only stare back at him in bemusement.

There was no fear. She knew in the deepest recesses of her soul that Abram would never hurt her. He would never lift a hand to threaten her. But there was something in his gaze that warned her to beware, that there were far worse things to be frightened of than his anger.

But she also heard, felt, and saw the hunger in his gaze that assured her that he hadn't been lying about burning just as she did. He wanted her. He was aching for her.

"Do the other women make the need any less sharp?" she whispered painfully. "Tell me, Abram. Does taking another lover ease that hunger?"

Would it ease hers? Would it stop the fantasies and make the restless need go away. Would finding her own lover help to stop each impulse of hunger that had her teasing him at every opportunity.

"Don't." There was no lessening of the anger, or the iron-hard determination in his expression. But what did change was the addition of painful knowledge that crossed his expression.

He knew exactly what she was asking. Just as he knew exactly why she had asked it.

"Answer me." She forced him to move back or risk touching her as she came up, kneeling in the bed to stare back at him with her own anger now. "Does fucking those other women make it easier to bear the pain? Will acquiring a lover rather than saving my virginity for someone who doesn't want it, make it easier to bear?"

For a second, for just a second, shock gleamed in his eyes.

"A virgin?" he seemed to choke on the words before he gave his head a hard shake and moved away from her. "Save your virginity for someone who deserves it." Self-disgust competed with the anger in his expression as he straightened and stared down at her, his jaw flexing, the muscle working furiously as he obviously fought whatever he was forcing himself not to say.

"You're absolutely right," she said, her throat tight with the knowledge that it was something he may want, but he had no intentions of accepting.

She could want him until hell froze over. She could ache, she could need. And at this moment she might even hate him. Because it didn't matter how much she needed him, or how much he needed her, and she could see that need in his eyes, but he would walk away no matter what she said. No matter what she felt.

"I'm right about what?" he seemed to bite the words out.

"You're right, you don't deserve it," she said bitterly as she forced herself from the bed, found her panties and clothes and dressed hurriedly. "You don't have to tell Khalid I was here. He'll only worry."

"Did you come to see Khalid?" he questioned, his arms going over his chest as a glare settled on his face.

"Actually, I did." Buttoning the snug jeans she pushed her feet into her sandals before lifting her head and staring back at him, refusing to feel any shame or embarrassment. "I came, because he hadn't told me you were here, and I just wanted to see you." The pain in her chest was overwhelming as emotion clogged her throat. "How insane was that?"

"Insane," he snapped, his expression like stone.

She nodded to the response. "Exactly. So I'll just return to the house and pack. We're returning to Greece tonight." Regret welled inside her when his expression didn't even shift. No regret, nothing. "I guess I won't be staying in Virginia this year after all." She let her gaze flick over him scathingly. "There's no reason whatsoever to stay."

She had to get out of there before she lost control of the tears that tightened her throat and threatened to fill her eyes. Turning on her heel she quickly unlocked the door before rushing out of the room and heading for the door and the hall that led to the elevator, and below, back to the safety her parents' home represented.

Her body still hummed with pleasure.

Her clit was still so sensitive and swollen that each step was an agony of sensation as it rubbed against the silk of her panties.

One more year. She would stay away from Virginia, her brother, and her dream of working in America for one more year. And pray it was enough time to rid herself of the emotional and the physical complications Abram Mustafa caused within her.

Because if she didn't, then he just may well end up breaking her heart.

Abram watched her leave.

Staring from the window of the bedroom Khalid had given Paige for her visits, he watched as she appeared on the sidewalk, her white silk oversized blouse flattening against her slender body as the breeze whipped around it.

Flame-red hair whipped around her, like strands of burning silk, it blazed around her face, adding a splash of color to the otherwise dull reality that existed around him.

And with each step she took he could feel the bitterness growing inside him as he braced his palms flat on the high windowsill and buried the insane impulse to follow after her. If he did, he would drag her back to this bed and fuck her until nothing else existed for either one of them.

But reality would return. He couldn't delay it long enough to sate himself with his need for her, or to ensure her safety.

How much more was he to lose? How much more could one man bear to see broken in his life before he finally ceased to exist?

Paige was his last weakness, he thought, answering the question for himself. She was as bright as the sun that rose in the desert, warming those who existed around her, becoming the very essence of their lives if they gave her the chance. To allow his life to break her would be a far greater sin than any he may have committed so far.

To allow his sexuality to break her—her innocence and her dreams—would be the killing stroke. Because the need that would rise inside him to see her beneath a third, one Abram knew he could depend upon to protect her, to pleasure her, to ease her should he ever cease to be, would destroy the romantic dreams he knew Paige had. How could a woman accept that he never wanted to see another man fuck her with the same hunger that he felt to have her beneath him himself? How could a virgin accept the desires he fantasized of fulfilling with her?

Of seeing her beneath Tariq, watching as his dick buried in the sweet, fist-tight grip of her pussy. Of being inside her himself, filling her little cunt, experiencing the ripples of response in the too-tight muscles as Tariq filled her ass with his cock.

His entire body tightened with the thought of it. Of feeling her pussy pulse and flex and milk his dick until he couldn't hold back his release any longer. Until he came with the vicious, pounding spurts of seed that incited a pleasure so deep, so all-consuming it could never be forgotten. And he wanted nothing with any woman, especially with Paige, that could be forgotten.

She may have been aroused, she may be curious, but he couldn't see her craving that pleasure as he would crave giving her the pleasure, had he not gone as far as he had.

There was also the knowledge that the dark sexuality that was so much a part of him would accept nothing less. It was his own personal torment, that need that drove at him like an addiction he couldn't kick.

How could he tell her, explain to her, that to see her pleasure, to watch her as she slipped into that realm of sensuality that he had only seen a woman find when she was overwhelmed by two lovers, was more than he could deny himself. It was more than he could deny his lover.

That as long as there was a third, one as strong, as determined to protect her as he was, then what had happened to Lessa wouldn't have as great a chance of happening to her.

It was the mistake he and Khalid had made with Lessa. Abram had fought that side of him, fearing Lessa gave into his brother's touch because she knew it was what Abram wished. He had refused Khalid the privileges he would have given a third as well as the responsibilities of one. He hadn't told Khalid that he would be away from the province the day his brother had been caught unaware, beaten and left for dead, before Ayid and Aman had gone after Lessa.

But, as Khalid had warned him the day he realized Abram had seen Paige as a woman, she deserved more. She deserved a man who knew possessive love, who understood it. But even more importantly, a man who did not bring with him the shadow of death.

"She's gone?"

Tariq stepped into the room behind him, his voice somber as he posed the question.

He, too, had seen her standing at the door, her eyes wide, face flushed, that look of drowning sensuality filling her expression the moment they had spilled their release into another woman's body.

In that expression he had seen the knowledge that it didn't matter the woman they were with, it didn't matter how he fought it, how he strove to deny it, each time he stepped foot in the U.S., there was only one face he searched for now. There was only one gaze he avoided with everything inside him.

"She's gone," he stated, wondering if he had effectively hidden the regret that surged through him.

"She was angry?" Tariq probed.

Abram gave a quick shake of his head. "Surprisingly, no."

No, she hadn't been angry. It had been disillusionment. It had been bitterness. It had been the knowledge that girlish dreams never came true no matter how desperately she fought to bring them to fruition.

They died. Painfully. Hurtfully. They were tromped beneath uncaring feet and left to wither by a world that didn't know true warmth.

And he had done no more than contribute to the cold that filled her gaze now, the disillusionment.

She was a woman searching for the dreams that filled her soul, and he couldn't be the man to fulfill those dreams, no matter his own wishes.

"Has our companion left?" he turned to Tariq, seeing the intent look on his cousin's expression.

Tariq had been watching him too closely of late whenever they were in Virginia, especially whenever Paige was present. As though he were searching for something, some affirmation of a suspicion.

Abram refused to give into the question in his third's gaze. They both desired her, and yet, he refused to act on that desire, or in Abram's case, that hunger.

"She's showering." Tariq shrugged his shoulders beneath the expensive cotton shirt he wore. "She seems discontent with your lack of attention now that your pleasure has been attained."

Now that his pleasure had been attained? His cock was still as hard as it had been the moment he stepped off the fucking plane. And it was still as hard as the moment he had stepped into Paige's bedroom to see her fingers preparing to thrust inside the heated depths of her pussy.

He had never imagined she was a virgin. Never imagined it, and now, had no idea how he could force himself to forget it.

"See her home, Tariq," Abram ordered. "I'll await your return before leaving to meet with Director Jennings and Senator Mathews. I'd like to give them the information we've attained on Ayid and Aman quickly, before Azir realizes we have left Saudi entirely."

His brothers, Ayid and Aman. Younger half-brothers. Twins who shared a rabid rage and intellectual cruelty that never ceased to amaze him. And Azir, his father. How had he ever believed his father could have the smallest iota of kindness inside his blackened soul? Now, six months after the death of the wife Azir had forced him to marry, and the child she had carried,

Abram found it almost impossible to keep from killing the old bastard. Especially after he learned exactly how involved his father had been in ensuring there were no heirs other than Abram before he turned thirty-six.

If there were other heirs, then Abram's death would not result in allowing Azir to turn the province over to the sons he preferred. The sons who shared his warped vision of the future of the world.

That vision had seen to the death of Abram's first wife, when he had been no more than twenty. It had seen to the death of his second wife, and his unborn child, two years later. And it would destroy any other woman Abram ever allowed himself to care for.

Just as Ayid and Aman would see to the death of any woman Khalid could love, other than his sister, Paige.

They were cursed. The eldest sons of Azir bore the hatred and the fruits of malice that sprang from not just Azir, but also his youngest sons.

As Paige stepped into the back of the car in which she'd ridden into the city, the driver closing the door solicitously behind her, Abram turned and met Tariq's gaze.

"She's gone." He hadn't meant the words to pass his lips, or the thought to torment him as it did.

Watching her leave, watching that innocence, that hunger and zest for life, and for him, disappear, had driven home the fact that she could be taken forever if he weren't very, very careful.

Tariq's lips quirked in amusement though, the bitterness and realization that tormented Abram wasn't a part of the other man's present thoughts.

"She won't be for long," Tariq assured him. "If that mark on your shoulder is any indication, you've given her a taste of what you both hunger for. I have a feeling, Abram, Miss Galbraithe will return sooner than you think."

The mark?

His gaze jerked to his shoulder before he moved to the mirror atop the dresser next to him.

There, on his shoulder, just as Tariq had stated, a love bite that marred his flesh deeper than he would have imagined she could have given without his knowledge.

It marked him far deeper than flesh alone.

He forced himself to turn away.

He forced himself to leave her bedroom.

He forced himself to forget those few, precious moments when his lips had caressed the softest flesh he had ever known, when his tongue had tasted pure, fiery ecstasy.

A taste that would linger in his senses forever.

And a regret he knew he would never outrun.

He hadn't expected this, he thought, it had caught him unaware the day he had arrived to help her and her family celebrate her eighteenth birthday. When he had seen her in that simple sundress on the sunny Greek island where she and her family lived part of the year. With the tops of her breasts rising above the bodice of the dress, the tiny straps stretching over slender, graceful shoulders, and the red gold of her hair hanging to the middle of her back.

"Abram," she had whispered his name with a breathy little sigh. *"I've missed you."*

Stars had gleamed in the emerald green of her eyes. Her face had flushed beneath the soft hint of the Mediterranean-bronzed flesh. Her skin wasn't as dark as her father's, but neither was it as light as her mother's. When combined with the silken flames of her hair, the combination was enough to daze a lesser man.

It was that day he had seen the woman she was. It was that day his cock had swelled, becoming so engorged, so torturously hot and tight he swore he'd been on the edge of dizziness.

He almost grinned at that thought.

Almost. Because, he knew the fate that would await her.

He knew the hell he would revisit and this time never escape.

He couldn't have her, he couldn't allow his need to corrupt her, or his legacy to endanger her.

And he couldn't keep his hunger for her from raging . . .

1

EIGHT YEARS LATER

He was home. Finally.

Paige Galbraithe moved from the chaise positioned next to the balcony doors of her bedroom and stared at the lights that swept over the lawn.

The limousine moved with an almost stealthy slowness along the curved, oak-bordered drive. The lights swept over the landscaping like a cat burglar's penlight as the car neared the garage. The bright gleam disappeared into the three-story mansion Khalid owned in the heart of the exclusive section of Alexandria, Virginia, designed as Squire Point.

After ten days captivity in her brother's home, the rat had finally shown up. It was about time. She was rather sick of cooling her heels in the luxurious comfort of her brother's home rather than in her own apartment.

Collecting the silk robe she had left lying on the back of the chaise, Paige pulled it on quickly, covering the ankle-length, matching deep-violet gown she wore. Anger and determination made her movements jerky.

Ten days. She had waited ten days to confront him.

He wouldn't answer his cell phone—his fiancée Marty was running interference—but still, her brother wasn't talking to her. Marty assured her daily that she would get to tear a strip off his hide in person, and each day, he was a no-show.

"Relax for a while, Paige . . ."

"Khalid will call soon . . ."

"You'll have explanations when Khalid arrives . . ."

Even her parents refused to tell her what she needed to know, what she demanded each time they called to see how she was doing.

She was fed up with it. She was twenty-five years old; she wasn't a teenager. She was Khalid's sister, not some damned prisoner he could control. She was easy to work with, and she considered herself a very understanding person. But her patience had begun wearing thin a week ago.

Belting the robe furiously as she turned on her heel, Paige stalked across the bedroom and eased open the door before stepping into the hall. Moving to the stairs she stopped and waited, listening carefully.

She wasn't about to let him think that she was still awake and waiting on him. He'd been slipping into the house after he was certain she was asleep, doing whatever he did, then slipping back out before she awoke.

The damned coward.

Abdul, or Abbie as she called him, his Saudi man-servant, was always abjectly apologetic that he hadn't awakened her before Khalid left, as she had asked him to do. He had a million excuses, but she knew the truth. Khalid was his boss, and Khalid wasn't about to face her until she simply left him no choice.

They were working together—Abbie, Marty, Khalid's security team, and even Khalid himself—to keep her in place and completely in the dark as to why she was suddenly being held in what her brother called "protective custody." Even the U.S. marshal service wasn't this damned diligent.

Even her parents were refusing to help her. Her mother's fear for her only daughter, her "baby" as she called her, had Marilyn Galbraithe going along with whatever her son had cooked up this time.

And that son hadn't even given his sister the courtesy of facing her and giving her a clue as to how long this would last, if there was an end in sight, or the details involving the danger she was facing.

She had a good idea. After all, she was well aware of the fact that his brother, Ayid, had finally played his final hand and attempted to murder Khalid and his fiancée, Marty, less than a month before. Just as Ayid's twin, Aman, had gone after Abram in D.C. as he waited in a hotel to meet with FBI Director Zack Jennings and the Homeland Security Director to declare his U.S. citizenship based on his mother's status as an American citizen.

Instead, Khalid had killed Ayid, and Abram had killed his youngest brother, Aman. Though, to keep Abram's defection to the U.S. a secret, Khalid had taken the blame for both deaths.

She suspected this was why she was placed in isolation in the monstrous mansion her brother now owned.

The mansion that same father, Azir Mustafa, had bought for him.

She wanted to hear it from him, though. She wanted to know exactly why Azir Mustafa thought threatening her was going to gain him anything. And she wanted to know why the hell Khalid thought that destroying the life she was building for herself was going to help.

She'd been all but imprisoned by her overprotective parents for far too many years. Her mother had been so terrified Paige would be kidnapped or taken, that she would disappear as had once happened to her, that she had kept Paige always in sight.

Bodyguards. Security-enhanced private schools. Private tutors. She'd been so overprotected she had nearly smothered to death.

Escaping had taken every ounce of strength she had, because she loved her parents. Because even in their attempts to ensure her safety, she had always been aware of their love for her. Just as she had been of the nightmares they suffered from a past haunted by the horror of her mother's kidnapping, forced marriage and rapes at the hands of a monster. That monster had been the father of her half-brother and the father of the man she couldn't push out of her mind or her fantasies.

"Stay away from me." His eyes blazing with black fury and none of the sexual satisfaction he should have felt after spilling himself only moments before into the lover he had shared with his cousin, Tariq. Only moments before he came to her. "For both our sakes, Paige, stay the fuck away from me!"

That had been eight years ago. Eight years since he had buried his lips and tongue between her thighs and threw her into an ecstasy she still hadn't felt again. Not before and not since. Eight years since he had fucked her with his tongue yet, he had never even kissed her.

In those years she had taken a lover, she had finished college, and she had begun a career that she enjoyed. But still, there was a regret that lay inside her like a weight. The regret that came with so many "what might have beens."

Moving from her room to the stairs, she waited. Standing back from the steps just far enough that he couldn't see her, Paige peeked into the shadows below as he moved to the second floor, turned, and a few seconds later, she heard the door to his suite close.

Her lips tightened into a hard smile.

Ten days. It was ten days too long and she was damned tired of waiting, of being patient and fighting to understand why her parents and her brother had to live in fear of the day that Azir Mustafa or one of his family members would come after her.

Moving quietly, swiftly, she made her way to the second floor and the door of the master suite.

No lights shone from beneath the door, but that didn't mean anything. She'd seen Khalid move in the dark as though he were born to it.

His brother, Abram navigated it as though he owned it though.

She shook that thought away. She was not going to think about Abram tonight. She was not going to allow the rest of her night to be as restless as her days had been with the fantasies and the memory of those stolen moments in her bedroom all those years ago.

This was the reason she refused to settle back and

relax while she was here. It was the reason why she pushed herself to the point of exhaustion each night after work. To keep low the fires of arousal from building any higher.

Thinking of Abram was always a mistake. And desiring him showed a complete lack of judgment and had nothing to do with why she was here or why she was getting ready to skin her brother alive.

The worst thing she could do at the moment was allow thoughts of Abram to interfere with her determination to get the answers she needed, and to find a way to balance her family's fears with her own determination to have a life.

She needed a life. Without it, all she could think about, dream about and remember, was Abram and the feel of his lips sucking hard and tight at her clit as his tongue—

She shook away the thought again.

Gripping the doorknob she checked it slowly, quietly. It wasn't locked. He wasn't busy with his fiancée, or having wild monkey sex with her. He was obviously there alone, because she couldn't hear him talking and Marty didn't move as quietly in the dark as Khalid did. Besides, the door to his suite was always locked when they were in it together.

Easing the door forward stealthily, she all but tiptoed as she began to enter the room. Inside was dark, shadows lengthening through the narrow slits between the curtains, providing the barest hint of moonlight. Determination clenched her teeth a second before the door was jerked out of her hand, a manacle wrapped around her wrist, and in the next second she found herself flat against the wall as the door slammed closed.

Fight or flight.

Flight wasn't possible, and for the briefest, shocked second, she had no idea the identity behind the hard, masculine body pressing her into the wall. Calloused and rough, a broad hand covered her lips, muffling her cry as her knee slammed upward, almost but not quite managing to connect and slam her attacker's balls straight to his throat.

Instead, she found her knee blocked by a hard, extremely muscular thigh as it shoved its way between hers, pressed into the juncture and lifted her to her tiptoes. In the same breath she felt her attacker's head bend, strong teeth nipping her ear and drawing a shocked gasp from her throat.

"Hello to you too, hellcat."

She froze.

It had been so long since she had heard his voice. The rich, dark, foreign flavor of it wrapping around her senses and sending a heavy, heated lethargy to settle in the depths of her sex.

Memories washed over her.

His hands, calloused and strong, so dark against her thighs as his black hair, like roughened silk falling over her flesh as his lips moved over her clit. They had surrounded it, sucked it, lit a fire to it that had exploded through her system into an ecstasy she longed to revisit every second of her life.

Abram.

Beneath his palm her lips parted to drag in a hard,

heavy breath as her body began to soften, to shape to the harder, stronger contours of his masculine body.

She shouldn't be doing this. He had avoided her for years, slipping in and out of Khalid's home and her life, and she had seen him only briefly, and always in the company of others.

Without volition her hips relaxed, the mound of her pussy pressing against the hard upper leg shoved between her thighs as she felt her breasts harden, her nipples so sensitive they actually ached.

Pleasure skated through her system as her tongue peeked out to touch her lips, to touch his palm. Slightly salty, male, the taste of him exploded against her tongue as he jerked back from her just as suddenly.

Staring up at the darkened shadow of his face, seeing the glitter of his gaze, feeling the heat of his body, Paige found herself, probably for the first time in her life, unable to speak. She couldn't find the words, she couldn't fight past the emotions or the tightening of her throat as she stared back at him.

The need for his touch was a craving she couldn't resist. She couldn't deny it. It was like a drug and she had gone far too long without a fix.

Her lips parted, but no words came out. She couldn't let them, because she was terribly afraid those words would be a plea. That she would beg for things she wasn't certain how to ask for with this man. Things she knew she was probably better off without.

Her body sure as hell knew how to ask though. She was shocked, flushed with heat and had to forcibly keep her hips from rubbing against the hard flesh pressed into the mound of her pussy.

And he knew it. His leg was tense, but each time her hips shifted against the firm muscle she swore he tightened further against her.

And he wasn't letting her go. If anything, he was holding her tighter, perhaps, if she weren't mistaken, his leg was pressing more firmly against the suddenly heated, swollen folds between her thighs. And oh yes, it felt so damned good. That heated, slow rub against her, stroking her clit, sending bursts of incredible sensation ratcheting through her.

She had known over the years that this was coming. At the first opportunity. The moment he touched her, the very second they found themselves hidden from curious gazes. She had known this would happen. That the need and the hunger would rage out of control.

"Why?" squeaky, weak, her voice was nothing as it should have been. It didn't sound determined or confident as it usually did. And it sure as hell didn't sound independent and strong.

Swallowing tightly she tried again.

"Why are you here? Where's Khalid?"

She tightened her fingers against the hold he had on her wrists, though she found herself stopping short of actually straining against his hold. After all, if she protested too loudly, or struggled too much, he might actually let her go.

"Khalid and Marty are with her parents." Deep, dark, she swore she actually trembled as he spoke. "They are completing the plans for your protection."

Her protection? Right now, all she needed protection from was the brilliant heat she was helpless against.

"He should be here." Oh man, she was dying here.

She could feel her blood racing, her flesh heating, her clit throbbing harder in demand with each second.

The longer she lay there beneath him, the more she wanted him. The more she wanted the sensations, the pleasure she had only had the briefest taste of eight years before.

"Should he be?" His fingers tightened, then relaxed against her hip a second before his palm cupped it, shifting her, moving her against his thigh. "I think at this moment, it's a very good thing that he isn't here. Wouldn't you say?"

A flash of fire streaked through her pussy, clenched the tightened muscles and almost stole her breath. Pleasure raged through her body, but it was a painful pleasure, an achy, needing-so-much-more sensation type of pleasure that it weakened her knees and had her breathing in roughly.

"He kidnapped me," she breathed out roughly. "I'm going to kick his ass."

"Go right ahead," he murmured. "When he arrives. Until then, I believe it might be time to see if your lips are as soft and as sweet as they appear to be. If they are anywhere as sweet as that hot, luscious little pussy I cannot forget the taste of."

Her entire body clenched in excitement at the declaration.

Then his head lowered.

Paige felt her lashes drift close, lips remaining parted, breath suspended as his lips brushed against the edge of her face, sending a rush of exquisite pleasure washing through her again.

"You're trying to distract me," she accused him roughly.

"I'm not going to let you do it. Khalid owes me explanations, Abram."

He owed her. She owed herself. She couldn't let him do this to her or once he was gone, there would be nothing left of her.

"He's protecting you," he stated, though his voice sounded rougher, more strained as his lips moved to her ear, his breath stroking across the shell as he spoke. "You're in danger, Paige, you should have guessed that by now."

In danger of screaming in need. Of begging for his touch. Of whimpering with the painful hunger she couldn't control.

"Guessed what?" She hoped he didn't actually expect her to be able to think at the moment, because it wasn't happening. But she couldn't imagine a single reason why she would be in danger.

Unless it was in danger of dying of arousal. As of this moment, that was definitely a consideration. In all her adult years she had never felt this way with another man, had never ached or lost her breath, or felt on fire as she did now. And never had she been so certain she may lose herself in another person.

"That you're in danger." There was a thread of amusement in his voice now, the knowledge of it sweeping through her with the same force the hunger had swept through her moments before.

Amusement was the last thing she could have felt as he held her, as the thrill of touching him, of being touched by him, held her captivated.

Clenching her teeth she tensed, trying to pull back, to put just a breath between their bodies as she attempted to find her control somewhere in the morass of aching hunger and need assailing her.

Wasn't it just her luck to be so aroused by a man while his own arousal, his own needs, were so obviously distant, just as they had been before. It was the story of her life where Abram was concerned. From the time she'd realized she wanted those devilish, sexy lips of his on her, he'd been either furious or amused by her.

"In danger of killing Khalid perhaps," she forced out. "Would you please let me go now? Get off me, Abram. I'm not in the mood for your games."

He rubbed his cheek against her hair as though considering her request for long moments. "Perhaps, I like you fine as you are," he finally stated. "I like how you feel against me, Paige Eleanora Galbraithe. Do you know how the memory of those very few stolen moments have tormented me?"

"And perhaps I think by now I know better," she whispered hoarsely. "Stop playing with me."

"Ahh, Paige, love, this is far beyond playing. This is the reason why I have fought against your touch. Because I can feel my control going straight to hell just from the simple act of holding you against me. How can I convince you how much I enjoy the feel of you against me?"

How she felt against him? Or the fact that for the barest few moments, she'd been unable to tell him what an ass he was being?

At the moment, he wasn't being his normal, mocking self, but she could sense that beast ready to spring forth. And once it did, their confrontations could turn brutal. His mocking, hers loud. They'd been known to rip at

each other for hours, like little children poking at each
other to gain dominance.

"I can tell," she said. "You're on the verge of laughing your ass off, Abram. Let me go."

His grip tightened on her wrists for a second as she
felt tension hardening his body further. Against her
lower stomach his cock felt harder, hotter, his body more
insistent as he seemed closer, blanketing her like a sensual, muscular beast.

"Not at you." His voice was suddenly lower, the feel
of his heart racing at her breast as he pulled her closer
against him with the hand at her hip. "At myself, hellcat. Because no matter how hard I try to pull away from
you, I want nothing more than to sink inside you."

The second the words passed his lips they were covering hers. His body shifted, his free hand pulling her
farther up his thigh, working it against the swollen folds
as her gown pooled around his leg. The silk of her panties saturating with her juices as she strained closer to
him. Her clit heated with a fiery intensity. Her pussy
clenched, tightened, the muscles ached with a desperation to be filled and every cell in her body sizzled with
the need to be touched.

Pleasure rose fast and hard inside her. Heart racing, blood pounding through her system as her lips
parted, her head falling back as he possessed her with
his kiss.

Every thought of protest flew out the window. Past
angers, conflicts, and confrontations were gone. With
her wrists secured to the wall, his thigh pressed between
hers, and his lips and tongue caressing and owning
every pulse of sensuality, he was drowning her. Paige

could feel herself weakening into the promise of the remembered ecstasy.

Dominance swirled from him. It was a wave of heat
wrapping around her and sinking into her flesh as his
lips rubbed and caressed hers. His tongue licked at hers,
dipping in, tasting and caressing until Paige found herself arching up to him, moaning for more.

The only place his hands touched her were at her
wrists, and again at her hip. The rest of his body stroked
her though. His hard chest against her breasts, his thigh
pressed between hers.

Each flex of his leg stroked the hard muscle against
her pussy, her clit, sending incredible pleasure racing
through each nerve ending as she arched to be closer.

She had to get closer to him.

The need for the heat, for the pleasure was rushing
through her like a tornado. She was dying for more of
him. For another taste of him. His kiss was like an aph-
rodisiac, spicy and addictive as his lips slanted over
hers and he kissed her with a pure, sensual hunger that
she couldn't have dreamed existed.

The restraint at her wrists should have made her nervous. No man had ever restrained her. She would have
never allowed it until now.

Until Abram.

Until the feel of him against her, until his hands restrained her and his kiss made her like it.

But that didn't mean she was submitting easily. Even
amidst the incredible starbursts of pleasure. On a primitive, primal level, Paige could sense the battle that could
brew between them. The one that had been shaping for
years now.

How dominant he could be.

How submissive she would never allow herself to be.

She nipped at his tongue as he licked over hers again, causing his head to jerk back, his gaze to narrow in the darkness.

"You're playing with fire." There was a growl in his voice that sent a shiver racing up her spine.

"And what are you playing with?" It was all she could do to keep the tremors from her voice, from her fingers as he held them above her head. "I didn't start this, Abram, you did."

"You started this eight years ago, Paige," he rasped. "Eight years and the taste of the sweetest pussy I've had touched my tongue to. You torment me. And now, there is no choice but to anger you in our attempt to ensure your security."

"Do you think you and Khalid can just kidnap me and get the hell away with it? That you can kiss good enough to make up for it?"

She had to force herself not to let a shiver of pleasure race through her body as his fingers moved over her hip before inching closer to her thigh. To where the silk of her gown fell away from her flesh at the point that her knee had bent, lifting to clasp his thigh, to rub herself against him.

She had to fight to maintain her senses, to control the need to sink back into his kiss, to allow him to sink into her, however she could convince him to do it.

But she knew this man. Dominant. Powerful. A force to be reckoned with in a world so different from her own that it may as well be an alien planet.

"Kidnapped you? I?" Amazement filled his voice,

and perhaps just a hint of anger. "Had I kidnapped you, hellcat, you would well know it," he finally scoffed, and the anger was readily apparent just as his accent became stronger.

Thankfully, his fingers relaxed. He stepped back slowly before reaching to the side and flipping the lights on as he released her.

For a second, she was blinded. Her eyes snapped closed and when she opened them again a second later, he was halfway across the room and heading for the bar.

For a drink. She was tempted to join him.

He moved like a predator.

Paige watched as he stalked almost lazily across the expensive, pearlescent carpeting to the bar on the other side of the room.

Without turning back, he poured a whiskey from the looks of it, and if she wasn't mistaken, it was Khalid's finest.

His head tilted back as he took a hard drink. Thick, heavy black hair fell nearly to his shoulders, the blue-black strands silky and glistening in the bright overhead light.

"Get out of here before I insult Khalid by fucking you in his bed," he snapped.

"Talk about a mood change." Her eyes rolled as he shot her a hard, half angry look from the corner of his eyes.

"Not nearly enough of a change to keep from fucking my brother's sister."

Paige blinked back at him. "Damn, that sounded almost depraved, Abram. Would you like to rephrase?"

He turned. Male grace and predatory strength. And pulsing, blazing, male lust.

She could feel her pussy creaming, saturating her panties further and sensitizing her clit to the point of painful need.

Just the sight of him was enough to make her ache, to make her crave with a strength and a power that made her knees weak.

He was tall, broad, and muscular. There wasn't an ounce of fat on his six-four frame, or beneath the exceptionally soft white shirt and well-worn jeans.

Finishing the whiskey he sat the glass on the bar behind him, his gaze never leaving hers. She could feel that look through every inch of her body. Sensitized and aching for his touch, her skin felt too tight, constricting as she tried to still the rapid rise and fall of her breasts.

"Rephrasing isn't the only thing I'd like to do, or may attempt to do." The heavy warning in his voice was followed by a heavy-lidded glance along her body.

Hell, she may as well have been naked. Unfortunately, there was a part of her that wished she was naked.

Paige didn't have to look down to see that her nipples were trying to burrow their way through the silk of her gown.

She didn't bother to tug the robe over the swollen curves or even pretend a shame she didn't feel. And it wasn't the first time she'd been forced to face Abram as an independent woman rather than the submissive child he often expected her to portray.

Unfortunately, he was rarely shocked by her anymore.

"And what makes now any different from the past years? There was a time when I would have welcomed your touch, Abram, but now I can't help but be suspicious. What the hell is going on?"

"Besides your determination to acquire that spanking I keep promising you with?" He spoke as though he were serious.

"Promises, promises. My ass stopped tingling in anticipation years ago." She waved the comment away. "That doesn't change the fact that unless you tell Khalid's goons out there to get out of my face and let me go home, I'm going to have every one of you brought up on charges. That wouldn't please your daddy, Abram. Last I heard old man Azir was already pissed because you were refusing to remarry for the sake of a child."

Her ass had stopped tingling in anticipation? Abram nearly came in his damned jeans with that comment. His cock hardened to pure iron, the head throbbed, and if there wasn't pre-cum in his jeans, then he wasn't iron hard.

Paige watched his black eyes flare with renewed lust. A perfectly arched, perfectly male black brow rose lazily. "Are the phones in the house not working?" He all but smirked as he ignored her last comment.

Her lips thinned. "I'm trying to be nice about this, Abram. Don't make me call the authorities."

He waved his hand toward the phone on a nearby desk in invitation. "I didn't kidnap you, Paige. Daniel Conover and his security team did so, at your brother's orders and with FBI Director Zachary Jennings's approval. Would you like to call the authorities now, hellcat?"

She glared back at him irritably. "Stop calling me that . . . .And it would likely do just as much good to call the cops now as it would to call Khalid," she snapped. "Get me out of here, Abram."

She was desperate. If she had to stay locked up even one day longer she was going to go crazy. There was nothing to do here. No way to focus her energy or to stop fantasizing about this man who seemed intent on dancing through her mind at all hours of the day and night.

If she didn't find a way to return home, to get back to her job—knowing now that Abram was the one slipping into the house at night—then she might end up making the biggest mistake of her life. . . . begging him to take her to his bed and to finish what he had started eight years before.

"Take me home." She crossed her arms over her breast and stared back at him firmly.

"I can't do that." He shook his head, his expression suddenly somber. "Relax, Paige. Enjoy a nice vacation for a few more weeks—"

"Weeks!" Her eyes widened as amazed disbelief flashed through her and rejection instantly snapped through her mind. "Hell no!" Her hands went to her hips as she confronted him furiously now. "I have a job, Abram. I have a life . . ."

"Not if you leave here." His tone was suddenly ominous, his expression hardening as though he knew the danger she would face, whatever it may be.

She was damned glad someone knew what was going on, because she sure didn't.

"What the hell do you mean by that?"

She could feel a premonition of danger then, even stronger than what she had felt in the past ten days.

Khalid wouldn't just kidnap her without a reason. A

part of her had known that whatever was going on was more than simply a suspicion of danger. It was more than a threat against Khalid and Abram.

Abram moved back to her slowly, his expression flashing with frustration, irritation, before slowly smoothing out to an icy calm that sent a chill of dread racing up her spine.

"Why can't I leave, Abram?" she whispered as she fought the edge of fear threatening to spread through her now. She knew her brother had been having some problems with his and Abram's two younger half-brothers, but surely those problems didn't extend to a threat to her? Besides, weren't they dead now?

"Because your name was found among papers of a certain terrorist, Paige. Until we learn why—" His voice lowered, his expression becoming heavy, sensual, and filled with hunger. "Until we know for certain, you are too precious to risk."

Something flashed in his eyes, something dark and dangerous as his hand lifted, his fingers sliding beneath the shoulder of her robe, the calloused, heated pads of his fingers caressing beneath the silken material.

"Abram." Too precious to risk? He'd said it as though he meant it, as though she were actually precious to him.

And she couldn't let herself believe that. She and Abram had had far too many confrontations over the years to ever believe she was anything more than an irritant, and for the moment, perhaps, a desire.

Focusing on the intimate touch, on the pleasure, was something she eagerly embraced now as she fought to distance herself from the information he had just given her. The knowledge that a terrorist had somehow focused on her.

The question of why raged in the back of her mind as she deliberately forced herself to focus on the desire instead.

She didn't think she wanted to know why. Not yet. Not until she could still the horrible foreboding, the fear threatening to overtake her.

Throughout the years she had teased, irritated, and deliberately provoked him. She winked at him when he was somber, blew kisses at him when he was angry, and that was just when she had been little more than a child and he an eighteen-year-old man of the world in her eyes. And now, he was the man she couldn't get out of her dreams, or out of her fantasies.

Paige stood still, silent, as Abram's fingers caressed from her shoulder to her neck, stroking her flesh as though he enjoyed the feel of it. His gaze locked with hers, his eyes somber, intent, and a flash of fiery hunger filled them as he pushed his fingers into her hair.

He cupped the back of her head, holding her in place as his head lowered slowly. Paige felt her lips part, her heart striking harder against her chest as it raced out of control.

"Let me taste you again, Paige," he whispered, his lips nearly touching hers. "I see you staring at me with such innocence, and with such hunger. All that's saved you these past years has been Khalid's diligence in keeping us apart." His lips touched hers. "Khalid isn't here now to save you, precious."

Paige felt her lips part helplessly.

"He wasn't there eight years ago," she whispered. "And you took another woman instead."

"And yet, all I remember of that day was how wet and sweet you were," he retorted sensually. "Are you still as sweet?" His lips brushed against hers. "Are you still as wet?"

She should be questioning him. She should be outraged. She should be frightened and trying to figure out a way to stay safe without remaining a prisoner in her brother's home and for the moment in Abram's arms.

Instead of questioning him, though, her lips were parting for him, a shaky moan leaving them as he pulled her to him firmly and deepened the intimate possession. A kiss that lacked the dominance of moments before, as well as the demand. This kiss seduced, it cajoled. His lips and tongue rubbed against hers, tasted hers and within seconds her hands were gripping his shoulders, nails biting into his flesh as she fought to get closer to him.

This was a side of Abram that he had never allowed her to see. This gentle, seductive side. The dangerous eroticism that existed just beneath the surface and was now flowing free as his lips, tongue, and hands began to stoke the searing flames of need through her entire body.

His hands slid to her shoulders, gently sliding the sleeves of her robe down her arms until the silk caught at her elbows.

His lips slid from hers, his tongue peeking out to taste the sensitive skin of her neck and sending shivers racing through her body. Paige gasped for breath, a low moan escaping her lips. She swore there was an electric current beneath her skin, brought alive by the touch of his lips as they stroked and kissed their way to her shoulder.

The calloused tips of his fingers moved to the thin strap of her gown, easing it over the curve of her shoulder as his lips continued to play, and to melt her resistance like butter. If there had been any resistance, which Paige was certain she couldn't have even attempted to fake.

She'd wanted him for far too long, ached for him for too many years to even consider rejecting this touch.

She had never had a man's touch burn through her as Abram's did now. She'd never known such abandoned pleasure, or ached to the very core of her body as she did now.

"Abram." The moaning whisper seemed torn from her as she felt the gown slide down her arms, then past the swollen, heavy flesh of her breasts. "You make my head spin."

The silk rasped over the tender tips, the sensation surging through her with a wicked rush of ecstatic pleasure as she allowed the words to escape her lips. She knew better. She should hold them back, hold a part of herself back. There was no strength to do so, though.

Her nipples peaked and hardened, rising and falling erratically with her heavy breaths as Abram stared down at them. Paige swore she could feel the very air stroking against her, the invisible currents touching her like a ghostly caress.

"How pretty." The dark, accented stroke of his voice against her senses had her arching to get closer to him, to feel him touching her breasts in some way, in any way, to ease the ache radiating through her flesh.

She'd fantasized about this. She had dreamed of it.

"What do you want, little hellcat?" His hand moved, his fingers moving over the curve of her breast as her lips parted to drag in air. "What touch do you wish against such pretty flesh?"

Oh God, how was she supposed to deal with this? To handle the sensations that were tearing through her, and the pleasure that made it impossible for her to consider anything but the culmination of the hunger raging through her.

Paige stared up at him, her gaze heavy-lidded as a sense of sensual bravado overcame her.

Her hand smoothed between them, up her stomach to the mound of her breast. Cupping it, she lifted it to him in invitation as his gaze flared in overwhelming hunger. His lips parted, his tongue touching the tip of the tortured flesh.

"Son of a bitch!"

Shock. Horror.

Paige's head jerked to the side as Abram's lifted quickly, turning even as he jerked the gown's straps and her robe back over her shoulders to cover her naked breasts.

Khalid.

Her brother stood just inside the doorway, his black eyes almost bulging in shock, his expression, for the briefest moment, slack with complete amazement before it morphed to complete fury.

God, he *would* show up at the most inopportune time

and catch her doing the one thing he'd forbidden her to do years ago.

Don't mess with Abram, he'd ordered her. Don't cause such trouble with the only brother he accepted, the only true friend he had ever known. Because it would make enemies of them if Abram took her to his bed.

And what had she done? What had she plotted to do for years? To find herself in Abram's arms, his lips and hands caressing her. To find herself in his bed, his moving over her, inside her.

Oh hell, Khalid was so pissed.

Slowly, Abram backed away.

Her head turned back and she stared up at him as his gaze turned back to her, his black eyes, darker, more intense than Khalid's were enigmatic, as Abram straightened her robe over her breasts then began distancing himself fully.

"Go," he said softly, his tone suddenly remarkably gentle. "You don't need to be here for this."

"Paige, what the hell is going on?" Khalid's tone was coldly furious and striking across Abram's whispered, though gentle command.

Paige rolled her eyes, stepped back, and finished fixing her gown and robe herself as she turned back to her brother. She couldn't let herself look at Abram, couldn't afford to show any weakness now.

Brothers were like wild animals. Show that first hint of weakness and they could be merciless. Rather like an animal at that first scent of blood.

"Get over yourself," she told him as though unconcerned as she looked behind him and watched as Marty

fought to hold back her grin. Khalid's fiancée was nothing if not laid back and more or less amused by all of
them. "What happened Marty? Did aliens kidnap my
nice brother again and leave the asshole in its place?"

The "nice brother" referred to his general good mood
in the past weeks since he and Marty had become engaged. She'd rather hoped it would last a while.

"The 'nice brother,' as you call me, was doing exceptionally well until I walked in here," he snapped, his
arms going across his chest in the classic, arrogant pose.

Just how many times had she seen that pose in the
past ten years? Possibly every time Khalid caught her
so much as looking at Abram.

Paige glanced between the two men.

It was incredibly easy to tell they were related, to
tell they were brothers actually. If she didn't know
better, she would have sworn they were twins rather
than half-brothers. But she did know better. Abram was
five minutes older than Khalid, and his mother had
delicate blond hair rather than the vibrant red hair of
Khalid and Paige's mother. Khalid and Abram's father,
Azir Mustafa preferred American wives. Kidnapped,
terrified American wives.

Abram wasn't her brother though. He wasn't even her
half-brother. But Khalid refused to see the distinction.

"Neither of you have answered me." Khalid stared
between them, his nostrils flaring in anger.

"I would have thought it was pretty self-evident,"
Paige replied archly. "You're not exactly a virgin,
Khalid, so unless that question was simply an exercise
in arrogance, then you're well aware of exactly what was
going on."

"It was a mistake," Abram said then, the shock of the statement ripping through her consciousness.

Paige swung around to stare at him in disbelief.

"What did you say?"

"It was a mistake," he repeated as he turned back to Khalid. "It will not happen again."

She could only stare at him. Disbelief warred with a sense of betrayal as he turned back to her, his expression cool and composed, no hint of the hunger, or need, he'd shown only moments before.

"A mistake?" she whispered, feeling her throat tighten as she felt both Marty and Khalid watching.

How shameful. To have them witness such a rejection. How impossibly stupid of her not to have realized exactly what was coming though. He hadn't stayed away from her, ensured they were never alone together over the past years for no reason.

"A regrettable one," he answered. "I apologize to you as well, Paige . . ."

"Save it." Flipping her hand out to him dismissively she turned on her heel and headed for the door.

Once reaching the exit she turned back, her gaze meeting Khalid's as anger burned bright and hot inside her. "If I don't see you in the morning, then you better tell your hired goons to watch their damned backs because I won't stay here any longer. And you damned well better have an alternative method of protection because I'm not a child to be locked away. Nor am I too damned stupid to understand what the hell is going on when the situation is eventually explained to me."

She didn't give him time to speak. She didn't want to hear his damned explanations at the moment and she sure as hell didn't want to see the pity in his and Marty's eyes. She wanted to get the hell away from all of them.

She was a mistake. A regrettable one.

Her teeth clenched furiously as humiliation washed through her.

He could excuse himself until hell froze over but it wouldn't change the fact that he wanted her. He had wanted her with almost the same destructive hunger that burned inside her whenever he was around.

He didn't want to admit it? He wanted to ignore it?

That was just damned fine, because it wasn't over. She'd seen his gaze. She'd seen what he'd wanted to hide behind that deceptively calm, unemotional mask.

She'd seen the hunger burning so hot, so deep that it possibly went even deeper than her own did. She'd felt it. She'd tasted it in his kiss. He wanted to devour her.

She knew herself that denying it simply didn't work. When he was done with the denials, when he was finished pretending he didn't want her to keep Khalid's little protective instincts calmed, then he'd better be damned careful.

She just might show him exactly how rejection felt.

As the door closed quietly behind her, Abram almost flinched. The near silence of the action spoke volumes. Had she slammed the door, it wouldn't have been nearly as effective.

It had been the pain he'd seen in her eyes though, that sense of betrayal that had driven home to him exactly how deeply he had hurt her.

She didn't understand.

Touching her had been the worst mistake he could have made, because it showed her to be a weakness he could ill afford.

And responding to him eight years before, when his lips had buried between her thighs, had been the worst mistake she could have made.

Even now, Abram couldn't get the taste of her out of his mind. He couldn't get her pure, uninhibited response to him out of his system.

Her eyes had been filled with such hunger. The long swath of pretty fire-reddened hair cascading around her. Her pale flesh flushed with her need, and those perfect breasts. Those sweet, firm mounds had risen to him, the pale innocently pinkened nipples tight and hard, and responsive to his touch.

Taking her would be like immersing himself in fire. He could see it, feel it.

Iron hard and throbbing in fury at his refusal to take her, his cock had swelled to painful readiness, his balls drawn tight and painful. He couldn't remember ever having ached with such desperation for a woman's touch, or needing to touch one as he needed to touch Paige.

"Have you fucking lost your mind, Abram?" Khalid rasped behind him, his voice hoarse with fury.

"Evidently." Abram turned to him, careful to keep his expression composed, without emotion. "I won't be berated like a child, Khalid. You've known for years the desire that burns between us. You should have only been surprised it took this long to risk my control."

He inhaled slowly, evenly. Paige hadn't just risked his control, she had fucking destroyed it.

Yet, he couldn't blame his brother for his anger either.

Paige was Khalid's little sister; a treasured child that none in her family could see had been a woman for a good many years now.

"This is ridiculous," Khalid snapped. "You have enough women, Abram. Stay the hell away from Paige."

Abram glanced at Marty and allowed a somber smile to touch his lips. He well remembered the years Khalid had been tortured and tempted by this woman. The nights his brother had spent simply talking about the delicate little FBI agent trailing him.

"Marty and I are an entirely different matter," Khalid growled as he followed his brother's look. "Marty isn't related to me by blood."

To that Abram simply had to laugh. "And what blood do I share with Paige, Khalid?" he questioned him. "She is the daughter of your mother, while I am the son of your father. Where do you believe we share blood?"

Khalid could be amazingly stubborn, and attempted to arrange reality to suit him rather than arranging himself to suit reality. It was a fault of his, and one Abram had learned over the years to ignore. Because no matter how Khalid tried, he had yet to force the winds of fate to turn to his hand.

"Both of you need to stop arguing over this. Your main audience has left, so there's no longer anyone to impress or posture to." Marty shot them both a disgusted look. She was definitely a woman that believed in speaking her mind.

And she was right. In ways, they had been playing to a perfect audience for years. But as Abram realized now, Paige rarely stayed to listen to the arguments or paid any attention to the undercurrents of tension that existed between himself and Khalid whenever she was around.

Paige had grown tired of the game, though he and Khalid still played it. It gave Abram something to focus on rather than his desire for Paige during those odd times when he could no longer avoid her.

Abram finally sighed wearily. "I didn't come here to lose my control with Paige, or to argue with you," he told his brother. "I'm returning in a few hours for Saudi."

The shock was palpable. Marty's gaze widened and Khalid's expression suddenly turned icy. He understood the quick anger, the disbelief. They had planned his move from Saudi Arabia for years. To have Abram back out now, at the last moment so to speak, was little more than an insult.

"You only just arrived," Khalid finally stated. "You're not giving Immigration enough time to examine your mother's birth records as well as your own. Give it time."

Abram gave his head a quick shake. "There is something I must do first, Khalid."

He had known his brother would never understand this move he was being forced to make.

"And what the fuck could be more important than your life?" Khalid suddenly snarled, the fury cracking past the ice. "Azir Mustafa will never let you live now. Goddammit, Abram, we just killed two of his sons. The blackhearted little bastards he risked everything to protect over the years."

"Abram, my father is certain that your citizenship will be accepted within days," Marty stated from her fiancé's side. "There's no question of it. But if you return, there's nothing he can do."

He shook his head quickly, tightly. "I have to go back."

"Why, damned you?!" Khalid yelled back at him furiously as rage lit his black gaze once again.

"Because Paige's picture was found in the possession of a dead terrorist known to be a part of the cell Ayid and Aman commanded, just hours ago as he attempted to board a plane in Jordan. Your suspicions were right. She's in danger. And I'm going back to stop it, Khalid, one way or another. I've already lost two wives to those bastards. I won't lose my soul to their ghosts."

Paige. His soul. He'd lost his youth and his heart when his first wife, Lessa had been murdered. His second wife had been forced on him, and losing her and their child had taken the last bit of hope inside him. Their deaths had nearly finished him off. The thought of that innocent life, not yet born, taken so cruelly, had nearly cost him his sanity.

That child had been his daughter. The daughter he had planned to secretly smuggle out of Saudi Arabia after her birth and send to his brother's parents. Pavlos and Marilyn Galbraithe would have raised and protected his child as they had their own precious daughter.

But Paige, God help him, there was no way he would survive her death. It would destroy him. For some reason she had begun to represent something wild and innocent inside him eight years ago. When the future had appeared to be nothing but bleak, furious pain, it was always the image of her that brought him comfort. Her laughter, the sweet warmth that burned in her emerald eyes.

And from the looks of Khalid's expression, the complete disbelief and horror burning in his gaze assured Abram that it would destroy him as well. They had both schemed, plotted, and run interference with Azir Mustafa since the day the red-haired little beauty had been born. The birth of the child to his escaped forced bride had sent Azir into a rage that had torn through the Mustafa stronghold like a demon.

That day, two servants had died, and a third had fled into the desert in fear. The insanity that had begun infecting Azir had only grown since that day, as though it were a trigger of some sort that he had been unable to fight.

"I was going to send her home in the morning," Khalid finally stated, his voice a low, rough rasp. "God help me, Abram. I was going to allow her to leave when Abdul's cousin was unable to learn anything else."

Abdul, Khalid's manservant, had several cousins that worked within the castle and managed to send along information whenever they heard it. The threats against Paige, in retaliation for Khalid's killing of Ayid and Aman Mustafa, had begun the moment Azir learned of their deaths.

He knew Khalid's weakness, just as he knew those of his other sons. Somehow, Azir had learned years before that Abram had formed a soft spot for Khalid's little sister. A place inside his heart that he'd believed was hidden from even the most astute gaze.

"You can't allow her to go." He'd kidnap her and have her locked up somewhere safe himself if Khalid dared to allow her to leave. "I've fought to stay away from her, Khalid, as you ordered. But if you allow her to return to her home, then I promise you, all bets will be off."

He didn't wait to argue. He turned and walked away. His control was too shaky, he was too frightened for her, too certain that if she was unprotected for even a second, then his father, Azir el Hamid Mustafa would exact his vengeance in the worst way.

Abram now had no choice but to return. No one yet knew he'd left Saudi to defect from his homeland and to refuse the legacy so tainted by blood, death, and nightmares. Azir Mustafa had become a scourge that even the Saudi government wanted to be rid of. Unfortunately, until Azir revealed the blood on his hands, there was nothing they could do to step in and deflect the misery he created.

Abram had given up on saving his father light-years before. The day he found his wife in a desert shack, bloody, tortured, her face frozen into an expression of such abject pain and horror that it had taken him to his knees. He had known the rapists, the inhuman scourge that had taken her life were the half-brothers he had taught to ride horseback when they were boys. The same that had been such sweet, laughter-filled children before Azir had taken them to his wing of the castle to raise them himself.

From that day, the change had been overwhelming. As though Azir had known what to do to release the soulless cruelty that existed within them.

Entering the garage Abram strode for the limo as Tariq, his cousin and coconspirator, stepped from the shadows to open the door for him.

"It's time to go now, Tariq," he stated as he stepped into the back of the limo. "He'll make certain she's protected."

"Azir has called the Saudi ambassador several times and he's demanding they search Khalid's home for you immediately." Disgust filled the man's voice. "I contacted him after the ambassador contacted me, just after you entered the house. I've assured him you're here to investigate the reasons for your brothers' deaths and that you are returning soon. He's certain you're here to help Khalid escape justice instead."

Tariq didn't give Abram a chance to comment. He slammed the door shut with latent violence then stalked around the limo to the driver's side door.

Abram watched as he slid behind the wheel, his gaze meeting Tariq's dark tobacco brown eyes in the mirror.

"And did he buy it?" Abram had no doubt Azir had. In his mind, no matter what he did, or who he killed, Abram wouldn't have the strength to walk away from the deserted, blood-drenched land of his birth.

Unfortunately for Azir Mustafa, his son shared few of his beliefs and none of his love for the land that had destroyed so many he loved. Abram had been all too aware that he was the last hope those he loved had of escaping Azir's cruelty. But only if Abram always remembered to never show his weakness, to never reveal he cared for anyone or anything outside the Mustafa fortress. Showing that affection was guaranteed to ensure, if not their deaths, then the ever-present risk of it.

"Shall we say he was a bit more than irate?" Tariq said with chilling calm.

Irate? Azir Mustafa was deranged. The fact that he had allowed his youngest sons' terrorist partners to take up residence in the Mustafa fortress proved it.

Jafar Mustafa, son of Azir's youngest brother, and

cousin to both Abram and Tariq, was surprisingly one of the lieutenants within the terrorist cell Ayid and Aman had commanded.

Abram's disappointment to learn Jafar was as corrupt as Ayid and Aman had been, went deeper than he'd expected. Once, he'd had high hopes for Jafar. Abram had fought for him to attend college in America, to work with the oil companies rather than joining the insanity Azir was breeding.

Azir Mustafa hadn't escaped it. As a matter of fact, he had helped exacerbate the insanity within his sons, and now, he couldn't accept that they were dead. He couldn't accept that Abram, his eldest son and heir could have defected as Jafar had informed him, or that Khalid, the son he'd given Ayid and Aman permission to murder, had actually survived.

His sanity seemed to be coming more into question by the day, but the one thing the old bastard hadn't forgotten was that in less then a month, Abram would turn thirty-six. Then the Saudi king would send his emissary to the Mustafa lands and take Abram's vow to guide the people and the land to prosperity.

Azir had, with his determination to protect his youngest sons, managed to force the royal house to cut off all funds and aid to the boundary lands until his legal heir was thirty-six. Those funds had been funneled into the coffers of the very terrorists they were fighting against.

The king's punishment had come with one ray of hope for Azir. If Abram would vow to protect and preserve the people in accordance with the law as well as pledge his loyalty to the throne on his thirty-sixth birthday, then money would flow into the Mustafa lands once more.

In all his crazed determination Azir thought he could then see the dreams of his dead sons completed once that was accomplished.

It was a vow Abram couldn't make. But, until he learned why Paige was a target, and how pervasive the terrorists now were in the city he had once called home, he had no choice but to return.

The fact that his cousin Jafar was reported to have moved into the fortress in the past days to console Azir, greatly concerned Abram.

Jafar had, until now, managed to fool Abram. He'd gone to college in America, vacationed with the rich and notorious in their playgrounds, and had once, years before, even spoken to Abram about defection himself. That same man had returned to Saudi Arabia three years before, disappeared from the public, and was rumored to have joined one of the newly formed terrorist organizations protesting Western modernization in the Middle East.

Jafar's belief that the ills of the Middle East stemmed from America was something that Abram hadn't expected.

"I called several contacts and they've reported Jafar has brought several more of his men into the castle," Abram began. "The terrorist who was supposedly killed in Jordan was seen at the fortress two nights ago. He slipped across the border, met with Jafar, and collected a file from Azir. It's reported to name the target he's chosen to exact his punishment for his sons' deaths on."

He had to give it to Jafar. So far, he was a damned

sight smarter than Ayid and Aman had been. He did nothing over e-mail, and rarely used the same courier twice when sending out reports or orders to soldiers. There was no way to gather the evidence needed to arrest him, and no way to figure out whatever plans were in the works.

And that was why Abram was returning. To protect Paige. To protect the last bit of innocence left in his life, the woman he couldn't get out of his fantasies.

"Contact Anwar," Abram ordered him. "Inform him of our arrival time at the landing area and tell him to be prepared to give me a thorough oral report."

Nothing was put on paper. Like Jafar, Abram knew the danger of ever leaving evidence.

Returning was killing him, but he knew if he didn't, Azir would strike against Paige, ensuring Abram suffered for it. And if it wasn't Azir, then it would be the terrorists he had given his allegiance to. Before he left, Abram knew he would have to commit to memory the face of every threat that could return to haunt him, Paige, or Khalid.

The prediction Khalid had made when he had been no more than eighteen seemed to be coming true.

Khalid had stated Azir would force his eldest son, his heir, to kill him to escape the Mustafa lands. Khalid had stared into the hot desert sun as he and Abram had been returning to the forest from a hunt and spoken the damning words.

Abram was finally realizing just how right his brother had been. And God help him, if Paige was harmed he'd also lose what was left of his own sanity.

He hadn't touched her until tonight, but in his fantasies, in his dreams, he touched her nightly. He touched her, and he watched as his third touched her. He possessed her, and he watched as his third possessed her.

He heard her screams of pleasure, watched her emerald eyes darken in ecstasy, and heard her beg him for release. And he woke with his dick so painfully hard, the need to possess her so strong, that no amount of masturbation could ease the hunger.

"Abram, are you sure about this?" Tariq asked as he turned the limo from Khalid's drive and headed for the private airport. "It's not too late to change your mind. Go back, convince Khalid to allow us to protect Paige ourselves. If Azir and Jafar refuse to give us peace, then we'll kill them ourselves."

As a plan, it was simple, perfect, and it would complete the dark stain spreading across his soul.

"And we'll always know we were the ones that killed him," Abram reminded him. "His murder would unleash secrets both of us would prefer were never known, Tariq. We return, learn of their plans against the throne and Paige, take them to the emissary before he arrives in Mustafa lands, and allow the government to take care of him from there.

"The lands will be repossessed by the government. Azir will either be beheaded for treason or placed in a facility for the insane until his death. Either way, our secrets remain secret, and we'll have a much better chance of safety when we return."

"That or certain death," Tariq stated tightly. "Mustafa lands are drenched in as much blood as their hands. They're saturated in it. The name is synonymous with nothing but death, greed, and such cruelty against our women that neither of us have known anything but shame since the day our mothers committed suicide. I don't know how we've refrained from killing that old bastard before now."

"Because we've always known that we would have only one chance at happiness, Tariq. I won't allow him to win by taking that from me." Abram stared out the limo's darkened windows to the sliver of light beginning to filter through as dawn edged in.

This was how he felt. Hope was there, edging into the shadows when he'd learned he would have to return to ensure Paige's safety. She was his. Since the death of his first wife so long ago, Abram had known very little hope. He couldn't turn away from it, he couldn't allow Azir to risk it.

"There are very few of our men left," Tariq reminded him. "Only those who hadn't yet been able to slip over the borders. I managed to contact four, and they'll see if they can find the others."

"We'll have to make do." Abram glanced at the mirror and met Tariq's gaze again. "We have no other choice, Tariq. We will have to make do, and we will have to succeed."

Because defeat meant not just his death, but Khalid's, Marty's, and Paige's. He would kill Azir himself before he would allow that to happen.

2

THREE DAYS LATER

"Paige, you're more than welcome to come to the party with us tonight," Marty said as she stood in the open doorway of Paige's suite, resplendent in her amber evening gown and topaz jewelry.

Shoulder-length blond hair was swept up to the top of her head with artfully arranged wisps falling from the topaz combs. It lent a charming disarray to the effect.

Paige set her book aside before uncurling from the chair and faced her brother's fiancée. She was still amazed that her dark, cynical brother had managed to capture Marty's heart. She had hoped the woman would help him chill out just a little bit. So far, though, it wasn't happening that she could see.

"I'm really not in the mood for a party, even one of Tally's." She grinned.

Tally Conover was becoming known as a premier hostess and seemed to enjoy it. The fact that Tally found the patience for it managed to surprise all her friends.

"Tally throws a damned good party," Marty reminded her. "She also somehow managed to secure a promise from Anger Thornton to be there. I want to see if he actually arrives."

Anger Thornton, CEO of Thornton Holdings and Acquisitions rarely attended anyone's parties but his own. And even those, he was known to be absent from.

"That's almost tempting," Paige agreed. "I think I'll finish my book instead."

Attending the party meant being civil to Khalid. She just didn't think she had it in her at the moment. They had existed in a state of warfare for the past three days, and Paige didn't see that changing anytime soon.

"Finish the book or continue to ignore Khalid?" Marty finally asked.

Paige stared back at her. Her lips pursed and her teeth clenched for one angry second.

"It's better that Khalid and I have the least amount to do with each other as possible, Marty," she finally stated.

The other woman shook her head, the wisps of silken hair brushing about her face as she chuckled lightly.

"You two are just too much alike," she accused. "And as I understand it, Abram Mustafa is just as bad. Khalid, Abram, and their cousins, Tariq and Jafar are all cut from the same cloth, trust me."

Paige rolled her eyes. She knew all four men. They were so much alike they all could have been brothers rather than cousins. Hell, they could probably be clones—at times they were so equally arrogant and conceited.

"They're all four equal pains in the ass," Paige stated.

"So I've heard." Marty nodded. "But there are still other pretty interesting men in the world. Abram isn't the only one out there, Paige."

Paige pulled her legs up, knees bending, her feet pressing into the cushions as she looped her arms around her knees.

"There are many interesting men in the world, and if I were sexually interested in them I'd be out there looking for them."

Marty glanced behind her, making sure no one was close enough to hear what was being said. Most likely ensuring Khalid wasn't there. As though their conversation was any of his business, still, they were both aware he would make it his business.

"He isn't rational and you know it," Paige informed her, the irritation she was feeling impossible to keep hidden. "Do you know he's lectured me every time he's seen me since Abram was here? Talked to me as though I were a child and didn't know how to run my own life. It's damned insulting."

Marty grimaced, as her hand rubbed her temple. Her expression was amusingly sympathetic and only exacerbated the aggravation Paige couldn't fight or hide anymore.

"He worries, Paige," she finally stated softly. "He's terrified that perhaps you're not fully aware of what you're getting into sexually with Abram. Besides, you're his sister, his baby sister, and Abram is his brother. The dynamics of that are making him crazy."

"Dynamics are always making Khalid insane." Paige waved the explanation away. She didn't even bother hiding the fact that there wasn't a chance in hell she was going to fall for that one. "I'm amazed the dynamics of being in love hasn't had him pulling his hair out. Or causing you to pull yours out."

"It has been getting a little thinner." Marty laughed, her gray eyes sparkling with pure happiness. "But it doesn't change the fact that he does have reason to worry at the moment. Be a little patient with him."

"I've been patient with him my entire life," Paige scoffed. "Do you realize he's lectured me twice today already? He's treating me as though I'm not well aware of the fact that Abram and Khalid both share a penchant for having a third in their sexual relationships. Or that I don't know damned good and well that Abram Mustafa can be a complete dominant asshole."

There was a look of genuine shock on Marty's face before complete laughter filled her eyes and a throaty chuckle left her lips.

"You surprise me, Paige," she admitted. "And here I thought a sweet little innocent like you wouldn't notice the signs or understand the rumors if you heard them."

"What does innocence have to do with anything?" Paige rose from the chair and paced back and forth across the room. "Would that exclude me from understanding what a threesome is or how it works? Come on, Marty, remember Courtney Sinclair is one of my best friends. I knew what a threesome was when she called me sobbing about the inexhaustible Ian Sinclair having sex with her maids and calling them by her name. Do you know she would spy on him when he visited her parents' home?"

Marty wasn't having an easy time holding back her

laughter. Courtney Sinclair and her husband Ian had one of those fiery, wonderful relationships most women dreamed of having.

"Come on, Paige, you have to admit with everything that's happened, Khalid has a right to worry. Abram is ten years older than you, and on top of that, he does often have a third as I understand it. But while Khalid doesn't want your heart broken, he also helped raise you. Accepting that you have sex is probably something he's never going to do."

"He needs to worry about something other than whether or not I intend to fuck his brother and if I let his cousin join in."

Marty howled with laughter. Paige was about to join in but Khalid chose that moment to step into the room.

The laughter broke off immediately.

His expression was dark with anger, his black gaze snapping with it.

"Do you even have a clue what a man like Abram could be like?" he growled. "Do you think he's going to be a gentleman? Be sweet and ask nicely to make love to you as his third pets you sweetly and whispers sweet nothings in your ear?"

"Don't use that tone with me, Khalid," she warned him calmly. "I didn't invite you into this conversation, so if you don't like it, then you can leave and keep your opinion to yourself."

Marty turned to him, her expression concerned now. "Khalid, we were just joking, darling. You two enjoy poking at each other a little too much."

"I wasn't joking," Paige informed them both as she crossed her arms over her breasts and glared at her brother. "The only reason I'm not trying to slip into his bed right now is because he's not here."

Khalid's lips thinned. "I'll be damned if I'll argue with you over this."

"Of course you won't," Paige agreed mockingly. "It's so much easier to have a little man-to-man chat with Abram." She let her eyes widen. "Oh but wait, that didn't work so well either, did it? The first chance he had, he ignored that too."

She could feel years of anger rising inside her now. For as long as she could remember her parents had deferred to Khalid regarding her protection, and in any choices that they had to make in her life.

Khalid had chosen the schools she attended, the bodyguards she had as a child, her first ugly car, and was behind her father's refusal to allow her to date her first boyfriend.

"She's not a child anymore, Khalid," Marty reminded him softly. But Paige knew her brother, and he wasn't about to listen to anyone but himself. She was simply at the end of her patience.

"Do you even care how much it hurts or humiliates me to have you step in and play lord of all you survey with my life? I lost my job today, Khalid, because I haven't been there in two weeks. Now, I can either lose my car or bum money from you or my parents. I'm twenty-five years old, not eighteen, and I enjoy taking care of myself," she cried out furiously.

"And I enjoy waking up each morning knowing you're alive and safe," he bit out, his tone dark with anger. "Do you have any idea of the danger you are in at the moment, or the man you are tempting to take you into his bed? The two are entwined, Paige. Being with Abram draws you front and center into Azir's attention, if you weren't already there. And I know, beyond a shadow of a doubt, that no matter what happens, Abram will break your heart. He will not be an easy lover, Paige, nor will he understand your independence and your determination to do as you wish."

"And none of this is your choice to make." She dropped her arms to her sides and faced him without the anger she knew she should be feeling.

She was tired of arguing with him. She was tired of the lectures and she was tired of trying to force him to treat her like an adult rather than a child.

"Paige, would you come between Abram and me?" he finally questioned her harshly.

"Khalid!" Marty gasped as she turned on him furiously. "That's low, even for you."

But Paige wasn't surprised in the least that he had attempted such emotional blackmail. It was reminiscent of her childhood years when he had used her emotions to get what he wanted every time she attempted to defy him.

"Would you really lose me over this?" she asked in return. "Because that's what will happen if you keep standing between me and Abram. Whether or not he wants me, or I want him, shouldn't be tainted by your demands that we stay away from each other. Because honestly, Khalid, there have been times when the very fact that you didn't want me to do something made it all that more appealing. Do you really want to chance that in this situation?"

"So I'm to just stand by and watch him break your

heart when he becomes the man he is and he tries to subjugate you as we both know he will? He may have different ideas on sexuality and women's rights on the surface, Paige, but trust me when I tell you that only in your sexuality will he be more accepting. He is still a product of the culture he was raised within."

Paige could only stare back at him incredulously. "How little you know your brother, or your sister for that matter," she told him, pity and anger converging together. "Does he beat his women, Khalid? Does he lock them up, or demand that they have no life outside of him? Does he have six wives and twelve children that I know nothing about?"

Khalid's frown deepened. "You know he would never do such things."

"Then your only objection is that you're worried Abram may try to curb my independence?"

"You'll forget the meaning of the word *independence*," he told her.

"Has Leyla forgotten the independence you taught her?" Leyla was one of the six young women Khalid had raised after his father sent them to Khalid as teenagers. They were young women Azir had bought and then given to his son to begin his own little harem.

Leyla was engaged to a young man who had come to America with his parents from Saudi Arabia.

"Leyla's fiancé is much younger than Abram," he snapped. "Don't you understand that, Paige? Abram is a full-grown man who has spent much of his life in the Middle East. A man that will never—"

"Stop preaching at me," she demanded roughly, her head practically ringing with the list of objections he was repeating from earlier. "You say Abram would attempt to make me live by his rules? What the hell do you believe you're doing? You're trying to force me to do what you want, whether it's what I want or not."

And that was beginning to piss her off. She had tried to avoid these confrontations for the past few days. Several times she had simply left the room only to have him follow her and continue the argument.

"Paige, I'm trying to protect you," he snarled. His frustration was readily apparent but she couldn't make herself feel sorry for him, or even suggest they agree to disagree.

"Go to your party, Khalid. I'm sick of your lectures and I've had enough of your judgmental attitude. Now leave my room."

She didn't wait for him to leave. Paige turned and stomped to the bathroom, slamming the door behind her.

Then, the tears she'd only barely held back filled her eyes and began to fall down her cheeks. She didn't sob. She remained silent, pressing her hands to her lips and tried to stop the tears as she had so many times in the past.

She loved her brother. Khalid had always been a mainstay in her life, even if he had frustrated the hell out of her. He'd been amused at her father's nerves when she rode her bicycle without training wheels, and laughed at her mother's fears when Paige got her driver's license.

He had always acted damned strange about Abram though, despite the fact that Abram had been married the first time Paige had met him and his wife Lessa.

Paige had been drawn to Abram from the first

moment. She'd been fascinated by this man who looked so much like her brother, who her brother called a brother, yet he wasn't her brother. She'd only been nine when she first met him, and he'd been nineteen and already married.

The relationship between him and his brother had at first confused the hell out of her. After all, Khalid was her brother, so why wasn't Abram?

That confusion had amused her parents and Abram's wife Lessa, but Khalid hadn't seemed nearly so amused by it.

Paige liked Abram's wife, Lessa, enjoyed her laughter and her quiet manner the few times she'd been able to spend any time with her. Lessa was murdered several years after Paige met her, and Paige's heart had broken for Abram.

He'd loved his wife, there had been no doubt of it. Over the next few years, he'd been a regular in her life. He'd visited when her family vacationed in Cairo, and joined Khalid in Greece when he returned for their mother's birthday.

She was eighteen when things suddenly changed, when he had looked at her for the first time and hadn't seen a child. When his gaze had flicked to her breasts, encased in the bodice of the strapless ball gown she had worn.

He had danced with her, his hand riding low on her back and pressing her closer to him than any of the younger men she had danced with had done.

Her heart had raced so hard she had thought it would tear from her chest. He'd stared down at her, somber and intense, holding her eyes as she swore she saw some message swirling in the depths of his own.

And against her hip, hard and thick, she had felt his erection, proof that he was seeing her as a woman, and that she wasn't alone in the sensations surging through her.

It was the first time she had creamed her panties. The first time her clit had become so swollen and sensitive that it only took her seconds to come when she had masturbated in her bed later that night.

From that night, she hadn't been able to get him out of her mind, or her fantasies. She hadn't even tried to keep him from stealing her heart as the years went by.

Khalid was equally determined to keep anything from happening between them. Even during those first years when Paige had been determined to go to college and get her degree before allowing any relationship to develop too far, still, Khalid had begun arranging Abram's visits to keep her from seeing him.

It didn't always work.

And nothing had ever stemmed the need that only grew with each year, with each moment spent with him. And with each acknowledgement that her brother was willing to alienate her rather than see her with Abram.

Sniffling quietly she wiped at the tears and tried to stem them. If she stayed here, then they were going to end up saying things that couldn't be taken back.

She didn't want that. She didn't want to lose her brother. That left only one other option. To leave his house, at least until they could learn to agree to disagree where Abram was concerned.

It had been almost two weeks since Khalid's security team had practically kidnapped her and brought her to the mansion.

Today, she had lost her job. Her savings weren't nearly enough to keep her rent and utilities going, along with her car payment, for more than a few months. She would have to find a job, and there was no doubt she would have to ask her parents for money or borrow from her trust fund. A fund she had wanted to save for a time when she really needed it.

Getting another job wasn't going to be easy. The advertising firm she had worked for had already informed her that there would be no reference forthcoming.

Her entire life had been changed because of this and on top of it, she was losing Khalid because she couldn't get his brother out of her mind, or out of her fantasies.

She shared no blood with Abram. He was no relation to her. He was the man that made her heart beat faster, made her womb clench violently, and her pussy throb in need.

She wasn't a virgin, despite Khalid and Marty's obvious beliefs. She'd had a few lovers, two to be exact, in her attempts to forget the one man that fascinated her as nothing or no one ever had.

And to be with the man she wanted more than anyone, she was going to lose the brother she had always idolized, despite his autocratic attitude.

That knowledge had her heart clenching in pain again as fresh tears fell from her eyes before she could wipe them away.

"Paige?" A soft knock at the door followed Marty's gentle voice.

A second later the bathroom door opened and the other woman stepped inside. Paige quickly wiped at her tears.

"Oh, Paige." Sympathy filled Marty's voice as Paige hurriedly dampened a washcloth with cold water to wash her face. "He didn't mean to hurt you like this." She sighed.

"I'm fine." Raspy, tear-roughened, her voice sounded like hell. "Go to your party, Marty, and take your fiancé with you. Hopefully, if he's out of my face for a while, I can find a way to remember the brother he used to be, rather than the bastard he's becoming."

"He's so worried, Paige," Marty whispered. "He's pacing the floors day and night trying to keep you safe and worrying that Abram won't return. He's not a man that's able to sit back and allow those he loves to fight the battle Abram is fighting, alone. But he can't join him, he can't protect you if he isn't here, and he's terrified Azir will go after your mother as well. He has to stay while Abram is in danger, and sometimes he feels as though he's fighting ghosts in trying to protect you."

"Do you think I'm not aware of the stress he's under?" Her breathing hitched as the tears threatened again. "Just take him to the damned party, Marty. I'll be okay if I can just get away from him for a while."

Just long enough to call a cab and go home for a few hours.

She needed her home for just a little while. The comfort of her surroundings, the soothing warmth of her fireplace.

It was an electric fireplace, but still, it was hers. It was warm, and it looked close enough to the real thing. Like her vibrator. It did the job, even if it did lack the qualities or the warmth of the real thing.

She needed it. She needed to get out of here for just a little while.

"Once he thinks about it, he'll realize what he's doing," Marty promised. "You know how he is. He gets overprotective and ends up pissing us off. But he still loves us. He'd still die for us, Paige, and knowing he's hurting you is killing him. He just doesn't know how to fix it."

"I know this," she cried out in frustration. "Just give me a little while, Marty. I'm trying to adjust. I swear I am."

Marty breathed out heavily. Paige turned away and held the cold washcloth to her face.

"All right then," she said slowly. A second later Paige heard the door close behind her.

Marty had left, and there hadn't even been an accepting hug before she departed. God, that sucked. She could have used a hug today.

Paige shook her head before turning back and tossing the cloth in the sink. Maybe it was just time to accept that she wasn't the woman or the adult that those she loved really wanted.

Her mother was upset that she was working, her father was disappointed that she refused to head the charities his companies oversaw. Her brother disagreed with the men she wanted as lovers, and the lovers were pissed because she wanted to be independent and still live with them.

It was a no-win situation.

Maybe it was time to stop silently begging them to

accept her. She needed to find a way to live and stop hurting like this. Khalid had threatened to either disown his brother, or her. Either one would simply break her heart.

Moving back to the bedroom she changed out of her comfortable sweats and T-shirt and pulled on a pair of jeans and a sweatshirt. Warm socks, sneakers. As she tied the leather running shoes the lights of the limo lit up the darkness outside her bedroom window.

Khalid and Marty were going to their party. They were leaving, and they were leaving her alone. Just as she had asked.

Picking up her cell phone she called a cab, then grabbed her purse and made her way quietly downstairs to wait on the transportation, and hopefully to keep anyone else from turning it away.

She didn't have to wait long. The intercom from the front gate pinged at the wall next to the door. Stepping to it, Paige accepted the summons.

"A Plus Cabs," the voice on the other end announced.

"Come on up to the house." Paige pressed the security lock and before the cab was passing through the open gates Daniel Conover was walking into the foyer from the back wing of the house.

"You can follow me, or you can wait for me to return, your choice," she informed him as he leaned against the wall opposite her, his dark blond head tilting to the side as he regarded her curiously.

"You know I can't allow you to leave," he stated.

"But you will," she told him. "Otherwise, I'll call the authorities next. I'll have you charged with kidnapping and imprisonment."

She wasn't serious and she had a feeling he suspected it. But he wasn't certain, and that was what mattered.

"I'll be right behind you," he finally sighed. He flexed his broad shoulders beneath the cotton shirt he wore and straightened from the wall. He looped his thumbs in the back pockets of his well-worn, just-snug-enough jeans and gave her a curious little smile. "You're as stubborn as your brother, you know."

"So everyone says," she sniffed. "Funny, he always seems to come out the winner though."

Paige moved past him as he opened the door for her. She walked outside to the cab.

Just a few hours, she promised herself. She wasn't going to worry her family unnecessarily. She wasn't going to risk her life or her bodyguards. But she needed to go home to recharge away from the too-big, too-empty house she was usually in alone.

And she needed the space to figure out how to sit back and accept her brother's protection, her father's offer to pay the bills while the situation was being resolved, and to decide which was more important. Following her heart, or obeying the brother she would lose if she didn't walk away from Abram.

She had a feeling that decision was going to be impossible to make.

3

Her apartment was simple, a kitchen and living area, a bedroom and a bathroom with a large soaking tub. That bathtub had been the selling point for her. The electric fireplace sat in front of the overstuffed couch and was the focal point of the room.

The kitchen was small, but roomy enough to cook and entertain a few friends in.

It was hers. She paid the bills, stocked the cabinets, and lived comfortably and happily on the salary she earned at the advertising firm she had gone to work for after graduating from college.

The floors were hardwood, gleaming around the large area rugs beneath the small kitchen table and the coffee table in the living area.

She didn't have a television, yet. For entertainment she used her laptop, which she had left at her brother's. She'd been so busy in the past year that she hadn't really had time to watch television or enjoy movies as she once had.

She'd missed her home while she had been at Khalid's. Her brother's home was too big, too private perhaps. The suites were self-contained except for eating, and his house staff was always more than happy to fix a meal and bring it to her room.

She'd been lost there, and lonely. At first, she'd been sequestered there by herself, then with Khalid's return it had been one lecture and argument after another until she was ready to go insane.

As she placed her purse on the small table inside the door, her cell phone rang again. The ringtone was a set of strident cymbals. It reminded her of her brother's habit of demanding she answer the phone quickly.

She ignored it.

Pushing her fingers through her hair she walked through the apartment, checked each room, straightened a pillow on the bed then moved back into the living area where she turned on the electric fireplace and collapsed on the large pillows in front of it.

She felt exhausted.

Fighting with Khalid always left her feeling as though she had just run a marathon. It sapped her energy and made her question her own logic.

At the end of the day, what it came down to was the fact that whether it was logical or not, she was miserable living in that big house, unable to visit friends, unable to feel safe and secure in her own home because Khalid's father was a crazy bastard.

He'd kidnapped their mother when she was seventeen,

forced her to marry him and immediately raped her and forced her to conceive.

She'd been locked in a harem, forced to spend her days with only one pursuit, that of pleasing him.

Her mother had lived in hell while she had been imprisoned in the Mustafa stronghold, and only a stroke of luck had afforded her escape.

Pavlos Galbraithe, her then-fiancé and now Paige's father, had learned of the meeting between Marilyn and Azir Mustafa while Marilyn was visiting family in Cairo, Egypt. Mustafa, he had been told, had been insistent on meeting Marilyn. He'd been entranced by her flame-red, silky hair and brilliant emerald green eyes.

He'd made her so uncomfortable with his stares and his disapproval each time she spoke that she had excused herself and returned to her room. Only to have her cousin, upset and concerned by Mustafa's attitude, convince her to come back down because he was becoming so irate.

The next day, Marilyn had disappeared.

But still, Pavlos and his future brother-in-law, Henry Girard, wouldn't have had a chance of gaining entrance into the fortress or rescuing Marilyn if she hadn't found her own way out through a secret door in the stronghold's outer wall. A wall that had surrounded the private gardens of the Mustafa harem.

Paige's mother had in essence rescued herself and her newborn son, Khalid Mustafa. The baby Azir had forced on her, yet one she had come to adore.

Pavlos and Henry had been outside that wall, searching for the same secret door they had heard existed that led into the harem. They had been there as the stones seemed to part, push forward, and a slim, darkened figure had slipped out.

How her mother had managed to survive her time there, Paige had never understood. She knew Marilyn hated Azir Mustafa with a violence that could erupt into fury if his name was mentioned.

But she loved the son that had been forced on her. Khalid had been her salvation, she claimed. If it hadn't been for her baby, and the knowledge of what she feared Azir would turn him into, then she wouldn't have had the strength to keep searching for a way out.

To Pavlos's credit, he had endured Khalid. Paige was always aware of the fact that there was an underlying tension between her brother and her father, but the truce was one that had always stood.

He'd raised Khalid, looked after him and educated him.

When Khalid had returned to Saudi Arabia after his high school graduation for the agreed-upon stay with his father, Pavlos had been furious. It had been negotiated years before between Marilyn and the Saudi ambassador who had been sent to negotiate what had become an international incident after Mustafa had attempted to kidnap Khalid. But Paige knew her father had arranged with a CIA asset in the area to watch over Khalid and to ensure he came to no harm.

Staring into the electric flames of the fireplace, Paige readily admitted that Khalid was as hard as he was for a reason. That he knew the dangers, understood the monster that never seemed to stop haunting him, and worried constantly that Azir would strike out at his family.

The man was insane.

But Abram wasn't.

Khalid knew Abram, she understood that, just as she understood Khalid's fears in regards to her broken heart. God knew, she didn't want to face that pain unless she simply had no other choice. But the risk was one she was willing to take. She simply didn't believe Abram was going to lock her into a harem and beat her each time she tried to escape.

Shaking her head at the thought, she got to her feet. She moved back to the bedroom to pack a few things to take back to Khalid's with her.

She had only a few things of her own there. The way she had been snatched from work and taken to her brother's home hadn't given her time to pack.

She liked her own clothes, thank you very much. And the few things Marty and Khalid had collected for her hadn't been enough, nor had they been her favorites.

It looked as though she would be there for a while, so she pulled out the full set of leather luggage her parents had bought her and packed the things she needed.

Her overnight bag held her shampoos, conditioner, makeup, and feminine items. Several bars of the soap her father kept her supplied with, the scent created especially for her.

Clothes were harder to choose. She had only two large bags and one lingerie bag. She packed those, zipped them closed, then hauled them to the door before walking through the small apartment one more time.

She sighed wearily as she stood at the window, staring out into the darkened park across the street. During the day, it was alive with the sound of children's laughter.

At night, occasionally, she had glimpsed lovers walking hand in hand.

Damn, she hoped she got to come home soon.

Moving back to the kitchen she was reaching for her purse to call Daniel when a knock at the door had a grin twitching her lips. He was obviously becoming impatient.

A friend of Khalid's impatient? Go figure.

She moved to the door, unlocked it, and swung the door open.

Her eyes widened.

Her lips parted to scream.

A second later, the world went black around her.

TWO HOURS LATER

Khalid stood inside the living area of Paige's apartment and stared around, his chest feeling as though an open wound had been dug into it.

It was neat, like his sister was, sparsely decorated. She claimed she hadn't developed her style quite yet. The electric fireplace was still on, and everything appeared perfectly organized.

"The majority of her clothes and toiletries are missing." Daniel Conover moved from the bedroom, his expression foreboding, his blue eyes burning with rage. "Her bags aren't in the closet."

Khalid shoved his hands into the wool coat he wore, his gaze turning to where his lover sat in a comfortable easy chair, her hands covering her face.

She wasn't crying, though he knew she was upset.

Marty didn't cry often, thank God. But at the moment, he wished she would, because he couldn't.

"Would his men have packed her bags?" Daniel asked.

Khalid shook his head. Azir's men would not have taken the time.

"She would have." Marty lifted her head. "She was complaining she had none of her favorite clothes or her makeup. She could have packed herself before they arrived."

"If the bags had been sitting there, and if they were sympathetic to Abram or to myself, then they would have picked up the luggage," Khalid answered.

"That doesn't sound like terrorists," Daniel commented.

"Many of the new recruits are men and young boys who have been raised within the Mustafa province." Khalid sighed. "They know me, they know Abram. They would have grabbed her luggage along with her if there was more than one. They're aware this is something Abram would be furious over and they may want to garner leniency by providing her clothes."

He felt like howling in rage, in pain. He couldn't believe he had allowed his sister to be taken by that monster, and there was no doubt it was Azir who had taken her.

They knew Azir Mustafa had his men in the area, several of which were aligned with the terrorist cell Ayid and Aman had commanded.

"This is my fault," he whispered as he stared around the apartment again, aware of Marty as she rose quickly to her feet and crossed to him.

"Khalid, this isn't your fault any more than it's Paige's," she protested. "You could only keep her confined for so long. She lasted longer than either of us thought she would. He would have been waiting, no matter the circumstances."

His arms went around her, the need for her comfort like a beast raging inside him.

He had failed his sister.

"When Mother brought her home from the hospital, I stared at this ugly, red-faced little piece of a thing, and I swore I would protect her." A dagger was digging into his soul. "I swore she would not know what my mother had known. That she would not face that hell if I lived and breathed. And now, he has her."

"Then Abram will have her." She pulled back just enough to glare up at him. "Khalid, no matter what you believe about your brother, he will protect Paige. You know he will."

"What I believe about my brother." He sighed as he met her gaze. "I believe Abram is a good man, Marty. But even good men have their faults. And his fascination with Paige bothers me. He'll fight against Azir until hell freezes over, and he'll walk away from that land without a backward look, but he's still a product of the desert and how he was raised."

"Khalid, you know Abram would never do anything to hurt Paige."

He shook his head. "But he'll end up hurting her just the same. If he can get to her before Azir kills her."

And that was his nightmare.

The enmity between Khalid and his father was at a breaking point. Khalid had gone to one of the reigning princes and the Saudi ambassador concerning Azir's sanity and Ayid and Aman's attack against him. And he knew it was a matter that was being investigated. Azir would know it as well. He had his own spies within the monarchy, and his own ways of gaining information.

Thank God Abram hadn't officially defected after Ayid and Aman had been killed. If he had, there would have been no one there to protect Paige.

"It's been about two hours since I found the door open and Paige gone," Daniel stated. "We have all the airports covered and we're checking all the private planes on the ground. There are officers checking out the private landing strips as well."

Khalid shook his head. "They were in the air within thirty minutes or less of having taken her. She's gone, Daniel."

And it was his fault.

He looked down at Marty again, misery crawling through his body as guilt raked sharpened talons across his heart.

"I need to contact Abram." He sighed. "I can only do that from the house. The satellite link we've established can only be made from one location and only at certain times of the day." He checked his watch as Marty moved back.

Catching her hand with his he looked around the room once again. "It will be another two hours before I can send the message to Abram. Until then, I can still get ahold of a few contacts I have in Saudi and see what can be done."

"Someone needs to tell your mother and Pavlos,"

Marty reminded him gently. "They're flying into D.C. tonight. We should be there when they arrive."

His mother had been worried. She had been certain Azir wouldn't wait much longer to attempt to take Paige, and she had been right.

God, this was going to kill her.

Fragile, gentle, his delicate mother may not survive if her daughter never returned home to her.

He breathed out heavily.

"We'll meet them," he told her. "After I send a message to Abram. Let's get back to the house." He turned to Daniel. "Lock up the apartment. Check with her neighbors and see if they heard anything. We may not be able to catch them, but hopefully we can track down whoever helped them. They couldn't have pulled this off without help."

Daniel nodded, then paused. "I'm sorry, Khalid," he said, his voice low. "This happened on my watch, and it shouldn't have. I take full responsibility for it."

"As Marty said, he would have found an opportunity eventually," he stated, though a part of him blamed the investigator/security consultant. It had been his job to protect her and to ensure no gaps were open in her security.

It was a no-win situation though. Sooner or later, it would have happened, Khalid knew. Everyone had to blink eventually.

Holding Marty's hand, Khalid turned and headed for the door. He was almost there when something caught his eye. A glimmer of gold on the floor.

Stopping, he bent and picked up the delicate little

hoop with its fragile, dangling chains attached to tiny gold feathers.

The earrings Abram had sent to her for her twenty-first birthday.

He grimaced at the thought.

He'd fought to keep them apart over the years, even knowing it was doing little good, and that the day would come when nothing could stop it.

It wasn't that he believed Abram would hurt her, or even that he wouldn't be good for her. It was simply that Khalid knew his brother, and he knew, after the deaths of his first two wives, any lover he had would suffer the ultraprotective possessiveness Abram would feel.

Independence would go to hell along with the hearts. Abram wouldn't be able to control himself, and all that dark, tortured hunger inside him would become a ravening beast in the face of Paige's determination.

And this was where Paige would struggle.

There was no hunger strong enough, no love vital enough and no woman with enough patience or enough understanding to stand against a man determined to lock her away from the world.

Khalid had always feared that was exactly what Abram would attempt to do with the fiery independence that was so much a part of Paige.

And there wouldn't be a damned thing he could do to save her from it.

4

She was so screwed.

That was the first thought that drifted through her mind as Paige's eyes blinked open and she found herself in an unfamiliar room.

If she thought her suite at her brother's home was too expensive and opulent, then it was nothing compared to where she found herself now.

The room was huge, at least twelve feet tall with several motorized fans turning lazily overhead and creating the slightest breeze.

She was laying on a huge bed, its comfort unlike anything she had known before. Beneath her naked body she could feel the excellent grade and cool perfection of the silk sheets.

Laying over her was more silk, the sheet against her flesh airy and cool while the ultrathin cashmere throw laying on top of her added a measure of warmth.

Looking around, she saw velvet upholstery on the

chairs next to a fireplace, and what appeared to be a silk-covered chaise lounge positioned at the side of the room. There were large pillows tossed in front of the hearth in differing sizes and in different expensive materials.

The windows were high and arched with wooden shutters pulled closed against the sunlight. The slats in the shutters allowed the fragile, heated rays to slip in and pierce the dim light.

White stone walls peeked out from behind several large tapestries, reminding her of the ancient castles she'd visited in England.

Stone floors were covered here and there with matching tapestries, and in front of the fireplace lay what appeared to be a thick, cashmere rug.

Swallowing tight, Paige felt the gummy, sticky feeling of her mouth. She wondered how long she had been unconscious as she fought to keep her hysteria under control.

If she didn't concentrate on something else, then she wouldn't make it. She collapsed into a heap of pure hysterical fear.

Because she knew exactly where she was. She'd heard her mother describe this room so many times it was burned into her brain.

This was the room she had lived in during her stay when she wasn't locked in Azir's bedroom. She ate in this room, wept in this room, and plotted her escape from this room.

She was in the Mustafa stronghold on the Saudi Arabian and Iraqi borders. A wasteland of unproven ground, where even oil didn't reside.

Nothing of consequence lived here, as she had heard Abram and Khalid say, except the people who had been born here, worked here, and eked out their living here.

The fortress had been built centuries before, the castle a mix of both Middle Eastern and English influence well before the days of the Knights Templars and the holy wars.

She had seen pictures of it. Khalid and her mother had put together a map of sorts of the castle and the outlying areas around it.

There were ways to escape; Paige just had to find them.

Terror was crawling through her now. She hadn't believed Azir Mustafa would retaliate against Khalid. He'd threatened before. How many times had Paige been locked behind protective walls because Khalid and Azir were feuding again, or because Azir had, in one of his periods of insane fury, threatened to kidnap Paige's mother and bring her back where he believed she belonged?

There had been too many times to count. And he'd never done it before. Evidently he had grown tired of simply threatening.

He had actually managed to kidnap her, and evidently Abram had no idea. If he knew, he would have been there when she awoke, she told herself. He wouldn't have allowed her to face this alone.

Now he had her. A monster.

Her chest tightened, her throat nearly closing with fear and tears as she fought against it. She wasn't going to allow him to see her cry. It was a sign of weakness, and like any jackal, she couldn't allow Azir Mustafa to see her weakness. Or her fear.

Pulling the sheet and throw closer around her nakedness as fear began to send shudders through her body, Paige's breath hitched as she pushed back her screams.

She was stronger than this, she assured herself. Azir Mustafa would be looking for fear. And he might have her now, but not once Abram found her, or learned she was there, which would be as soon as Khalid contacted him. If he hadn't already.

No. Her hands tightened on the sheet and throw convulsively. If Khalid had contacted Abram then Abram would be here. He would be assuring her everything was going to be okay. He would be finding a way to get her home. And he really needed to get on that. Sometime before her heart burst from terror.

She was naked, in a bed. Breath hitching, gasping from her lips she began to check her body, to feel between her thighs. Desperation was an oily stain across her mind as she checked her body, praying to God she hadn't been raped, because she knew Azir Mustafa wasn't above drugging a woman to rape her.

There were no signs of it, but the fact that she was naked, that someone had undressed her to bare skin while she was unconscious was a violation as well. It made her feel helpless and out of control and that terrified her.

She'd always sympathized with her mother for what she'd gone through with Azir. She'd hated the bastard for it. But now, she understood much better exactly how her mother had felt, and she was scared.

She should have listened to Khalid and not left the house. If she had just stayed in place, this wouldn't have happened. At least not yet. Not this way.

Every time she ever refused to listen to him, she had paid for it. That was why she hadn't fought against him as hard as she could have when he first had her taken to the house by Daniel Conover. Because she knew Khalid wouldn't have done it without good reason.

Rising from the bed she moved around the room, searching for the clothes that had been taken from her. Her jeans and shirt, her underclothes. Her shoes. Oh God, she really needed her shoes. How was she supposed to escape without running shoes?

Se couldn't bear to be naked as she was. She felt too exposed, despite the sheet and throw she had wrapped around herself. The material didn't even begin to be protective. Not that clothing would have been.

She couldn't bear to feel this helpless. That was what Khalid didn't understand, and what she could never tell him. She had only been this helpless once before in her life and the memories of it sent a surge of terror racing through her again.

She tried to shake the memory away. Dealing with the memories of that night right now would shred what little control she had left over the hysteria bubbling inside her.

She had to clear her head. She had to be able to think and find a way out of this.

She had to find a way out. She had found a way out the last time she was this helpless and had escaped. She had to do it again. She didn't think her sanity could survive otherwise.

The door was locked. The shutters on the windows were locked. Her mother hadn't mentioned hidden doors or passageways in this room.

She couldn't find her clothes. There were no dressers and the four armoires in the room only held bedding materials. There were no clothes.

Her breath felt trapped in her lungs. Her heart was racing out of control and panic was beginning to close in.

She would go crazy in this place.

Abram sat back in the comfortable leather of the modified Land Rover as Tariq drove into the fortress compound. His gaze narrowed at the men and women milling around in the outer yards. The women were covered from head to toe in the required burka, while the men were dressed in fatigues or combat-ready pants and shirts.

The face of the Mustafa province was changing and he hadn't been able to stop it during the years when stopping it had mattered to him. All he did now was look on in regret.

Once, this land had thrived, if not from oil then from the small mines outside of town where precious ore was eked out and sold to the government. It had been a minimal income, but when added to the funds the monarchy had once sent, the lands and mines had been sufficient to keep the small farms pulling precious water from the deep wells and the crops growing.

The province had held a small but thriving area of trade due to those crops and the ore. Something it no longer held because of Azir's greed and murderous inclinations.

"Look who showed up." Tariq nodded toward the fortress castle where a lone figure stood at the top of the stone steps against the stone wall.

The tall double doors were his backdrop, emphasizing the slender, muscular form, his dark hair pulled back from a lean, Arabic face.

The man who had been slowly overtaking the Mustafa fortress even before the deaths of Ayid and Aman Mustafa. No matter how Abram had fought over the years, still, Jafar Mustafa—along with Ayid and Aman—had facilitated the steady introduction of men Abram was certain were no more than soldiers to the terrorist cell Ayid and Aman had commanded. A cell Jafar was now rumored to command.

First cousin to both Abram and Tariq, Jafar was the son of the youngest of the three Mustafa brothers who had inherited differing sections of the province from their father.

Until the two youngest brothers had died under highly suspicious circumstances. Abram had always suspected Azir had had his brothers killed, but he had never been able to prove it.

"He can't want anything good," Abram assured him as Tariq drew the Land Rover to a stop before the castle. Stepping from the vehicle Abram allowed Tariq to move in behind him and cover his back. They mounted the steps and moved up to the entrance where Jafar awaited them.

The dark arrogance in the other man's expression was a forewarning. Abram could feel the tension emanating from him, the animosity that had been brewing between them mixing to create a heavy, barely civil atmosphere.

The cynical amusement in Jafar's odd green eyes was a clue to the fact that he wasn't going to like whatever the other man had to say. Fortunately, there was at least a shred of information in anything Jafar said. He enjoyed the games he played and the fact that Abram couldn't do a damned thing to stop the steady infiltration of the terrorists moving in.

Like Abram and Tariq, Jafar's mother had been American. But unlike them, Jafar had actually inherited some of his mother's traits. His hair was a deep, dark brown, rather than black, and the celadon green of his eyes was damned off-putting in a land of mostly dark eyes.

The men of Mustafa seemed to have a particular fondness for pale-haired or redheaded women. Jafar's mother had been a Scandinavian blonde and like Abram and Tariq, he had taken his height from her ancestors.

It was a fondness their sons seemed to share as well, Abram thought.

"What the hell do you want, Jafar?" he growled as he topped the stone stairs and faced his cousin.

Jafar chuckled, the amusement in the sound matching that of his eyes as his gaze flicked between Abram and Tariq.

"Perhaps I just want to wish you a good afternoon, cousin. After all, it's been a while since we've visited. Don't tell me you haven't missed me."

"I haven't missed you," Abram assured him with a sneering lift of his lip. "Is that all you wanted?"

The smirk on Jafar's lips assured him otherwise.

It was too bad they seemed to have gravitated to opposing ends of their own beliefs. There had been a time when he and Jafar had been close. When they had both spoken of the dream of a far different future than the ones they had embraced.

Abram waited for long, tense moments for Jafar to reveal why he was waiting, but when he didn't, Abram's patience began to dissolve.

"Go to hell, Jafar," he grunted. "Let me know when you're doing more than fucking off."

Jafar's eyes narrowed at the deliberate vulgarity. He and his cousin had been in more than one battle in the past years over Abram's language or Jafar's deliberate disrespect. Many times their disagreements had almost turned violent and nearly resulted in a punch being thrown.

"Tell me, Abram, do you believe your friendship with the son of a prince will save you forever? Or the fact that the unpaid funds owed to the land of Mustafa can only return at your inheritance assures your safety from those who suspect your depravities?"

His depravities. What a damned joke. He enjoyed a good whiskey, a beautiful woman, and on occasion he was prone to enjoy watching his lover become a willing sensual feast for not just him, but a third as well.

Those were his depravities.

"Friendships rarely stand when you need them to, Jafar. I believe we're both aware of that." He stared back at his cousin mockingly.

Jafar's lips thinned. "I knew nothing of Lessa's crimes, nor did I know of the plans to punish her." It wasn't the first time he had denied the knowledge, and it wasn't the last time Abram would accuse him of it.

Because he knew his cousin had to have at least suspected.

"Nevertheless, I vowed I would never again have to depend upon those I call friends to aid me," Abram informed him. "That is a commodity that only a fool can expect."

Better Jafar believe to the bone that Abram expected no help from anyone should the religious police decide to actually take action against him for his suspected *depravities,* especially the son of a prince, the government contact in charge of investigating the terrorists taking over the Mustafa lands and focusing their attention on Paige Galbraithe.

Until he learned Azir's plans for her, he couldn't rest. And so far, he hadn't been able to learn anything except that Azir was definitely planning something.

Abram would take them all down to keep her safe. Jafar, Azir, the son of a prince, he'd see them all laying in the dust if that was what it took to keep the evil infecting his father from touching her.

"I'm busy, Jafar," he finally stated. He fought to push back his anger as he moved to pass his cousin once again.

"Abram." Jafar stopped him again as he moved to enter the castle.

"What do you want, Jafar?" he questioned impatiently, his teeth clenching at the anger he couldn't seem to stop from surging through him.

"Do you remember when we were sixteen and I caught you and that American student you were friends with at the whore's apartment?"

Abram's lips thinned. "She was no whore, Jafar."

They had been in America visiting with cousins who had lived in D.C. Abram had met up with friends of Khalid's and from there, had done his best to enjoy the time there rather than involving himself with a family that had escaped years before.

"She was taking two men into her body at the same time," Jafar reminded him mockingly. "In any culture, she is called a whore."

"Only in this one," Abram snarled. "Now tell me what you want."

"Answer me first," Jafar told him. "Do you remember?"

"I remember," Abram snapped. "Now what does it have to do with anything?"

Jafar's lips thinned. "I warned you about bringing your hungers from America to your home," Jafar reminded him. "And you brought them not just to your home, but to your wife."

"Don't make me kill you, Jafar." Even now, more than ten years later, the memory of what had happened to Lessa had the power to enrage him.

"Don't make me have to deal with the religious police, Abram," Jafar warned him in return. "Keep your depravities under control. The battle we are involved in together, I prefer to win fairly."

"There is no battle," Abram assured him seriously, and as far as he was concerned, there wasn't one. There would never be one.

Once Abram had achieved his objectives, then he was gone. If he hadn't found a way to keep Paige safe from his father before the king's emissary arrived, then he would simply take her and disappear until the bastard's death.

"There is always a battle between us, Abram," Jafar retorted. "And I am impatient. I may refuse to wait until the battle between you and your father has ended before I begin pushing for my own triumph."

Abram's lips thinned as he stared back at his cousin, attempting to figure out just what the hell he was talking about.

"There is no battle between us, Jafar," he told him again.

Jafar chuckled. "Tell that lie to the present your father has acquired for your early birthday present, my friend. Then tell me how you're going to survive the means he has acquired to win this war that wages between you. And I tell you once again, remember well the warning I gave you when we were sixteen, because I may not give you fair warning in time to save you from the consequences of your own sins."

Abram felt ice race up his spine at Jafar's words as the other man smirked back at him.

It wasn't possible. God help him, he'd done everything he could, used every contact he had to ensure he had warning before it happened, not after.

Fury began burning in the back of his head, engulfing his senses as he stared into Jafar's eyes and read the truth there.

Tension radiated through his body. His muscles began to tighten as though in preparation for a fight, his fists clenching in rage. A hard, warning sizzle began at the base of his brain as the red at the edges of his vision began to darken and push forward.

Murderous, all-consuming rage washed over him.

"What has he done?" he snarled back at his cousin.

Jafar's gaze flashed with what could have been a momentary regret before hatred filled the pale green orbs once again.

"What he always does," Jafar answered him. "He's plotted your destruction. Though, this time it may well be your final one."

5

She couldn't believe this.

There wasn't a single article of clothing to be found in any of the four armoires arranged around the stone room. There were sheets, throws, there were even pillows. But there wasn't a single shirt, pair of pants, or even a pair of socks . . . Would socks have been out of the damned question?

This was completely ridiculous. The least they could have done was left her something to wear.

Tucking the silk sheet between her breasts, she propped her hands on her hips and stared around the dim, sun-dappled room with a frown and narrowed eyes.

Her mother had never really said much about this room, other than it had belonged to Azir's first wife, Abram's mother, Shahla, as Azir had named her. Her actual name, as she had told Marilyn, had been Anna Bailey. She'd been on vacation in Saudi Arabia with her family. Her father had been an executive for one of the oil companies.

Paige's mother had contacted Anna Bailey's family as soon as she had been able to, but they seemed reluctant to believe her, or to do anything to rescue their daughter.

Pavlos had checked into it for the woman he still intended to marry, and learned that when Anna had been kidnapped, her father had received a large deposit to his account to cover excess gambling debts.

Marilyn had always suspected Anna's family had sold her, or perhaps accepted the payment to stop searching for their daughter and accusing the Saudi government of covering up her disappearance.

Both Anna Bailey and the French-born tourist Marilyn Girard would have been forgotten had it not been for Pavlos Galbraithe's determination to find his fiancée, and Marilyn's stubbornness in not giving up her plans to escape.

But, by the time Pavlos had put together a team willing to breach the fortress and rescue Anna and her son, Azir had killed her. According to Abdul at the time, Azir had strangled her to death in her own bedroom, in front of her three-year-old son, after dragging them both back from an escape attempt.

Abdul had recounted to her parents and to Khalid how the young Abram had screamed and even then, fought to free himself from the wooden crib he had been placed in. How the moment his mother had dropped to the ground, lifeless, he had stopped screaming, stared at her, then slowly sat down in his bed, lifted his eyes to his father, and simply stared back at him.

Now, more than thirty years later, Abram was still attempting to stand between his father and a woman Azir was trying to kill.

Where the hell was he now? She could use a little rescuing herself.

He had to be here somewhere. There was no doubt in her mind this was the Mustafa fortress on the Iraqi border. She hadn't been kidnapped and sold, she had simply been kidnapped by a madman. Didn't that just round out her week.

Turning, she walked back to the middle of the room where she stood looking around once more, trying to find something that would at least make her feel as though she were trying to escape.

As she started to move toward one of the armoires again, the wide, heavy wooden door was thrown open, a breeze surging past her. She stared at the apparition that entered with a nightmarish vision of terror.

The sense that this couldn't be happening almost overwhelmed her. It had to be a dream.

Azir Mustafa swept into the room, his black eyes locked on her, his desert-dark face worn and creased with bitter lines. The long white thobe, the loose, ankle-length garment mostly worn in the Middle East seemed to ripple around his broad, overweight body. The ghutra, or keffiyeh, the large white square cloth secured to his head by a black cord, swept out behind him only to reverse direction and swirl around him as he came to an abrupt stop. He stared back at her as though mesmerized.

His eyes appeared dazed and damp. His expression filled with deepening hope as he watched her carefully, as though frightened she would disappear at any moment.

He lifted a shaking hand as though to touch her from a more than ten-foot distance, before he let it fall limply back to his side.

"Marilyn," he whispered, his lips trembling as he took a step forward, bemusement and mesmerism slackening his expression. "You stayed so young, Marilyn. And I have grown so old. What trick is this that you return to me, the same as you left?"

Paige gripped the sheet between her breasts and stepped back, her eyes narrowing at the proof of Azir's weakening sanity. He thought she was her mother.

"I'm not Marilyn." Paige informed him cautiously. She didn't look that much like her mother.

"Marilyn," he whispered again. "My precious Marilyn. Why did you leave? Why did you corrupt my sons?" Pain, bitter and filled with a little boy's confusion, he watched her with tears in his eyes. "Did I not love you above all others? Did I not whisper my love to you each time I held you?"

Paige inhaled sharply. Her mother had said Azir was insane, even when he was younger. Paige had always argued that it wasn't insanity, it was criminal arrogance. Now, she wondered if her mother hadn't been right all along. It was obvious the man had some serious, delusional issues.

The crazed belief that filled Azir's face as he stared at her wasn't in the least bit comforting. He truly believed that somehow, Marilyn had returned to him.

Paige moved back another step as Azir came forward

the same distance. She felt like a mouse being toyed with by a very large cat, and she had no hole to hide in.

"Come to me, Marilyn." His expression tightened in anger as she kept retreating. "Do not test my anger, beloved. You know you will lose and I will feel remorse for the need to punish you. You are my wife. You may not refuse me."

He actually thought she was going to let him touch her? If he was playing a game, then he was doing a damned good job of it. And if he wasn't, then he was far crazier than anyone suspected and she was in a hell of a lot more trouble than she had imagined.

"There's been a mistake," she stated warily. "I'm not Marilyn. I'm her daughter, Paige."

Azir stopped and frowned at her, his body poised as though ready to jump on her. He eased back, his eyes narrowing on her before pure, furious hatred snapped into his gaze for a quick second. In the next second, his eyes cleared and he stared around the room as though wondering how he had found himself there.

He turned back to her slowly.

"Paige Galbraithe," he murmured, his rasping voice the sound of a nightmare in her mind. "The daughter of my faithless, adulterous wife and the whore's son that stole her from me. A diseased bastard daughter. You should have been stoned to death at birth."

As he spoke, his voice became louder, harder, and more furious until the enraged tone sounded grating and filled with the very insanity Paige had doubted he suffered from.

Oh, he was insane all right. There was no doubt in her mind now that he *was* bat-shit crazy.

"Mother wouldn't be pleased if you killed me, Azir," she told him with subtle, flippant mockery, as though he might really give a fuck. "She might never come visit you before you die."

"You mock me," he rasped. "No worries, I can have it done whenever I please. It is a matter easily taken care of. The sins of the mother become the responsibility of the daughter."

She couldn't believe this. It was a nightmare. He was past insane.

"I've committed no sin." Her fingers tightened on the sheet as his gaze flicked to her breasts then back to her eyes. She actually felt dirty from the look.

"Your mother did, that's enough." He smiled almost pleasantly. Pretty much crazily. "I could have you dragged to the courtyard and stones would be battering your weak body within minutes. I could take that very pretty face, so much like your mother's, and I could crush it." His hand lifted, his fingers snapping into a fist in emphasis.

She could see the rage in his eyes and in his face. He was flushed with it, his gaze becoming demented with it. There was a need glittering in his eyes to hurt her, to destroy her. He looked at her and he saw the mother, not the daughter. But he also saw what he called her mother's sins. Hell, she wasn't going to win here.

Strange, her horoscope hadn't mentioned to beware of crazy kidnappers or demented desert sheikhs this week.

If Abram didn't get here, really fast, then she was going to be in a hell of a lot more trouble than she could pull herself out of on her own. Maybe. It was kind of hard to find options that involved being dressed in nothing but a very expensive, very soft sheet.

It was apparent Azir thought he could punish the daughter because the mother had escaped him. And she didn't doubt he had all intentions of doing just that.

Marilyn Girard had escaped and taken his three-month-old son, and she had married another man and had a child by him as well. Paige was that child, and as he stared at her, she realized he could easily choke the life right out of her and never regret it. He could happily throw her to whomever would stone her, and feel nothing but cheerful glee as each heavy blow broke her body further.

Oh God, where was Abram?

"You have her eyes," Azir said as he stilled once again, his head tilting to the side to stare back at her with an odd smirk. "Eyes that mesmerize a man and fill him with the desire to do nothing but possess you."

"It could be indigestion. Trust me, possessing me is a very bad idea. It could be considered really irritating I've been told," she suggested brazenly, certain she was going to die at any moment, but she would be damned if she would go down without a fight.

She would not give this old, vicious monster the satisfaction of seeing her cry, or beg. Unless it hurt too badly. She might beg then, she thought irrationally. Anything was possible.

The shark's smile that curled his lips was filled with a pure, cruel menace as his expression turned mocking, threatening.

"Speak to me with such disrespect again and I will have your tongue sliced from your mouth before you have the chance to beg my son to aid you," he warned her, his monstrous voice grating with savage anticipation. "I will ensure he does not endure the disrespect of the daughter as I did the mother."

Okay, no more disrespect. She liked her tongue in her mouth, thank you very much.

She stared back at him silently, certain there had to be a weakness she could exploit to at least survive until she found a way to run.

Running beat standing here and waiting for him to choke her to death as he had Abram's mother.

"You know my son don't you, my dear? Both of my sons, actually. One is your brother, and what would the other be to you, I wonder?" He chuckled insidiously. "Are you a whore as your mother is? Do you lie down and spread your legs for any dog that would hump between them as well as the friends he would bring with him? Do you lie between two as easily as you would with one?"

The vulgarity of the insult had her eyes narrowing as anger began to swirl and tighten into pure fury. She bit her tongue until she thought she might bite through it as easily as the knife he had threatened to slice it off with.

She really didn't want to lose her tongue, and she had no doubt he wasn't dead fucking serious about the threat, but dammit, that was her mother.

"And your *brother*." He sneered. "His perversions infected my heir and my home until Abram gave to him the virtuous wife he had married. She spread her legs for them together and spoke such filth that she desecrated the marriage bed she was given."

Khalid was her brother. He pissed her off regularly, but she would die for him. If Azir kept this up, she would be losing her tongue for certain.

She stepped back cautiously as he took another step forward, his fists clenching and unclenching spasmodically as she breathed in deeply.

"Azir, this isn't a good idea." She was wasting her breath and she knew it. "Come on, I know many of your nephews and nieces. Several of your king's great granddaughters are friends of mine. Protests are already being filed with your government over this, if I know my parents and if Abram finds out you harmed me, he won't be happy, and you know Khalid will go crazy on you."

She could see the hatred in Azir's face as she said his son's name. Khalid had killed his two sons, but only to protect himself as well as Marty when they attacked him in his home.

Paige watched him warily as she tried to maneuver closer to the door, only to have him block her attempt to slide around a chaise and run for the exit.

He smiled in anticipation.

"If you die, then he will not risk God's displeasure, nor the retaliation of the Matawa for his perversions with you," he murmured. "You were seen, spreading your thighs, speaking the filth and begging for more."

She flushed, not in shame or in embarrassment, but in anger. Maybe, if she screamed for Abram, he would hear her? But if he were that close, he would have been here.

"Tell me, Paige, how is my bastard, traitorous son and his whore doing these days?" His lips curled in disgust. "I was actually surprised his brother Abram wasn't present in the bed with him and his little Jezebel, rather than that ineffective agent to your FBI that was fucking her instead."

How in God's name did Azir know these things?

Shane Conner, the FBI agent, was Khalid's third, that was the truth. He was also working with Daniel Conover's security firm to upgrade the electronic security on Khalid's estate.

But Azir's men hadn't managed to kidnap her from Khalid's estate.

Oh yeah, that's right, she was too fucking stupid to stay there. Azir's men had caught her in her own home.

Azir knew things that were going on in that house that no one should have known about. Shane Connor's role as Khalid's third wasn't a well-known fact, even among the few friends Paige knew they had, who shared that little sexual taste.

"You're not answering me." Malice flashed in Azir's face. "Did your mother not teach you to respect your elders, you little bitch? Or did she only teach you to be the whore she is as well?"

"My mother is no whore!" The words jumped from her lips as though they had a mind of her own.

He could have her tongue at this point. She wouldn't stand to hear her mother called such names. "I did not ask your opinion on whether or not she was the whore we both know she is. I asked you how that bastard brother and his Jezebel are doing. A simple enough request I thought, or are you too stupid to understand even that much?"

"Sorry, I don't know a bastard brother or anyone

called Jezebel." Brief. To the point. She had to fight the need to tell the dirty son of a bitch exactly where he could get off at.

His lips twisted in satisfaction. "Punishing you will be a pleasure."

"I have no doubt you'll find it the highlight of your old and wasted life," she muttered. "So why don't you tell me why I'm here rather than threatening me all day?"

He grunted at what she considered a very clear order.

"What of the less than charming Mr. Connor? Is he still fucking Khalid's trash up the ass or has he fulfilled his depravity and Khalid's, by actually taking Khalid like the animals they both are?" Azir watched her like a hungry wolf.

Paige could feel a chill of dread race up her spine as her skin crawled with distaste at the lustful interest in his gaze. Each time he mentioned Khalid and Shane sharing Marty, or any reference to their sexual activities, hunger flashed across his face.

She shook her head warily. "You must have the Shane Connor I know confused with someone else, not to mention the Khalid and Marty I know. Are you sure you haven't been sniffing the camel glue a little too often?"

Azir snorted sarcastically, his lips curling in disgust. "I should have killed him and his whoring mother when I had the chance. When I realized she was as faithless as the wind."

"All women are just whores to you, aren't they, Azir?" Good common sense was overridden by the continued insults to her gentle, compassionate mother.

Despite the time she had been locked in these rooms, raped nightly and forced to conceive the child of her rapist, still, she had adored her son and lavished him with love, just as she had her daughter.

"Your mother is a whore," he snarled. "She shares herself as her son shares the diseased flesh of his women. She corrupted my son's mind and his soul and turned him into a depraved animal."

"After you kidnapped and raped her, and forced her to marry you I'd say you're the monster and the animal, not my mother or my brother," Paige retorted scathingly. She could practically feel the knife against her tongue now.

"Your father stole what was mine. He is the kidnapper, the criminal. From my very home he tore my wife from my arms and turned her against me." He raged, his arms lifting, fingers curling to fists as he brought them to his chest as though in supplication. "Do you not understand what they did to me? To my child? They destroyed us."

"She was running for her life when my uncle and my father found her," she argued desperately. "She risked death to escape you, Azir. No one had to tear her from your arms because she had already done it for herself. She risked her life and that of her baby to get away from you, Mustafa!"

Hatred.

It was like a disease.

It overrode terror just enough to keep her from shutting her mouth and being prudent. Her temper was getting the best of her. It was her curse. She was a nice person, she really was, until someone ignorant decided to force that ignorance in her face, and then she just couldn't hold back.

"She belongs to me!" he screamed, his eyes widening, becoming crazed as he surged forward before she could escape him.

He caught her off guard as he backhanded her with what she was certain had to be the full force he possessed. It was enough force to make her feel as if the blow had disintegrated every bone in her head.

Lights exploded before her eyes as she felt herself all but fly across the room to collapse against the stone floor. Her head was ringing with a thousand cymbals, her gaze dizzy as she lost her breath. She felt herself trying to pass out from the coppery taste of her own blood.

The taste filled her mouth, and in a distant, horror-filled part of her mind Paige realized that this was the first time in her life that she had ever been struck.

"You are a disrespectful little harlot, just as your mother was. But she learned her place, and you will learn yours. Or you will die as I should have killed her."

He stood over her, raging down at her like a maniac.

"She escaped you though, didn't she?" She wheezed as she fought to breathe through the pain, her arms shaking as she tried to brace them under her. "She hates you, Azir. She hates you so much she'd kill you herself if she could."

If she was going to die, then she would be damned if she wouldn't inflict just as many insults as she could drag out of her ringing, pain-dazed mind.

"I could break you!" He sounded like a wild animal as she tried to focus on him. "I should show you how easy it is to break a little whore such as yourself. I could make you beg to die. Beg to call your mother a whore to her face just to make the pain cease."

"I'd kill myself first," she snarled back at him. She tried to brace herself against the floor, her arm losing strength and giving up on her as she fell to the floor once again.

A second later vicious fingers were curling into her hair, dragging her to her knees as she screamed.

Her struggles were weak, ineffective. She hadn't managed to get her bearings from that blow yet or the agonizing pain still roiling through her senses, and the strength was just slow returning, she told herself.

She could feel the knotted sheet between her breasts slipping. Suddenly, the knowledge that she would be naked before him seemed as bad as being raped by him. Someone had already undressed her, that violation was enough. She sure as hell had no intention of allowing him to see her again, while she was conscious.

She struggled to grip the sheet and hold it to her as Azir, gripping her arms, jerked her to her feet and began shaking her viciously. Her head jerked dangerously on her shoulders as she tried to dig her nails into his arms, but she was weak and dizzy.

"I trained that little bitch, just as I'll train you."

With the last word she felt the strength gather in his arms and a second later he had flung her away from him. Hard.

She wasn't going to be able to break her fall.

Paige braced herself as she lost her grip on the sheet. This one was really going to hurt and there was no way to stop it.

Hell, she was going to be naked in front of Azir Mustafa.

A sob tore from her throat as she felt herself flying. Fear struck every nerve in her body a millisecond before her flight abruptly ended.

Strong hands caught her, pulling her against a hard, warm body as the sheet was simultaneously straightened around her nakedness.

Abram!

Her fingers curled against his arm, feeling the softness of cotton over his flesh as he held her to him, the warmth of his body wrapping around her.

He was here. Finally. He hadn't really deserted her. Could he control Azir? How long would it take him to get her a T-shirt and jeans? Panties would be nice. She didn't like running around without her drawers.

Fractured thoughts continued to race through her mind as her senses spun violently.

"Are you okay, precious?" He held her against him, his head bending to whisper gently at her ear, his voice rough with rage and regret as she tried to lift her head, which felt as if it were teetering on her shoulders.

Hysterical amusement threatened to escape in a gale of laughter as she tried to hold her head straight. "Make the room stop moving, Abram." She blinked back at him. "This sucks."

"It's okay, baby." His voice was a gentle murmur. "I promise you, everything's going to be okay. I want you to go with Tariq for now, though. He'll take care of you until I'm finished here. Will you do that, Paige? Go with Tariq, sweetheart."

"No! I want to go home." Her fingers curled demandingly into the long, cotton tuniclike shirt he wore as she forced her eyes to focus, forced herself to find whatever little strength was left in her legs. "Call Khalid or Papa. They'll come for me." She wasn't about to stay here a moment longer than she had to. "This is insane. Get me out of here."

Her vision was finally clearing, the dizzying blurriness slowly evaporating to focus on the tormented, tortured expression on his face.

Black eyes glowed in feral rage as his face seemed curved from stone into lines of brutal disillusionment.

"Go with Tariq, first, Paige." He gripped her arms and eased her from him before moving her in Tariq's direction.

"No. I won't leave you alone with him." She stared up at him, seeing the pain in his eyes, the grief in his face, and she knew he had to be inconsolable with rage. She couldn't leave him alone with this madman. "What if it's contagious?"

His gaze turned back to hers, a subtle glimmer of bemusement glowing in the wicked, night dark depths. "What is contagious, hellcat?"

"His insanity," she whispered back at him, at once hearing the ludicrous suggestion, yet the need to make light of the situation couldn't be fought. That was her. Take it seriously and she could end up sharing Abram's fate herself. Azir Mustafa could drive a saint crazy, she guessed. And poor Abram, he lived with the old bat.

He had to hate this. This place, this room, it wasn't Abram. The way he was dressed, the expression on his face, it wasn't the man she knew. He would never countenance abusing a woman, or kidnapping one.

He was as arrogant as the wind itself, as the very desert that raised him, but he wasn't the vicious monster his father obviously was.

"I'm certain it's not contagious," he promised. "But go with Tariq for now. I'll take care of everything and I'll join you soon."

"You beg a whore to do as you ask?" Azir cracked behind her. "How you have fallen, my son."

Paige refused to glance back at him, rather she continued to stare up at Abram, willing him to leave with her, to refuse to risk himself in his father's demented company.

"Now," his voice was nearly silent, but there was no mistaking the dark command that filled it. "Go with Tariq."

Tariq Mustafa. She knew him. There were times he had come to America with Abram and visited with Khalid and her family. He had smiled. He had "almost" flirted a time or two, but Abram and Khalid's displeasure had been clearly apparent.

This time though, his expression was hard, cold, as though he had no idea who she was. There wasn't so much as a glimmer of recognition as he took her from Abram.

Her lips thinned, her displeasure unable to hide. He had no business lingering here when they needed to make plans. When they needed to get her out of Saudi Arabia.

"Come on." Tariq wasn't flirting with her this time as she forced the strength in her legs to walk to the door.

He acted as though he didn't know her, as though he had never met her. And she would find out why the minute Abram joined them.

Abram watched as Tariq drew Paige from the room, eased her around the doors and led her up the hall to his suite. Dark, emerald green eyes stared back at him, defiance and anger reflecting in her gaze before she disappeared.

He turned back to Azir, though God knew he didn't want to. He could feel the killing rage rising inside him, threatening the control it had taken so many years to develop.

For a moment he wondered if she could be right, if the Mustafa legacy of blood, death, and insanity, wasn't actually a contagion that infected each generation after the other.

Staring at his father, he felt nothing but the overwhelming hatred that he was in danger of allowing to spill from the depths of his soul.

He stared at his father, and he saw nothing but the ragged, agonizing pain his first wife had felt as she died, the fear of his second wife as she died with their unborn child, and his own fear when he had learned that Paige's life was in danger.

"She's the very image of her mother, isn't she?" Azir stated calmly, as though he hadn't just been throwing that vision across the room with enough strength to kill her if her head were to strike the floor when she fell.

The calm, almost rational tone of his voice only incited the icy rage burning inside Abram.

"Why is she here?" He could only barely force a semblance of calm in his voice.

Azir smiled. A mocking, triumphant curve of his lips as he stared back at Abram.

"She is my insurance, my son, and the gift I would grant you for your birthday. Tell me, do you think her mother is worried? Perhaps certain who has taken her daughter and imagining the many ways I could make her suffer for her mother's crimes?"

The pleasure Azir clearly felt at the thought of the pain only a mother could feel filling Marilyn Galbraithe, sickened Abram.

"I will be returning her home—" he began.

"Then she will die." Azir's voice hardened, becoming gravely and tinged with anger. "The moment you leave the walls of the fortress with her then the guards will haul her back and I'll have her stoned for her mother's crimes. She is no virgin. She was checked for such innocence as she lay unconscious. Convincing the Matawa to order the stoning will be no hardship."

Abram stared back at his father in shock and disbelief. Surely even Azir wasn't that insane. To take such an action would only cause the royal family to be forced to take action against them.

"Don't do this," he ground out, his fists clenching, adrenaline surging through him and demanding blood. Azir's blood. And he would be well within his rights to spill it. He should simply do it. How much better the world would be without Azir Mustafa's presence. "She's done nothing to deserve this."

"But her mother has," Azir snapped back, his grating tone rasping against Abram's nerve endings. "She committed adultery against me in her false marriage to another man. She stole my son and turned his heart against me even as she and her American courts ripped from me my right to have him returned to me."

Azir's expression twisted with fanatical fury. "My precious Marilyn. She turned Khalid against me, and because of him, you have turned against me. I blame her for the atrocities Khalid has committed against God in his sexual depravity and I blame her for the deaths of your brothers. And her daughter will now pay the price." He was screaming. Staring back at Abram, the rage infecting not just his sanity, but also his control over himself.

"They were no brothers of mine!" As far as Abram was concerned, this was the last straw for Azir. He would never again claim blood relation to Azir or to the bastards who nearly killed him and Khalid. The same two men had created the situation Abram now found himself in. "Had they still lived when I claim the province from the King's emissary, then I would have ordered their deaths myself."

Azir glared back at him, his expression working furiously, his face brick red with fury. The old bastard had never been rational where Ayid and Aman were concerned, no more than he had been rational where Marilyn was concerned. Rational or sane.

"You and Khalid were responsible for the deaths of their wives and still you would hate them for their retaliation?" Azir questioned him incredulously, as though he himself had had nothing to do with their vocation or their wrath. "They lost what they held dearest. Chaste, faithful wives and you bemoan a whore who willingly shared her body between you and Khalid as though she were no more than a bitch dog in heat? I should have turned the two of you over to the Matawa the moment I discovered your perversion instead of believing that you would learn your lesson with your wife's death."

Abram felt the clawing, black ice he continually fought beginning to build, to overtake him. That dark, inner core freezing over, obliterating honor, morality. He stared at Azir and all he could see was the bastard's blood on the floor, sinking in, staining the stone and forever marking his sins.

How easy it would be to kill him, Abram thought without so much as a hint of guilt. But killing him now would only cause more problems than it would fix.

He was aware of Azir watching nervously now. Abram could only stare, his entire being centered on not killing the evil old bastard.

He couldn't trust himself to speak, to move. Not just yet. Not until he could wipe away the image of his hands wrapped around Azir's throat, his bloated, fanatical expression slowly turning blue.

"Forgive me, Abram." Azir suddenly spoke nervously as though realizing how close to death he was coming. "That was never an option. Never would I see you turned over to the authorities."

Too little. And he would have preferred that if only he could have kept Lessa safe all those years ago.

"In three weeks the king's emissary will arrive to take your vow to oversee the lands and return to our family the payments they froze so many years ago. Before that day, I give you leave to bed the daughter of my faithless wife. Her bastard child is my gift to you until that day. I have spoken with Tariq and given him leave, nay, I have ordered him to assist you however you wish in the enjoyment of her corrupt body. Once you have given the emissary your vow, you may escort her back to her mother, or if you so choose, you may have her as the first addition to your own harem."

To his harem?

Abram could feel his stomach recoiling sickeningly. In what demented fantasy did his father ever believe he would actually give that vow and remain here to allow Ayid and Aman's legacy to continue to grow?

"Do not betray me again, Abram." Azir's voice was hoarse as he spoke. "Betray your king if you must and leave to join your brother and your whore when it is done. The account is held until your vow is given. It will be mine, or what happened to your precious Lessa will seem a blessing compared to the hell that bastard sister of Khalid's will know. I beg of you, do not test me in this."

If he had to stand here another moment and listen, then he might lose the last hold on his murderous temper.

Turning, Abram stalked from the room Khalid's mother had once shared with his own mother for a short time. His own suite was above it with a private entrance to the secured quarters that had once held Azir's harem.

Abram moved up the stairs with a deliberately calm pace. His fists clenched and unclenched at his sides while the tightening of his teeth actually had his jaw aching with a hard burn from the stress of the pressure.

He needed to regain control. He needed to still the rush of adrenaline and come down from the high of the black icy fury that had filled him while he was with Azir.

He had to do it before he made it to his suite, before he saw Paige.

Because there was another side of the black ice.

There were consequences to the thaw of that icy rage.

And if he didn't get a handle on it, then it would be Paige that felt the full force of it. .

6

The other side of black ice.

Abram had been forced to learn to hold back that killing, murderous rage the day he found his mother beaten to death, and knew it had been Azir's fists that had killed her.

He remembered feeling it. Freezing, like shoving his entire body into an icy black nothingness and forcing himself to stay there rather than trying to find the man he called father to shove the knife his mother had given him straight into his black heart.

How many times over the years had he wished he had done exactly that?

Retribution would have been taken. He would have been punished severely, maybe even killed himself. But had he taken that punishment then so many other lives may have been saved.

The Mustafa lands would have been saved for Abram as Azir's legal heir, and Ayid and Aman would have been sent away to be raised by aunts and uncles who would not have pampered their criminal habits nor risked their own families to aid their terrorist pro-clivities.

That icy nothingness had enveloped him, allowing him to see past the fiery, brutal pain and into the logic of his actions.

Punishment for Azir would be so thorough, so per-fect, if only he could follow through with it. Abram would be free of the land and the land itself would return to the monarchy and be given back to tribal control.

But allowing Azir to live was becoming harder by the day. And today. He stopped as he reached the top of the stairs and stared down at the fist his fingers were still formed into.

Today, he'd almost given in to the impulse.

Today, he had almost become a murderer and God knew that wasn't what he wanted. Not now, not this close to freedom. Because if he killed Azir, the monar-chy would have no choice but to punish him. Jafar and his men, supposed members of the Mustafa family, would eagerly step forward and demand his punishment.

Because Abram had plotted and worked against Jafar and Azir, and even though Khalid had taken responsi-bility for both Ayid's and Aman's deaths, there were those that suspected Abram had killed Aman.

And they would have been right. Fortunately, there were very few who knew the actual truth, but if his half-brother's co-conspirators had a chance to strike out in such a way, they would eagerly take it.

There was no doubt that he had run out of time. He

would have to find a way to get both Paige and Tariq out of Saudi Arabia and into America and take his chances there.

He didn't know what the hell Azir thought he could accomplish by kidnapping Paige and gifting him with her, or by "ordering" Tariq to aid him in whatever manner Abram required in bedding her. One thing was for damned sure, it wasn't out of the kindness of his heart.

More likely, the minute he made his vow to the emissary both Jafar and Azir would have the authorities waiting to arrest him, Paige, and Tariq for sexual misconduct. And that was a killing offense.

Tearing the keffiyeh from his head and bunching it in his hand, he inhaled deeply and moved slowly to the securely locked door of his bedroom suite.

The electronic security was the only defense he possessed in the fortress now. There were less than half a dozen of the men that had once been loyal to him and Tariq. Those men couldn't be identified or step forward publicly if anything happened because of their own families.

He couldn't trust the guards, and he couldn't trust the men he had grown up with, or those he had attended college with who had returned to the Mustafa lands after him.

Throughout his life there had only been Khalid, Tariq, and Paige that he could depend upon to accept him as he was. And two of those, Tariq and Paige, were awaiting him now.

He was moving closer to the door, closer to the woman he hungered for with an irrational strength.

Reaching the door to the suite he keyed in the code

to the security lock, waited for the click to indicate the locks had disengaged, then stepped inside.

The other side of black ice.

The second he closed the door it kicked in.

The black ice was cracking and burning inside him, heat whipping through his body as fiery, burning lust sizzled through the dark emotionless protective layer.

In a single, blinding second the adrenaline switched gears. Murder wasn't an option, but sex was.

He couldn't squeeze the life from Azir's corrupt body, but he could allow Paige's tight, hot little pussy to squeeze the release from his dick.

Paige was there.

Lush.

Exotic.

Sensual.

With the sheet still her only covering, she was curled at the corner of the couch as Tariq sat in the chair opposite her. He leaned forward, his entire demeanor protective.

Long, silken, red-gold curls cascaded around the bruised side of her face. The abraded, darkening flesh almost had him turning around and completing the murderous act, imagining Azir gasping for air as his eyes began to glaze in death.

Emerald green eyes stared back at him in defiance, and always, always, in hunger. In that instant, just that fast, his cock was brutally hard, the need to fuck thundering through his body with a force nearly double what the drive to kill had been.

This was the fallout. The other side of the brutal ice-encased fury was this overwhelming, desperate need to push every sexual boundary. To make his lover touch that point between pleasure and pain. To fuck her until none of them could move. And once his third had caught his breath, to begin again.

And there was Paige. The object of every sexual fantasy he'd had since she had turned eighteen. The one woman he knew he should never touch.

He was going to touch her.

He was going to touch her in ways that would shock her, that would send her juices spilling hot and sweet from the swollen folds of her cunt.

"Abram?" Tariq rose warily to his feet. "Is the situation being resolved?"

Will Paige be sent home? Abram could see the question in the other man's gaze. The worry and the concern. Oh yes, they both knew what Azir was doing, and they were going to have to figure out a way to put a stop to it.

"I may need a third," Abram answered, his gaze on Paige as her eyes widened in shock.

She knew what he meant, and she knew exactly what he was going to need.

She didn't protest though, and she didn't argue, she just stared back at him, wide-eyed and silent.

And hungry.

Oh hell yes, he glimpsed the sensual, sexual need that darkened her eyes and flushed her face and breasts.

They had been dancing around this since the day she turned eighteen. He had stayed as far away from her as possible rather than introducing her to a hunger, a passion that he feared she wasn't ready for. And now, there was simply no way to save her from it.

"Leave," he ordered Tariq, his tone guttural.

It was an order Tariq was expecting. Abram was going to need a third, but this first time, this first touch, was all his. He shared his lovers, but still, he was a possessive bastard. He secured their affection as well as their arousal before he ever brought his third into the bed.

He waited, listening as Tariq strode across the room, opened the door, and stepped out.

He would be going no farther than his own room across the stone hall in case he was needed.

Paige's fingers tightened on the sheet as though she feared he would jerk it away from her.

"Abram?" She questioned when he didn't say anything.

She rose slowly to her feet, facing him, not just with a hint of wariness but also a blaze of need that rivaled his own.

God help him, he hadn't wanted it to come to this. Not here, and definitely not now.

"You and Khalid shared Lessa, didn't you?" she asked when he said nothing for several moments.

"We shared Lessa," he admitted. "And that is a subject we don't need to discuss tonight, Paige. Tonight, there is only us."

And he believed that explanation was all she had to hear? She let her lips curl into a mocking, defiant smile. "You asked Tariq to be your third, Abram. I'm not a child, and I'm not completely ignorant of your sexual lifestyle. Don't think you're going to just push something like this on me and we won't be discussing it."

He grimaced tightly. "This isn't the best time to

discuss anything, Paige," he told her. "And I notice you're not refusing." His brow arched. "Do you think I'm not very well aware of the fact that if you weren't dying for it then you'd put me in my place so fast it would make both our heads spin?"

At least he knew a few of her incredibly talented abilities.

She stared back at him warily though. Abram could never be accused of being predictable.

"I'm not ready to allow anyone to touch you but me," he stated. "Before we go further than you and me, we'll discuss it, I promise. But now isn't the time to do it. Now is the time to take that damned sheet off."

"Make me." He was entirely too arrogant for his own good, and if she was going to handle even the most distant relationship with him then she would have to establish her own boundaries quickly.

"What did you say?"

She had heard him though. Shock filled her voice. It widened her eyes again, but her response flushed her face and her nipples were just barely detectable beneath the sheet over her chest.

"Drop the sheet, Paige," he growled, stepping closer to her, unable to keep any distance between them.

He expected a fight. He thought she would curse. He was certain she would rage.

What he didn't expect?

"Kiss my ass," she scoffed. "Why don't you try putting me on a plane home first? Then we'll discuss the subject." A graceful shoulder shrugged as she stared back at him challengingly.

He had known she wouldn't come easy. But that was

just fine. Because he sure as hell never cared much for easy.

"Then I guess I'll just have to remove it myself."

Paige saw the battle raging within the rich black depths of his gaze. The taut expression of his face was primal, sensual. His lips had a more sexual, erotic curve. He suddenly looked like a sex god ready to seduce and ravish.

A sensual, dark aura seemed to suddenly surround them, washing through her senses and sensitizing her, preparing her for his touch.

She'd never felt anything like this at any time. She'd been dating for years. She'd dated some of the most arrogant, most dominant men in the world, but Abram had always had them all beat.

Her hands tightened on the material of the silk sheet between her breasts. His gaze dropped to her fingers as he gripped the clasped ends at the front of his tunic-like robe and pulled at it, parting it to shrug it easily from his powerful shoulders.

Dark, toughened skin stretched over powerful muscles.

He kicked his boots off as he reached for her, then stood, simply staring down at her for long, heated moments.

She expected seduction. Perhaps a bit of teasing. She should have known better.

She didn't expect what was coming. Before she realized his intentions he'd jerked her to him, lifting her, his lips coming down on hers with surprising gentleness. The certain, determined lick of his tongue against the seam of her lips surprised her into parting them. A quick indrawn breath, a wealth of pleasure, and he was inside.

His lips slanted over hers, his head tilting as a moan escaped her throat and Paige knew she was on the losing end of determination this time.

But this was Abram. She couldn't say no to him, she had no idea how to do it.

As his lips and tongue caressed and cajoled, she felt him holding her against him, her feet off the floor as he moved to the huge, silk-covered bed on the other end of the room.

She had to force her eyes open as he laid her back on the bed, his hands catching her wrists as he forced them above her head. Holding her wrists to the mattress, his knee pushed between her thighs, parting them, the soft cotton of his loose trousers caressing the bare skin of her inner legs as he stared down at her with hungry demand. His knee pressed upward against her pussy, rubbing and grinding against her clit.

The strong, heavy muscles were heated as she gripped the sides of his leg and arched to him. Each stroke against the swollen bud made her weaker, made her want to sink into the pleasure and never come up for reality.

She felt her heart racing. Blood thundered through her veins, throbbing in her clit as she struggled against the hold he had on her.

His head lowered once again, his lips careful in case her lips were sore. Thankfully, Azir had backhanded the side of her face, not her lips.

He didn't give her a chance to protest or enough breath to say no, and he made certain she was unable to outright reject him.

Did she want to protest?

Did she want to reject him?

How was she supposed to know? He wouldn't give her a chance to speak or a chance to think. But he let her feel.

Paige moaned, the sound seeming torn from the depths of her soul as his lips rubbed against hers, possessed hers. Licks and nips and his tongue pumping into her mouth, stroking against her tongue and sparring with it as she strained to get closer and to take control of the sumptuous pleasure.

The pleasure. She'd always wanted the pleasure of his touch, the exquisite ecstasy of his kiss. She swore pure white-hot flames were licking at her sensitive flesh and the delicate tips of her tight, hard nipples.

Her clit was swollen, throbbing. She wanted to rub against the power of his heavy thigh, to ease the agony of need pounding at the bundle of nerves.

His kiss was like a drug. It was addicting. She wanted more and he wasn't giving it to her.

Paige struggled against the hold on her wrists. Arching closer to the hard hips settling between hers, she cried out into his kiss as the thick, heavy length of his cock pressed into the folds of her pussy.

"Oh God, yes. Abram, yes, please." Tearing her mouth from his she gasped for breath, her head arching back as she rubbed her clit against the heavy head pressing into it.

He was so hard and hot.

Her pussy creamed heavily, her juices easing along the clenched muscles of her vagina and spilling to the thin, cotton-covered wedge of his cock as his hips rolled against her.

Curling her fingers in pleasure as he continued to re-strain her wrists, Paige lifted one leg, her knee bending to move closer and clasp his hip as he rubbed against her again.

Her thighs clenched and tightened. The hunger for the rising orgasm was building inside her like a flaming conflagration she couldn't control.

And she didn't want to control it. She wanted it to keep racing out of control, to keep burning through her and leaving every inch of her body so sensitive that each touch was rapture.

Forcing her eyes open she stared up at him as his free hand caressed up her side to cup the curve of her swollen breast. The touch of his calloused palm had her nipple tingling almost painfully until the pad of his thumb stroked across it.

"Oh yes," she moaned as sensation raced straight to her womb where it clenched and sent a surge of electric ecstasy racing through her pussy.

Each stroke of the roughened flesh against the tight bud of her nipple was an agony of pleasure. Brilliant streaks of fiery sensation tingled and built until she was arching tighter to him, the thought of his lips and tongue surrounding the peak making her crazy for the feel of it.

"Abram." She could hear the weak plea in her voice now, but she had no idea how to ask for what she needed. How to beg for it.

"Should I stop, love?" he crooned as his head lowered to her shoulder and his tongue licked over it.

Her hips jerked into his, the friction against her clit causing her to moan in building ecstasy.

"No. No, don't stop," she gasped.

"The taste of you is like the finest wine." The sound of his voice, guttural and rough as his lips moved along her neck, her jaw, had her shivering in pleasure.

The sensations were so intense she wondered if she would actually manage to orgasm before he even thrust his cock inside her.

His head moved from her jaw, down her neck again, to the smooth, sensitive flesh above her breasts. She was dying for the touch of his lips against her nipples and he was killing her as he continued to hold that caress from her.

"Abram, please," she begged, her voice raspy.

"Please, precious," he crooned in a dark, black velvet tone. "Please let me touch you. Just for this moment." There was no plea in his tone despite the words.

There was nothing but pure, dominant demand.

One hand still held her wrists, his fingers locked around them to hold her in place. His lips lifted from her upper chest, his black eyes flaming with heated hunger as he stared down at her.

The expression on his face had her hips arching involuntarily, desperate for more now.

She couldn't get enough of him. Each touch had her flesh tingling, aching for more.

The long, powerful fingers cupping her breast lifted it, his gaze holding hers as his head lowered, lips parting, his tongue peeking out to curl around her nipple as his lips met the flushed, swollen flesh.

"Yes," she hissed roughly as she watched, mesmerized by his lips closing on the tip and the feel of his mouth suddenly drawing on it, his tongue rubbing and stroking the nerve-laden tip. "That's so good." She arched again, her back bowing as she pressed her pussy into the heavy heat of his cock. "It's so good in your mouth, Abram. So hot."

She was afraid she was going to come from this alone and she didn't even care. She just wanted to come. She wanted the explosion tearing through her senses and throwing her into a pleasure she knew was going to leave her aching for more.

Sensation was racing to her clit, to her pussy. Her womb clenched hard and tight, rippling with nearing ecstasy as she moaned and fought desperately to get closer to him.

The heated, heavy juices of her arousal were saturating her pussy now, as well as the cotton that covered his leg where it pressed into her.

A cry tore from her as his teeth pressed against the hard nipple, sensitizing it further. He raked them against it, then drew it back, sucked it inside, and licked over it.

The different sensations were killing her with pleasure.

"What are you doing to me?" she gasped. "Oh God, Abram, it's so good. So good."

His head lifted to allow his lips to smooth over her nipple. "I'm pleasuring you, baby," he growled. "And how I've dreamed of pleasuring you."

Paige pushed her head deeper into the pillow behind her as she lifted, trying to get closer.

"I can't think," she cried out. "Let me think."

She wanted to scream, but she couldn't. She couldn't draw in enough oxygen to push the sound free.

As she fought for breath, fought to find a way to think, to consider what she was doing, she felt his hand move from the curve of her breast, his fingers stroking, rubbing, easing slowly down her torso, over her lower stomach, then brushing against the light growth of curls at the top of her sex.

Her fingers curled against his hand as his fingers slid through the slick, saturated slit of her pussy. He parted the swollen folds, the roughened fingertips rubbing and stroking until his fingers found her straining clit, drawing another cry from her lips.

She loved it. Each touch. It was incredible.

It was like little flares of lightning piercing her clit each time he stroked around it, sending flames to caress her pussy.

Her hips jerked, pushing closer, feeling his fingers rake against the opening of her saturated cunt. She could feel her juices, thick and heated as they coated the folds and then his fingers.

The need for more, the need to have his fingers filling her was making her crazy.

"What do you want, Paige?" he groaned, his voice rough. "Tell me, baby, and I'll give it to you."

"You know what I want," she protested weakly.

She couldn't think. She couldn't make sense of the impulses surging through her system.

"Let me hear it," he demanded roughly. "Tell me what you want. How should I touch you?"

She shook her head, imperatively. So many fantasies. She wanted so much, needed so much. How was she supposed to settle for just one touch?

"How sweet and soft your pussy feels, Paige." His

lips moved against her nipples again. "I love the feel of it against my fingers, but I want to feel it on my tongue. The way your juices feel, the tug of your pussy as I fuck my tongue inside you. The feel of you coming on my tongue—"

"Oh God!" She was so close.

She nearly raced over the edge of completion; she was that close, that sensitized.

She wanted to feel his tongue as she felt his fingers now. Licking over her, stroking her past reason.

"Let me touch you." She breathed out roughly. "Let me go, Abram."

"Not yet." His teeth raked against her nipple. "Just take the pleasure, Paige. Just for a minute, sweetheart."

It was too destructive. Being effectively bound, restrained, and touched with devastating results.

"I want to touch too," she demanded roughly.

His fingers waited at the entrance of her sex, two broad, strong digits tucking against the clenched opening as she stilled. She stared up at him and fought to breathe as he began pushing inside the snug depths of her pussy.

Her hips surged upward. The feel of his fingers stretching her, pushing inside her, would have had her screaming in violent pleasure if she could have just breathed.

As his fingers tormented her pussy, thrusting in, stoking an erotic, blazing heat through it, Abram moved his lips to her other breast, found the tight peak of her nipple, and sucked it in.

The alternating sensations, the flashes of electric pleasure surged from her nipple to her clit with each draw of his mouth, from her pussy to the rest of her body with each stroke of the two fingers inside her.

"Lick it," she moaned, needing that particular stroke against her nipple. "Lick it, Abram, just a second."

She wanted to come. She needed to come now.

Her hips arched and rotated, working her pussy on his thrusting fingers as rapid, desperate cries fell from her lips.

His tongue licked over her nipple, rubbed it.

"Don't stop," she moaned, her head thrown back as her hips thrust into his fucking fingers.

"Do you like it, precious? Do you like my fingers fucking inside you? Filling your tight little pussy?" His head lifted, his lips brushing the peak as his fingers stretched and burned her flesh.

With powerful, controlled thrusts his fingers reached inside her, stroking against nerve endings never touched, never pleasured before and sending her senses rioting. They scissored, stretched her, worked inside her. Blinding, elemental sensation tore through so many nerve endings it nearly sent her into sensory overload.

"More . . ." she cried out.

"More what, Paige?" He whispered against her lips as she dragged her lashes open to stare into the burning depths of his eyes.

"Your fingers," she gasped. "Fuck me harder, Abram." She arched, blinding pleasure searing her as she fought to find release. "Please. Please let me come."

She was so close. The need to come was screaming through her now. Her hips jerked, grinding into each thrust, her thighs tightening on the powerful legs holding hers apart as his fingers tortured her.

So close.

She gasped, her breath catching. Whimpers fell from her lips, then a startled, agonizing cry as he pulled back.

Suddenly her wrists were free and before she could do more than cry out his name his shoulders were between her thighs, his mouth on her pussy.

His tongue licked through the sensitive folds, the tip flicking and probing at her clit as she gasped, arched, and felt the flames rising inside her tortured pussy.

If she didn't come she was going to die from the need.

As his lips moved over her clit and surrounded it, his fingers slid against her entrance again, probing, rubbing, the two tormenting digits working inside the slick, juice-laden tissue.

A haze of blinding lust filled Abram's head as his fingers worked inside the velvety tissue as it clamped tightly on his fingers.

Ripples washed over his fingers as the muscles tightened and spasmed on his flesh.

"Abram." She moaned his name, the need in her voice pushing the blinding haze of lust higher and ripping at the control he was fighting to hold onto. "It's so good. Your fingers . . ." Her hips lifted and flexed into each thrust he worked inside the gripping flesh.

Damn, she was hot. Her pussy clamped and sucked at his fingers, as he imagined his cock buried inside the snug, fist-tight flesh.

"Fuck me," she whispered, desperation filling her voice. "Please, Abram, fuck me. Make me come."

For a second, just a few fragile seconds, he lost his grip on his control.

He sucked her clit tighter into his mouth, his tongue

working it, licking against it as his fingers began to thrust deeper, harder, feeling her tighten, then a second later, feeling her explode.

It was the most incredible sensation for him.

Never while pleasuring a woman had he spilled himself to the sheets simply from his lover's pleasure, but as Paige's pussy tightened on his fingers with a strength that had him groaning at the thought of it wrapped around his dick, he couldn't hold back.

As she came, her flesh rippling and clenching, he let his fingertips stroke a tiny spot deep and high inside her pussy, extending her climax and the shudders of release.

With each hard jerk of her body he let her ease down. Slowly, because he wanted to relish it. Drawing it out, because the thought of letting her go was suddenly abhorrent.

Paige's eyes were open, unseeing, dazed. All she was aware of, all she could process was the hard, brilliant flashes of light and pleasure rippling through her. It burned, exploded in flashing points of ecstasy that had her tightening to the breaking point.

She could feel every nerve ending in her body sizzling, burning in rapture.

She gasped, fighting to pull oxygen into her lungs as throaty, ecstatic moans escaped her throat.

She had never known herself to make such sounds. She had never known such pleasure or that pleasure could be so destructive and yet so filled with satisfaction.

As the last pulsing wave of release eased through her body, she blinked, feeling his fingers ease from her as he moved up her body, his chest rising hard and fast with his accelerated breathing, perspiration gleaming on his flesh.

His gaze looked almost satiated, his face flushed. There was a dominant, possessive expression that had her stilling while watching him warily.

"While you're here, until I can get you home, until I can ensure your safety you will stay within this suite. You will sleep in my bed and you *will* belong to me."

Well hell, and here she thought she already did.

But she kept her lips wisely closed and simply stared back at him defiantly, even if she really didn't feel that much defiance.

And her reward?

His gaze flamed with lust again.

His expression tightened with it.

And if she wasn't mistaken his cock was harder, thicker beneath the damp cotton of the loose trousers he still wore.

"Are you on birth control?" Abram asked as Paige pulled on the long, winter-warm gray thobe he had handed her moments before.

The loose dresslike garment flowed around her rather shapelessly but it covered her, and it was warm.

"Paige." He repeated her name, obviously expecting an answer.

Lifting her head she stared back at him, still amazed that she had, less than an hour ago, climaxed in his arms as though she were exploding from the inside out, and he still hadn't fully had sex with her.

"I'm protected," she replied. "I'm the one that can get pregnant, so I'm the one that makes certain it doesn't happen."

"I'll need to have whatever you take collected quickly," he told her. "Give me the name and dosage so I can have Tariq acquire it."

She stared back at him implacably. "You make it

sound as though I'm going to be stuck here indefinitely, Abram."

He moved slowly from the other side of the room, his expression brooding as he watched her, intense. "It may be a while," he finally told her. "And I don't want to take chances."

"I'm not staying here a while." A frown jumped between her brows. "Call someone. Khalid or my father, either one could have a transport here to fly me out within hours."

"And Azir will have you killed the moment he learns that a transport is heading in this direction."

Paige stared back at him miserably. She couldn't risk staying here. God, why had she left Khalid's home?

"Tell me what I need to know, Paige, then we'll fight over the rest of it later."

Her lips thinned. She knew that expression on his face. The hard, steely-eyed expression that assured her he meant exactly what he said.

If she wanted to discuss going home, then she would tell him exactly what he wanted to know.

Once she got home, if he decided to resume whatever started here, then he would have to rethink these stubborn tactics of his.

"I only take the medication once every three months," she finally told him, though she hated the necessity of it. "My last dose was just before your less-than-sane father had me kidnapped."

Crossing her arms over her breasts, she all but stomped to the couch positioned in front of the fireplace and plopped into the amazingly comfortable cushions. That comfort didn't make up for the fact that the Abram she was facing right now was little more than a stranger to her.

"Now, when am I going home?" she questioned him.

"When it's convenient to send you home." He shrugged as though it didn't matter, as though she were there for a friendly visit rather than being brought there forcibly.

"When it's convenient?" she asked him carefully. "And when do you think it might be *convenient* to take care of that little matter?"

"Once I've satisfied my hunger for you?" He tilted his head to the side as he answered her with a question rather than allowing her to know exactly what was going on.

That wasn't like the Abram she knew. Of course, there was always the chance she hadn't known him as well as she thought she had.

"That's not a satisfactory answer, Abram."

His eyes were cool and hard. She hated that look, that impassive, emotionless look so similar to Khalid's. A look that had been honed in the hellish existence where they had fought to survive, here in this foreign desert.

"That's the only answer I have for you at the moment. But I will have some answers from you. How did Azir's men manage to kidnap you?"

Paige crossed her arms over her breasts as she leaned back in the couch and glanced away from him.

"I went home," she finally answered, knowing it was the wrong time to become stubborn.

His expression tightened further, this time in anger.

"Are Khalid and Marty safe?"

She nodded jerkily. "They were at the Conovers'. Tally's party."

He closed his eyes in frustration before wiping his hand over his face and giving his head a brief, hard shake. When he looked at her again, he didn't bother to hide the anger heating inside him.

"You were told to stay safe." He growled as the irritation rose. "What happened, Paige? Don't try to tell me Khalid attempted to throw you out either."

Paige wanted to laugh at the comment, but the expression on his face didn't exactly invite amusement.

Instead, she dropped her arms, her hands clenching into the the couch cushions as she leaned forward, her own anger surging inside her.

"Do you realize I've lost my job because of this mess?" she snapped back at him. One hand lifted to wave at his room to emphasize the situation. "I haven't worked in over two weeks now, I have bills to pay and responsibilities to meet. Do you think I was meeting those responsibilities by playing the cowering puppy at my brother's home? Do you think my landlord is going to just nicely wait for me to pay my rent?"

"Since when did your parents refuse access to your trust fund, Paige?" His tone was chillingly uncompromising and unforgiving.

It was her own fault she had been taken and she knew it; she wasn't trying to claim otherwise. But he made her feel about two inches tall and responsible for the fall of the modern world with that look and tone.

"I didn't say it was the smartest idea I'd ever had," she burst out furiously. "But for God's sake, Abram, it had been two weeks. Khalid and I were at each other's throats and starting to go for blood. I just wanted to go home long enough to figure out how to handle him and his insistence on running my life."

"And that did you how much good?" He grunted irritably as he shot her a look of complete male frustration. "You were being protected and you insisted on leaving that protection. Now you can settle in here for the next three weeks and twiddle your thumbs until I can send you home."

She stared back at him in shock. "Abram, I can't stay here for three weeks," she whispered. "I have to go home."

"Khalid will take care of your bills and any problems that arise, and I'm certain he'll have a nice little discussion with the owner of the company you worked for so you can return. You have no choice but to cooperate here, Paige. Attempting to make me feel guilty for your situation will do you no good."

"You could send me home," she retorted angrily.

"If I could send you home I'd have you on a transport now," he snapped back as anger flashed across his face. "Unfortunately, that isn't possible at the moment, trust me on this."

Her lips thinned as she glared back at him. "Then let me call Papa. He'll come get me."

"Oh, there's a good idea." His smile was tight and hard. "Let's call Pavlos Galbraithe and have him arrive to antagonize Azir further." His bark of laughter was filled with sarcasm. "I can see that one working out well."

So, maybe that wasn't the wisest course of action, but staying here for three weeks wasn't acceptable either, not when old man Mustafa was bouncing around the place trying to find his little lost Marilyn.

The thought of it was sickening.

It sickened her and God only knew how her mother was feeling at the moment.

Raking her fingers through her hair she stared back at Abram in frustration, wondering where the heated, hungry lover of earlier had gone.

With that thought came another. Why, once she'd come until she thought she was going to die, hadn't he taken her fully and achieved his own release?

"Do I have your agreement to behave?" he asked her.

"I agree to follow the rules I know about." She shrugged. "But I think you know this is going to suck."

"Sucking or not, that's the way it is," he informed her, his voice as hard as the black onyx of his gaze. "And sucking beats dying, wouldn't you say?"

She had to look away from him.

She couldn't imagine how he had survived within this world. He was a man who enjoyed tastes, textures, touch, and laughter. She couldn't imagine there was much of a chance of those things existing in the cold, stone confines of this fortress.

Crossing her arms she rubbed at them, trying to bring a little warmth back to her body as a chill raced through her.

"Why did he do this?" she finally asked, wondering why his father would take a vendetta to this extreme.

"To punish Khalid for killing Ayid and Aman, no matter how they deserved it." Regret and guilt flashed across his gaze. "To punish your mother for escaping and in an attempt to find something or someone that he believes is my weakness."

"And of course, I'm no weakness of yours, am I, Abram?" The tone of his voice, the remoteness of his gaze as he spoke sent a spike of aching need tearing into her chest.

"I can't afford a weakness." He sighed. "Unfortunately, you can be used as one, simply because your presence here will be more of a temptation than I can resist. We learned that earlier, didn't we?" He nodded to the disheveled bed where she had lain gasping for air as she orgasmed violently in his arms.

A flush washed over her face and she shot him a hateful look. "It's not as though I tempted you too far," she shot back. "You still haven't . . ." She ran out of words, flushing heavier. It was much harder to say as she faced the distance he was placing between them.

His brow arched. "I still haven't fucked you?" he murmured.

Her pussy just had to respond. It just had to clench and ripple and spill her juices, again, to saturate the bare, swollen folds.

She needed panties before the dampness began easing down her thighs. But at this rate, she would end up using all she had within hours.

She stared back at him though, holding his gaze despite the response that flooded through her and the anger beginning to build.

"I'll get around to it," he promised her. "I first wanted to make sure you were on birth control, and secondly—" His lips twisted ruefully. "I may not have come, Paige, but you had me so fucking hot I spilled myself in my pants. Something I promise you will not happen again." His gaze flickered over her, heated now, aroused. "The next time, I'll spill in that sweet tight pussy, or buried in the snug clench of your ass. Either way, I promise you'll not doubt the fact that I've definitely taken you."

"I don't think so." She had to draw in a hard, tight breath to push those words past her lips, because it truly was hard to deny what her body so wanted.

A single, black brow arched with an arrogance that set her teeth on edge.

"Not while we're here, and not while you're acting like my jailer rather than my lover," she explained tightly, nerves trembling in her voice as she fought to keep it firm, strong.

The smile he gave her was triumphant, dominant. "We'll see about that." He held his hand up as her lips parted to deliver a blasting retort. "Before we get into this argument, Tariq will be bringing in our dinner any minute and I know your appetite is affected when you're angry. Let's enjoy our meal, Paige, then you can tell me the ways you're going to resist my touch while you're lying in the bed with me nightly." He leaned forward then, his expression no longer distanced but suffused with sensual hunger. "Tell me, Paige, how will you resist when you're lying not just with me, but with Tariq as well? And the one thing I can promise you can have while you're here is all the pleasure we can give you in that bed. More pleasure than you could ever imagine."

Abram watched her face, her eyes. No matter the anger that could spike through Paige, it was her eyes that always told the truth of her emotions. The fear that had filled them as he forced himself to remain distant, to lay out the situation for her, had tightened his chest until he wondered that he could breathe for it.

But the minute he'd allowed his hunger to show, the only emotion, the only response he could give her, that fear had slid away and a matching, feminine need had blazed in her emerald eyes.

Sensual and warm, she was a woman willing to explore her hunger, but even more, she would be willing to explore his.

And before Tariq arrived with the meal he had prepared, he wanted her primed and ready for the hungers that raged through him. Knowing the situation, knowing from where the pleasure may well come later, would keep her off balance and hopefully, keep her too involved to attempt to escape before he and Tariq had a plan in place.

Until then, he had to be certain that the line he was forced to teeter on didn't shift on him. He had to ensure it didn't throw him to the ground, broken and lost, again.

He'd been there once. He'd been at the precipice where nothing mattered but the blood of his enemies and the future was a vision he didn't want to face. He'd already lost one woman whose life meant more to him than any of his brothers, his compatriots, and the men and women who had died, and would die, for the future they dreamed of.

He couldn't let it happen again, because he might not manage to pull himself back again.

Azir had known that once Paige was here that she would become his main priority. Sometimes, Abram thought, the old bastard knew him better than he knew himself.

Azir suspected Abram's plans for defection, but he didn't know the plan he and Tariq were laying in to escape with the information they had amassed since Jafar's arrival at the fortress.

As though his cousin's presence was all it had taken, the roaches were coming out of the woodwork. Suspected militants and terrorist organizers were roaming the streets and discussing in public in small groups what should only be discussed behind closed doors and in secure bunkers.

But even more, Azir was braver, more confident and more secure now in acquiring the funds that had been frozen more than twenty years before.

As dinner was finished and Tariq cleared away the dishes and prepared coffee behind a screen at the small kitchenette Abram had had installed, he leaned back in his chair and watched as Paige wandered back to the fire.

She was nervous. Not frightened, and definitely not really wary, but she was nervous, her senses hyped and adrenaline coursing through her body.

She was trying to ignore both of them and to ignore the declaration he had made earlier.

He almost grinned as he considered the night ahead. He had no intentions of taking her yet, not yet. There were a few matters that had to be taken care of first, and precautions established to ensure their safety before he and Tariq took her together.

The hunger for it was beginning to build in him though, and he could see it building in Tariq. They'd shared enough women, seduced enough to know each other's responses as well as their woman's.

"Azir and Jafar have made plans to take a ride in the morning," Tariq told him as he carried the coffee back to the table. "They believe you and I will be too distracted to know that they've left." Tariq nodded to Paige.

"Do you know where they're going?" Abram lifted the cup to his lips as he murmured the question.

Tariq gave a quick shake of his head. "The equipment in Jafar's room is just as good as ours, but I wasn't close enough to the door to hear everything being said."

"You know who to contact." Abram dropped his voice as he spoke. The room was equipped with audio detection scramblers but he didn't like taking chances. "If there's a way to follow them, then he can figure it out."

Abram frowned thoughtfully. Azir and Jafar had been bitter enemies until the months before Ayid and Aman had attempted to murder Khalid and Abram. Now, less than three months after the deaths of his youngest sons, Azir was conspiring with his nephew. The nephew whose father Azir had murdered more than twenty years ago.

"He definitely kidnapped her just to distract you," Tariq stated as he nodded to Paige. "If we're trying to protect her then we're not following him. And he knows you'd never leave her here alone."

"I wouldn't trust her safety to just one of us either," he said quietly. "Not this close."

That was the catch. They were a team, and they had been working efficiently together for several years. But now, with Paige here, it would be impossible for Abram to be confident that either of them could protect her alone if Azir conspired against them.

If his cruelty extended to having Paige taken and circumcised as Ayid had had his manservant's wife circumcised several years before. Or if the authorities arrived to have her—or all three of them—arrested for depraved or indecent sexual acts.

Azir wasn't above either of those, or any other number of extreme acts to keep Abram from leaving Saudi Arabia.

"He doesn't know we have help. At least in following him," Tariq murmured as he leaned closer.

Eyes in the sky were what they had. A little help from their friendly neighborhood CIA asset. In the event of an extreme emergency, that asset could get them out of the fortress and to an extraction point, but it wouldn't be easy. It would compromise positions and covers and that was something no one wanted to do unless they simply had no other choice.

If Azir moved in a direction that would compromise Paige's safety, or her life, then he would call them in, and it was that simple.

If he had time.

Abram glanced at her again, the fiery red-gold of her hair as it spilled around her shoulders, the relaxed position of her body indicating she was at the least, dozing.

As the day had worn on, Paige had become worn out. The drug used on her, the confrontation and abuse inflicted by Azir, and the stress of the day had culminated into complete exhaustion.

"Azir timed this personally," Tariq stated as he followed Abram's look. "And the perfect weapon to strike against you. How did he know?"

Tariq watched Abram, seeing the normally hardened expression as it softened almost imperceptibly. For the first time in far too many years, he was watching a woman affect Abram, and that scared the hell out of him. Because now just wasn't the time for this.

"Who the hell knows how he found out." Abram breathed out roughly. "But he did, and now we have to deal with it."

"Do you have a plan?" Tariq asked, nodding toward Paige as her head slipped deeper into the cushion behind her.

"Keep her safe and alive," Abram stated roughly as he turned back to his coffee and sipped at the brew. His expression remained savagely intense. "Stay one step ahead of Azir where she's concerned and make certain he doesn't get the jump on us. Until we can get her out without compromising our contacts, then we have no other choice."

"And if we can't?" Tariq had a feeling he knew the answer to that question.

"If we can't then all bets are off." The look Abram turned on him was more than savage now, it was primal, murderous.

Tariq barely controlled a flinch as he stared back into pure black icy rage. And he couldn't say he blamed Abram. He'd lost too much in the years past, had watched too many hopes and dreams fall at his feet and buried too many friends, as well as two too many wives, one of which had owned him as much as any young man could be owned.

Abram wasn't a young man anymore though. He was an adult in his prime, and the heart he possessed was a man's heart, with all its scars and driving hungers.

It was one Tariq understood, because he too possessed such a heart.

Glancing at the young woman Azir had ordered him to aid Abram in pleasing, he wondered if sharing a woman with another man would always tempt him. Would the day come when he would come to crave his own woman, his own life? Or would his own scarred soul refuse to give the world enough trust to love again?

"When she turned eighteen she asked me if I'd ever love again." Abram drew his attention back.

The look on his cousin's face was remote, but his eyes were alive with the memories of the pain he had suffered. "Aleya had just died with our child." He shook his head with a quick, rough movement. "I told her only if hell froze over."

But Abram loved the girl now sleeping in his room, Tariq thought. He wouldn't admit it, not yet, but it was there in his eyes.

"And what would you tell her now?" Tariq asked, suddenly wishing he could have slipped some of Khalid's fine whiskey into the fortress.

If ever a man needed a drink, it was now.

Abram finished his coffee and rose to his feet before answering. "I would tell her I wouldn't dare tempt fate a third time," he whispered, his voice as tortured as Tariq knew his soul was. "I don't think I could survive it again."

Abram moved to the couch then, picked his delicate

lover up in his arms, and carried her to the huge, custom-made bed at the other end of the room. It was conveniently situated close to the hidden door that led beneath the harem and into an underground cavern at the base of the mountains beyond.

A tunnel they both prayed no one else had found in the years since Abram had. They suspected not, or else Azir would have had it filled in and destroyed like the others that had been discovered.

His harem had once been sacred to him. Until he had lost the funds the government once paid him and no longer had the gold or American cash to pay for the kidnappings or the American women occasionally auctioned off in the slave markets.

"Stay, Tariq," Abram told him as he lay his burden in the large bed before undressing and laying down beside her.

Silk sheets and the thin cashmere blanket were pulled over them as Paige turned and curled into the warmth of Abram's chest.

Such trust, Tariq thought as he turned out the lights, set the secondary security, and moved to the bed himself.

Undressing as well, he crawled in beneath the blankets, rolled onto his stomach, and settled into the comfort of the bed.

He was aroused, there was no doubt. Merely the thought of what was to come with the woman he had always been so curious about was enough to make him harder than hell.

But, like Abram, he was damn worried.

Azir was striking hard and fast and now moving in ways neither Tariq, nor Abram could anticipate.

If he continued in this vein, then they could easily end up on the losing end of the war they were now involved in. A war centering around one delicate, red-haired, green-eyed woman that Tariq knew he would have to guard his heart against.

8

Paige stood at the high windows of the bedroom and stared through the crack of the partially opened shutters to where Jafar and Azir stood on the other side of the fortress wall, barely visible.

The two men had their heads close together as they stared at the ground as though looking for something, the metal detector Jafar carried so shadowed that at first it had been hard to tell exactly what it was.

Their dark thobes, the loose, long-sleeved, ankle-length garments, unadorned and plain, rippled at their legs from the winds sweeping from the mountains. On their heads, the ghutra, a large square cloth of cotton, dark in color to match the thobe, was wrapped around their faces to protect them from the cold wind and secured with the thick, double black cord.

Azir seemed to teeter ever so often, and in the two hours she had watched them surveying the natural bank that split the land along the length of the fortress, she'd seen the old man almost topple over more than once.

Jafar kept close to him, catching him whenever he stumbled and staying close to him whenever the crazy old goat seemed to wander from whatever they were doing.

They were searching for something as far as she could tell, and evidently having little success in finding it.

"What are they looking for?" she asked Tariq as he worked on a piece of electronics at the small table across the room.

A muttered sound resembling a male grunt met her question. "Azir has spent years trying to find all the hidden tunnels coming in and out of the castle," he told her. "Each time he finds one he has it dynamited or filled in in some way to make it impossible."

She stared back down at the men with a frown. Why would they worry about hidden tunnels?

"To keep Abram from escaping," she murmured almost to herself.

"Pretty much," Tariq agreed. "Azir is fanatical about keeping him here until the king releases the funds he had frozen over twenty years ago. If Azir can get them returned, then the government has to pay out, no matter what, for the next ten years or risk breaking a treaty with several of the tribes that were a part of the original pact. They'll go to any lengths to keep from doing that, and Azir knows that."

Greed. Power. That was what it all came down to, one way or the other. Azir was hungry for it, just as his sons had been. Those who didn't hunger for it tried peaceful means at all costs, and kept their demands clearly stated.

Azir wanted nothing more than to fund whatever fanatical regime he was supporting, and nothing mattered but his wants. Not even the heir who seemed to be his last hope of a comfortable life in his old age.

She continued to stare out the window, watching as they began to track the ground with the metal detector once again.

"How does a metal detector help them find underground tunnels?" she asked without turning back.

"It's not exactly a metal detector," he answered. "It's specially modified to pick up pockets beneath the ground, vacancies that would indicate a cave, a cavern, or a tunnel."

"Is there a tunnel where he's looking?" She glanced back, but rather than searching for his eyes her gaze moved to his naked back once again.

"Not that we've found," he told her with a quick shake of his head. "Abram and I have searched high and low for tunnels that haven't yet been found. So far, we haven't found anything."

She turned back to the scene below to see Jafar gesture angrily to Azir with a frown. She would have never believed he was as deceitful as it appeared he was, or that he could have been a risk to her. Learning he had helped conspire to kidnap her had been a disillusioning blow.

There had been a lot of surprises in the past four days though, things she had truly never expected. She'd known Khalid's cousins most of her life. At one time or another she had been introduced to them under various circumstances outside the Saudi regime. Until perhaps five or six years before, his Saudi cousins had been regulars at many of the vacation spots her parents had visited, for either business or pleasure.

Then, the positions they had held within the Saudi government had been dissolved, Paige had learned.

Because of Ayid and Aman, Khalid had told her. Once the king had received proof they were still involved with terrorist activities, all the males working in the Riyadh government had been asked to return to their own province. Ayid and Aman had destroyed the regime's trust for the entire family.

Jafar and Tariq had actually held very lucrative positions within imports and exports, allowing them to travel all over the world. Several of Jafar's family members were still in the U.S. attending college on student visas he had arranged while they were still very young.

But Tariq and Jafar were here now, rather than jet-setting and representing their country financially.

Turning, she stared at Tariq once again, her gaze straying to his smooth, bare shoulders. He was dressed only in the ankle-length loose trousers that he and Abram wore beneath their thobes.

Once the two men entered the rooms, the first thing they did was strip off the thobes. She'd seen Abram pull on well-worn, lovingly faded denim the night before like a man pulling on a favorite lover. She swore his lashes almost fluttered in pleasure for a second.

Tariq's bare shoulders were the only part of his back that was smooth though. Unlike her mother's description of Azir with his heavy pelt of body hair, Tariq actually sported very little, as did Abram.

But his back was crisscrossed with what had to be hundreds of very fine, thin scars that went from his shoulder blades to beneath the drawstring waist of the trousers.

"What are you doing?" She cleared her throat uneasily as she moved toward him.

He'd been working on that piece of equipment for two days now.

"Someone found one of the GPS trackers I've been using on the Land Rovers and managed to scramble the signal," he murmured as he continued to peer into the electronic control board. "I'm trying to alter the device rather than attempting to steal the tracker itself back. If I can get it to remotely change the signal, then I'll have them again."

"Who are you trying to track?" She stared down at the intricate array of tiny wires, nodules, and electronic relays with a frown.

He looked over his shoulder at her, his milk chocolate–brown eyes faintly amused as he gave her a glance of male appreciation. "The new soaps Abram brought in for you smell nice."

She was that close to him. Not touching, but close enough that he had no problem smelling the very faint scent of rose and sandalwood.

She moved back, a sense of nervousness invading her as he continued to watch her for several seconds before turning back to the electronic device.

It was merely another variation of the same theme that had played out in the past two days that Abram hadn't been present. The looks of interest, the silent reminder that Abram had already asked him to be his third and that he shared that huge bed with them every night.

For the past two nights she had gone to sleep with Abram's arms around her, only to awaken with Tariq's holding her. It was creating an intimacy she couldn't seem to escape.

Restraining a frustrated sigh she turned back to him, her lips parting to comment on Abram's absence when a hard, imperative knock sounded on the heavy, thick wood of the door.

Paige flinched with near violence, her heart jumping into her throat as her gaze flew to where Tariq was quickly folding a square of cloth over the device he had been working on and rising from the chair.

He pointed to the connecting door that led to his suite as he moved to it quickly.

He was leaving?

"Where are you going?" she hissed.

"I'll be listening," he promised quickly, his voice so low as to be nearly silent. "See who it is, and don't let them know I'm here."

He handed her the scarf that Abram had given her in case Azir showed up to use over her head and around her neck as a hijab.

The knock sounded again, harder, and this time, more impatient.

"Who is it?" she called out as she quickly secured the scarf around her head as Abram had taught her.

"It is Jafar, Paige. I have someone here who wishes to see you." His voice came through the door quietly.

Dammit, where the hell was Abram?

"Abram isn't here, Jafar," she stated from the seam of the door and frame. "He told me not to open the door to anyone."

She heard Jafar's laughter through the heavy wood. "Put your scarf on and simply open the door. I do not intend to enter the room."

She looked to where Tariq watched from the doorway of his suite. He nodded at her as she gave him a look of desperation and silently mouthed, "What do I do?"

He grimaced tightly before nodding again at her and disappearing into the other room.

Releasing the locks she opened the door several inches and stared at Jafar and the figure clothed in black from head to foot in the face and body covering usually only worn in the strictest of areas.

Behind the mesh screen of the burqa, feminine eyes stared back at her, though the shape and color were impossible to distinguish.

Behind the much smaller figure stood Jafar, as his odd, almost translucent pale green eyes watched her with knowing, mocking amusement.

Antagonism rose within her at the first sight of him and it was all she could do to keep her lips clamped closed.

"Such a look of anger." He grinned at her, a brow arching in a move of such arrogance that for a second, he reminded her of Abram.

"Stop trying to make her angry, brother," the feminine voice chided him with surprising tartness.

Paige's gaze jerked back to the shrouded figure and struggled to peer behind the mesh eye covering.

"Chalah?" she whispered uncertainly, hopefully, though suspicion was blooming inside her.

"I told you she would remember me." Soft laughter spilled from behind the dark covering. "Let me in, Paige, so I can get rid of my hulking brother, if you don't mind."

Paige's eyes flicked to Jafar once again. How cruel of him to bring the sister who had once been her friend to betray her.

She eased back slowly, allowing the door to open as she kept a wary eye on Jafar. She trusted him even less now. It was incredibly obvious he was attempting to use the sister he had once seemed to adore.

The lies of the past were piling up on his head, and she hoped the weight of them buried him. Quickly.

"It's about time." Chalah all but bounced into the room as Paige closed the door in Jafar's laughing face.

"I thought you were still in college," Paige stated as she locked the door, her brows lifting as the burqa came off.

This was Chalah. White sneakers, her long legs just dark enough to give her a perpetually tanned look. Cut-off shorts and a snug camisole that shaped her full breasts and emphasized her tiny waist.

"All about covering yourself today, aren't you there, Chalah?" she drawled.

Chalah rolled her eyes. "I hear the Matawa deserted this damned place about the same time the money left," she snorted.

The Matawa, or religious police were the terror of any woman unlucky enough to draw their notice.

"How in the hell did you manage to get your ass in

this situation?" Chalah propped her hands on her hips as she glared back at Paige.

Long black hair was confined in a thick heavy braid. Exotic, honey brown eyes, thickly lashed, were sparkling as her lips pursed in irritation.

"An argument with Khalid." Paige admitted a truth she hadn't even told Abram.

"It figures it was that oaf's fault," Chalah retorted as she crossed her arms over her breasts and tilted her head curiously. "Let me guess, he didn't handle catching you in that tight, hot embrace with Abram very well? Did he scream incest?" She waggled her brows suggestively.

Paige stared back at her in surprise as she drew the scarf from her head and draped it over the back of the couch.

"How did you know about that?" she asked suspiciously.

She knew neither Khalid nor Marty would have told of the incident. To do so would have endangered Abram and further threatened Paige.

Chalah turned, glancing around the room before casting Paige an impish look from the corner of her eye.

"Where's Abram?" she asked.

Paige shrugged. "He was gone when I awoke this morning. Now, tell me how you knew about Abram being at Khalid's that night."

Chalah shot her a dark look as she paced around the room as though looking for something. When she made her way back to Paige she shook her head, her expression pensive.

"Because Khalid either has one of Azir or Jafar's spies, or a very gossipy employee on his payroll." Chalah kept her voice low. "And if you dare let anyone know I told you that, even Abram, then I may not survive long enough to return to the U.S. and finish my degree."

Paige closed her eyes for a second before turning, her hand moving to rub at the side of her head wearily. Her temple throbbed with stress.

"Is it Abdul?" she asked as she turned back, knowing it would break Khalid and Mary's heart if it were the manservant betraying him.

"How simple would that be?" Chalah rolled her eyes expressively. "But, no such luck. I'm afraid all I know for sure is that it's a female. A very vindictive one who's either in the house or in the employ of the Conover security team. She's been funneling information to the commander of the terrorist cell Ayid and Aman led for a while now."

"I thought Jafar commanded those men," Paige said as she watched the other girl suspiciously and wondered what the hell was going on.

Chalah gave a brief shake of her head as regret twisted her expression.

"No, Paige," she whispered, her voice barely audible now. "Jafar has taken Ayid and Aman's place as a mere leader, but they were never commanders. Even Jafar doesn't know who the commander is, and he claims he enjoys living so he does not ask."

Pain flashed in Chalah's eyes at the admission of her brother actually being part of the cell.

"Does Jafar know anything about him?" Paige asked.

Chalah grimaced, grief flashing in her eyes.

"Jafar refused to discuss it with me," she sighed. "After Anwar's death he was so consumed with vengeance at first that discussing anything with him was impossible. Having him murdered as he was, and believing Azir was behind it consumed him."

Anwar had been Jafar's older brother by several years. A full brother that Jafar had idolized as a child. He had also been the heir to a third of the Mustafa province and had been petitioning the regime to reacquire the property with a vow that it would be run as the family of Mustafa had vowed to run it centuries before.

Paige knew both Khalid and Abram were still certain Azir and his sons, Ayid and Aman, were behind his death.

Chalah moved to the table and leaned against it as Paige watched her quietly for several moments.

"Why are you telling me this?" Paige asked her warily. "Wouldn't Jafar be upset?"

Chalah's expression sobered. "If he knew, then he would be very upset, and if Azir ever learned I told you anything, then he would most surely have me stoned," she revealed heavily. "But I don't think I have to worry about you telling anyone but Abram, do I?"

"Then Azir has known all along that Abram and Khalid weren't estranged," she whispered, her stomach pitching sickeningly.

"I don't know how long he's known, but Jafar has known for several years. Just as he's known that Abram and Tariq have had a lover to share each time they've been to the U.S." Chalah's gaze was curious now. "Was it you?"

Paige nearly choked on her own mocking laughter. "Khalid had a cow when he caught Abram kissing me.

Do you really think I could have gotten away with anything else?"

"Knowing Khalid?" Chalah's brows lifted. "It is rather doubtful."

And Chalah knew Khalid. Not as well as Paige did, and certainly not as a lover, but one of the young women Azir had bought Khalid years ago for a personal harem, attended the same college with Chalah, and the two girls had socialized often.

Chalah was considered a friend, as well as a cousin to Khalid, and he had made it plain more than once that if she ever needed anything then he had no problem helping her out.

Watching Chalah closely now, Paige still had a hard time believing the other girl was here, or that she seemed to be willing to help.

"Why are you telling me this, Chalah?" Paige asked wearily, not bothering to hide her suspicion now. "By your own words, the brother who has spoiled you all your life might allow you to be stoned, or murdered for giving me this information. Why would you risk that?"

"Because you would do it for me," Chalah said softly, her honey-gold eyes filling with pain. "And Khalid would do it for me. But even more importantly, for Jafar. Because if anything happens to you and Abram, and Jafar ever realizes the mistake he's made, then it will kill him. Protecting him from himself is the only way I can help him at this point."

"Even if you have to face being murdered by your brother? By your uncle?"

Chalah sighed heavily. "It isn't murder here, Paige, not to these people or to this land. And not to Jafar or

Azir. Betrayal isn't tolerated, especially by a woman, and Jafar and Azir both would see it as an unforgivable betrayal."

"And you would risk that for me, Abram, and Khalid?" Paige asked her again. "I'm having a hard time believing that."

Chalah wasn't lying to her. She knew too many truths, understood the situation too clearly. But was she really trying to help, or in someway lead Abram into a trap?

"Really?" Chalah drawled as she crossed one ankle over the other and tilted her head to the side. "Why else would I return to this sun-baked wasteland but to try to help your stubborn ass? Have you really forgotten how much I hate this place, Paige?"

Paige shook her head as she kept a careful eye on the other woman. "We've been friends for a long time, Chalah." She sighed. "But Jafar is your brother, and I know you love him."

"And I do love him." Chalah nodded sharply. "But Jafar is wrong, Paige, and I couldn't live with myself if anything happened to you because of him. And I feel guilty," she whispered miserably. "I knew he was up to something when he called and asked me if I knew why you weren't at your apartment any longer and if I had heard where you were staying. I should have called you then. I should have warned you he was looking for you."

But would it have really changed things? Would she have taken the situation even less seriously than she already had simply because she thought she could trust Jafar?

Paige lifted her hand to rub at her temple again as she watched Chalah thoughtfully. Everything she knew of the other girl told her that Chalah was being honest. That she was simply trying to help.

"I don't have to agree with my brother to love him, Paige," she said regretfully. "And loving him doesn't mean I have to let him get away with what he's doing to you and Abram."

"And how do you think you can help?" Paige sighed as she paced to the table and sat down wearily. "Neither of us have enough power here to protect ourselves, let alone our brothers. And you know that as well as I do. You should go home and be safe. If anything happens to you, you're only going to make Abram feel as though it were his fault. He has enough on his conscience."

"And you think Jafar won't have enough on his conscience when he realizes the mistake he's made?" Chalah hissed back at her, her expressive eyes burning with anger. "I came here to help, Paige. To help my brother and yours, as well as Abram. I need to know what to do."

Paige's eyes rounded in surprise. "And you think I'd know what the hell you can do?" she whispered fiercely. "For God's sake Chalah, I haven't been out of these rooms since the day I came here. I have no idea what the hell is going on or how to help anyone. I don't even see Abram until after dark, and when I do see him, he's exhausted. So why don't *you* tell *me* what I could do."

Chalah stared back at her in dismay. Then her jaw tightened and she stomped to the end of the couch before turning back in frustration.

"There has to be something, Paige."

Paige gave her head a quick shake as she kept her voice low. "Go home. Go back to school. If Abram has to worry about protecting you as well as me, then it's only going to fracture his attention further. He can't afford that right now."

And she couldn't afford it. Losing Abram would kill her, especially if she lost him because of his affection, his connection—whatever the hell it was—to her.

He had come back to Saudi Arabia rather than defecting as he'd planned after the deaths of his brothers.

He'd been forced to return to Saudi Arabia as a personal favor to the Saudi Arabian ambassador to take pictures of suspected terrorists. When he'd managed to get back to the U.S., he'd had to return again because of the threat to her.

He couldn't seem to break away from the bloody legacy his father was creating here, or the threat of death that resulted from the pleasure he found in sharing his lover sexually.

"Jafar didn't used to be like this." Chalah sighed in regret as her lips trembled with the painful emotion she was feeling. "He wanted to be an American. He wanted to have the freedom to do as he wished, as Khalid did, as he knew Abram did."

"He knew Abram wanted to defect to the U.S.?" Paige asked.

"Paige." Chalah stared back at her in bemusement. "Abram, Tariq, Jafar, and several other cousins planned to defect together. It's been their plan since Abram's first wife, Lessa, was murdered by Ayid and Aman. Jafar has always known his plans, because they made them together."

"And Jafar would know exactly how to block every move Abram made." She sighed.

"But Abram knows what Jafar is aware of," Chalah pointed out. "It's some sort of battle between them." The other girl frowned in confusion. "And I can't understand what started it or why they are at odds with each other."

It was the same problem Paige had, trying to figure out what had changed Jafar since the last time she had seen him. She had been vacationing with her parents in Greece, three, perhaps four years before.

As she watched, Chalah's expression turned somber.

"Jafar was a good man once, wasn't he, Paige?" she whispered, grief flashing in her eyes for just a moment.

Paige looked away for a second wondering if she should lie, of if she should tell Chalah how she felt in regards to good men.

"Men are what they are," she finally said softly. "They're either born mostly good, or they're born mostly bad, just like anyone else is, Chalah. But the bad is always there, and for most men, the good is always there as well."

"For most men?" Chalah asked with bitterness. Paige could see the need in her eyes for an affirmation that there was a chance that her brother wasn't mostly, or even worse, fully bad.

"Sometimes, some men are always bad," she said gently. "And then, there are those good men, those really really good men, Chalah, who just want everyone to think they're bad for whatever reason."

"And then," Chalah whispered, tears filling her eyes. "There are those really bad men who are really good at making some people think they're good."

Paige dropped her eyes and crossed her arms over her

breasts to hold back the pain she felt for the other girl, to hold back her need to comfort her.

She hadn't decided yet, was Chalah the young woman she had once known? The future pediatrician with a gentle, loving heart, or was she one of those people everyone thought was good, but who for whatever reason, knew the evil inside her personally?

She lifted her eyes as Chalah sighed heavily. "Go home, Chalah," she said softly. "If you really want to help Abram, if you really want to help Jafar, then go home."

"Because you don't trust me, and if you don't trust me, then neither will Abram," Chalah guessed.

"It has nothing to do with trust, Chalah, and everything to do with the fact that from the sound of it, you know more than I do about the entire situation. And I think you know that if you talk to Abram, then he's going to tell you the same thing I did. Go home."

Tears glittered in her eyes. "They're my family, Paige. They're all I have left."

What the hell could she say? She knew exactly how she felt. After the death of her uncle when she was still a teenager she only had her parents and Khalid left, and she'd always been aware of the crosshairs Azir Mustafa kept the family under.

She'd always been aware that any time, she could either be dead, or alone.

As her lips parted to attempt to comfort the other girl, the sound of a heavy knock on the door sliced through the room, causing both women to jump, and Chalah's eyes to flash with fear.

A fear far stronger than she should have felt.

"Chalah, it's time to go." Jafar's voice was far colder than it had been earlier.

Paige swung her gaze around to the girl, and watched in fury as a tear slipped from the corner of her eye. Slowly, she lifted her hand to the medallion on the necklace she wore, turned it around, and showed Paige the device on the back of it.

She'd seen enough television programs and read enough adventure-romance novels to know exactly what it was. An electronic listening device. And Chalah had waited until the last minute to show it to her.

Paige straightened slowly, her arms dropping to her sides as she flashed Chalah a look of promised retribution. One way, some way, she would repay her for this.

Go home! she mouthed. *Now!*

Because if she ever saw the younger girl again then she would ensure Chalah knew exactly how completely severed their friendship was.

Jerking the scarf around her head, neck, and finally tucking it around her face until nothing but her eyes showed, she moved with jerky fury to the door and wrenched it open.

Chalah had only just managed to pull the abaya back on and secure the mesh over her eyes when Paige found herself facing the stone-hard, pale-eyed monster that watched her with calculating eyes.

She didn't dare speak. There were rules and punishments, consequences and dangers to uttering even one of the curses tearing through her brain now.

Hatred welled inside her, blistering hot and searing her from the inside out.

What had Jafar hoped to gain by using his sister this way?

She stood back and turned slowly to stare at Chalah.

"Good-bye," she stated with a withering stare. A ring of finality clearly echoed as she refused to say anything more.

She wouldn't endanger the younger girl, but if Chalah dared to return then the rules would change.

"Good-bye, Paige," Chalah said softly, miserably. Before Paige could avoid her, the other girl wrapped her arms around her in a tight, desperate hug. She whispered, "I swear, I'm good."

Paige stepped back slowly, deliberately pushing her away as her gaze moved to Jafar once again. He had forced Chalah, there was no doubt, but she had still betrayed Paige, Abram, and Tariq. She should have shown her the device before they ever spoke.

"Tell Abram when he returns that it would not be advisable to leave at night any longer, for either him or Tariq," he warned evenly, his pale green eyes like glass, cold and unemotional as his gaze flicked over her. "Or, Ms. Galbraithe, for you."

He reached past her, gripped Chalah's upper arm, and all but jerked her from the room.

He hadn't gotten what he wanted, and now his sister would pay for it, and Chalah knew it.

Her head was down, her shoulders shuddering as silent sobs shook her beneath the heavy shroud.

Paige prayed that the beating she knew Chalah would take for failure was the only punishment she would receive before Jafar allowed her to return to America, and to school.

Chalah had one dream, to be a pediatrician in America. But Paige doubted Jafar would allow her to keep it for long.

Pulling his sister after him, Jafar turned and strode away, his long-legged stride causing Chalah to struggle to keep up with him as they moved around the bend of the hall and disappeared from view.

Paige closed and locked the door carefully before leaning against it and letting a silent sob ripple through her own body. How close she had come to trusting the other girl and attempting to ease the pain she had felt in her. How close she had come to destroying herself, Tariq, and worst of all, Abram.

"The listening device didn't work, Paige."

Jerking, she turned to see Tariq standing behind her, his expression creased with anger and his own sorrow. "I detected it the second she and Jafar knocked on the door." He lifted the device he had been working on. "I fixed it."

She turned and wiped her eyes. "That only detects it," she whispered painfully.

He shook his head. "I switched on a device beneath the table before I left that alters the audio signal, either analog or digital. I didn't disable it until I saw you weren't going to betray Abram. Then, I used the controls in my suite to allow enough out to whoever was listening to assure them that you weren't shit, even if you knew. Perhaps, Jafar will send her home now."

He moved closer as more tears fell down her face, as she sniffed back the pain that tore through her and the disillusionment that shredded her heart.

"I hate this place," she suddenly spat, though the sobs,

as quiet as they were, roughened her voice to a rasp. "Oh God, Tariq, I hate this place."

He stepped closer, his expression suddenly tired, and just as disillusioned as she felt. "And you aren't alone," he whispered as he tucked a heavy strand of hair behind her ear, his fingertips caressing her ear gently for a fragile second before they dropped away. "Trust me, Paige, in that, you will never be alone."

9

A day of dealing with Azir and Jafar's paranoia as he searched fruitlessly for the only contact that could arrange extraction out of Saudi Arabia had Abram in a less than pleasant mood when he returned to his room that night.

For whatever reason, and he was beginning to suspect those reasons, Jafar had convinced Azir that Abram needed to personally handle the drilling of a new water well outside of the fortress.

That well supplied water to the dozen or so families that lived outside the fortress walls and provided the Mustafa province with the few vegetables and animals used for their meals.

The problems with lines, pipes, and generators had led to more than one worker throwing his hands up in surrender at the seemingly unending problems and delays.

Two of those settlements farmed domesticated rabbit and lamb and sold the wool and small amounts of meat to other provinces as well. They had to have that water, yet it seemed something or someone had deliberately fouled the equipment to halt the pumping of it.

There were a few local incomes that Abram had been able to provide for the province, knowing that once he left the few benefits the regime provided would drain away.

To add to the problems, Abram had learned several of the men had spied Azir and Jafar testing the ground and the fortress wall behind his and Tariq's suites for tunnels and exits.

Azir had been searching for that tunnel since before Khalid's mother had escaped. And no tunnel had even played a part in her ability to slip from the fortress.

The part that worried Abram the most was the fact that Azir was certain the tunnel was there. There were no drawings or blueprints left to reveal or cause anyone to suspect any bolt holes other than the ones already filled in.

Entering the suite silently well after dark, he found Paige curled on the couch napping, and Tariq at the small dining table still adjusting the piece of electronics he had been working on for over a week.

Closing the door silently he watched as Tariq held a shushing finger up, rose to his feet, and motioned Abram to the connecting suite.

Frowning, Abram followed, wondering what the hell could have happened here in the suite today to cause the look of anger that gleamed in his eyes.

No doubt, it had something to do with either Jafar or Azir. The two men were beginning to irritate him to his last nerve, even more so than usual.

Closing the door to the sitting room behind them, Tariq turned to him, his lips tightening as his dark eyes flashed with silent, burning anger.

"Jafar brought Chalah here today and she was simply a fount of information." He sneered. "As well as carrying a tiny listening device attached to the medallion I fucking gave her for her sixteenth birthday."

There was the reason for the fury. Tariq had always been fond of his little cousin. That medallion held special significance for him, and for her to use it against him or Abram would seem the worst betrayal.

Chalah Mustafa, Jafar's half-sister. She was Abram's first cousin, and would have been Tariq's if it weren't for the fact that Tariq's father hadn't been Hussein Mustafa as everyone assumed it was. That bit of knowledge was something even Azir was unaware of. There were a lot of half-siblings, step-siblings, half-cousins, and half-families parading as Mustafas these days though. There were times the dynamics of it boggled his mind and he wasn't a stupid man.

Abram listened silently to the conversation Tariq had recorded. His mind turned with suspicions and possibilities as Chalah attempted to gain the details of his relationship with Paige, as well as any plans they might have for leaving. She had revealed the recording device to Paige before leaving though, which meant she hadn't been there voluntarily.

She had been forced.

Somehow, Azir and her brother had found a way to

make her attempt to betray those she considered family, as well as Paige, who had always been a friend.

Abram wasn't going to hold it against her, but neither would he ever be able to trust her again. Had she revealed the device before the conversation started, then he would have felt differently.

"What was your impression?" he asked Tariq as he rubbed the back of his neck in irritation when the recording ended. "Was she forced by Jafar, by Azir, or by both?"

Tariq grimaced furiously, his dark brown eyes burning with his anger and perhaps even a hint of betrayal. He'd always cared for Chalah, always watched out for her whenever she returned to the province. To have her do something like this, without warning them, would have struck him in one of the few vulnerable areas he had.

"Hell, Abram, you know both of them, your guess is about as good as mine. Besides, you know that little hellion as well as I do." He growled as his arms crossed over his chest and his jaw clenched with his attempt at control. "Let's say she sounded sincere in her offer to help as well as her worry. Enough so that she had Paige fooled until she showed her that device." Disgust filled his voice. "She had Paige convinced." He pushed his fingers through his thick, dark brown hair. "Of something. Hell, I would have believed her if I hadn't known she was bugged."

Yeah, it was damned hard to lose trust in someone he had known all his life, protected, and taken care of.

"Is she coming back?" He breathed out roughly.

Jafar wouldn't be satisfied with the information he

would have heard, what little Tariq had allowed past the jammer. He would have to try again.

He didn't need this. They didn't need it. Chalah was as wild as the wind and just as unpredictable, but she had never been a danger until now.

That danger was forced. She hadn't done it willingly, but still, she had done it before warning them. That was a deal breaker in the trust department.

"If she comes back, Jafar will be escorting her, and to be honest, I can't assure you Paige will have the self-control not to confront Jafar. Remember, she doesn't know him like this, in the setting he was raised in. If she attempts to berate him, he could have her arrested and sent to the Matawa in the next province. Which is what I'm beginning to fear they intend to do with us the minute you give your vow to the monarch's emissary."

It was no more than Abram suspected himself.

Hell, he didn't suspect it, he knew it. It was one of the reasons he knew he had to get the hell out of there before the emissary showed up.

"Hell, at the very least, he could punish her himself, or Azir could," Tariq bit out as he continued. "Either way, it would end in bloodshed."

If either of them dared to touch Paige, then bloodshed would be the very least of their worries.

He had to find his contact, and that wasn't an easy chore when combined with the need to sleep and to leave Tariq there with her while he fought against the bond he knew would come when he took her.

And that was the overwhelming reason why he was the one out there searching for the contact rather than

Tariq. That bond that he could feel growing night by night as he lay next to her naked body while she slept. Without moving, without speaking, she was invading a part of him that he had always managed to keep her from invading before.

She was like lightning, and there was nothing he could do to tame her, nothing he could do to keep her from burning into his soul if he gave her the chance.

Already, she was burning through his control and inciting a hunger inside him unlike anything any other woman could have touched.

He was so fucking hard and horny he was in agony. The past three days and nights had been hell.

As soon as she fell asleep he had to drag his ass out of the bed and do what he could to work their way out of an impossible situation. When he was done, when he couldn't go without sleep any longer, only then did he send Tariq out. And then, he was left with her, sleeping beside her, feeling her against him, her delicate limbs entwined with his as they lay together.

What should have been accomplished quickly if he and Tariq worked together was taking twice the time and had become twice as dangerous. And much of the danger stemmed from the fact that he couldn't keep his mind off her enough to ensure he wasn't making mistakes.

All he could think about was fucking Paige until he had to cover her mouth to muffle her screams of pleasure. Or of holding her, controlling the movements of her body as he watched Tariq take her. Watched his cock slide slow and easy up her sensitive, tight pussy, or better yet—

His entire body tensed with a brutal, unrelenting hunger.

Or watching Tariq stretch the tight, small entrance of her ass, pushing inside her with the heavy breadth of his cock as she tried to scream from a pleasure that she knew how to distinguish from pain. A pleasure that engaged every sense, that left her focused on nothing but the submission of the act, the feel of a man's dick pounding inside her body in a way that forced home the knowledge that she was taken. That they trusted each other just as deeply.

The sight of it had been incredible in the past, Abram knew. Sharing a woman with another man was to be able to experience his lover's pleasure as he couldn't do in any other way.

To allow him to watch her being taken. To see the primal, possessive clasp of her flesh as it stretched and took the invader pumping inside her.

The need for it was growing. The hunger for it was tearing at him even as he fought it, to delay it until he could get her out of Saudi Arabia.

Now, Jafar thought he could mess with Abram's life further, with his happiness, by involving his sister and garnering evidence that he and Tariq were involved in sexual indecency?

If Jafar and Azir took their suspicions to the Matawa, the religious police, with the audio proof of admission from Paige, then even the king wouldn't be able to save them. And for that, Abram would have to kill Azir and Jafar both.

He looked around Tariq's suite, aware of the other man watching him carefully. He fought to push back the fury that was becoming harder to tame with each successive day.

"I expect Jafar to bring her back, Abram," Tariq revealed. "He obviously has no problem with using her however he can."

"If he brings Chalah back tomorrow, then we'll deal with it. We can't let him see either of us in the room with Paige though, and by all appearances both of us have to be staying in your suite. Tomorrow, he'll be aware that we're both there if he shows up at the door again."

Tariq tensed, his eyes narrowing at the declaration and the knowledge that Abram had reached his limit. It was in his voice, in the tension building inside him.

They had known each other too long perhaps, shared too many lovers in the past. They knew the signs the other showed, and could gauge interest as well as that point where it couldn't be ignored any longer.

He wasn't hiding well either, Abram knew. The hunger for her was tearing him apart inside as he tried to give Paige and Tariq the room he felt they needed for Paige to become closer to the man he had picked as his third. Hoping, a part of him terrified, that she would find in Tariq whatever emotion it was that she was searching for in Abram.

Could he handle it?

Could he handle it if she didn't?

God help him, she was his greatest weakness and he couldn't seem to find a way to protect himself should the unthinkable happen.

"Is she ready?" he finally asked Tariq when nothing else was said.

Surprise filled Tariq's eyes. "Ready in what way?"

Surely his cousin couldn't be surprised by the question, or unaware why Abram had been leaving them both here, naked, in the bed together, each morning.

"For you?" Abram paused, his brow arching sarcastically. "For both of us? Why do you think I've busted my ass the past nights to do the work of two men? So you can catch up on your nightly beauty sleep, Prince Mustafa?"

He'd left them there alone for a reason. To allow Paige to acclimate herself to the man she would call lover as well. He sure as hell hadn't left the two of them alone together for his mental health, because the knowledge of it had nearly corroded the last of his control.

Tariq grunted irritably at the comment.

"What did you want me to do, Abram?" Tariq's arms crossed over his chest as he tilted his head and stared back at him with cynical mockery. "She stands in the window and watches for you. She waits for you as a new wife awaits her husband. Would you have me attempt to seduce her when she clearly shows no interest?" He gave a bitter, hard laugh. "Do I appear the fool to you? There is no desire that comes from her until she sees you. Only then does she begin to burn."

Abram's teeth clenched. This wasn't what he'd expected despite the ambivalent feelings he had toward Tariq seducing not just her body, but her heart as well.

"I haven't exactly been standing outside the fortress twiddling my fingers," Abram growled disparagingly.

"Why don't I go ahead and find our contact tonight and you can seduce your woman," Tariq suggested, distinctly annoyed. "Don't make the mistake I see you walking into, my friend. Because she is not a woman that will forgive you for it."

She was the type of woman whose memory of her kiss and of her touch would torment him for life.

"I don't know what you're talking about, Tariq," Abram snarled.

A dark chuckle met his protest as Tariq stared back at him knowingly.

"Yes, you do know," Tariq informed him. "You know you haven't yet taken her because you fear when you do, she will become a part of your heart. Should that happen, then what defenses will you have if Azir and Jafar win in this game as Ayid and Aman always won in the others? Especially with Lessa. You are afraid you will not survive losing her."

"We won't be here long enough to allow that to happen," Abram stated savagely. "And I haven't taken her yet because I've wanted her to have the chance to acclimate to both of us. This isn't a life she's used to, nor is it one her innocence will have prepared her for."

It was technically the truth, Abram told himself furiously.

"Do you really believe her feelings are transferrable?" Tariq grunted sarcastically. "She will accept me as a third, Abram, but this is all I will ever be to her. If you attempt to chance that, then you'll lose her. And I don't believe that's really what you want."

But was her heart, the knowledge, the acceptance of her feelings, something he could face?

Abram almost felt his hands shaking at the thought of it.

"Do you want a third, Abram, or do you want to be the third?"

Abram narrowed his eyes, restrained his anger.

The question had a surge of powerful, forceful adrenaline racing through him. Never in his life had he allowed himself to play the third. He wasn't beginning now.

"I am no third," he growled in a flash of dominance.

Tariq chuckled at the exclamation.

"Then you should seduce your love, Abram. Prepare her yourself for the third you have chosen. Otherwise you may find yourself missing the opportunity to create that bond that will secure her heart to yours, rather than leaving it drifting and wild and searching for a home."

Secure her heart to his? Abram rubbed at the back of his neck, his teeth clenching at the thought of everything that could go wrong in his attempt to get them out of the fortress and to the extraction point on time.

The transport wouldn't be able to wait on them for long. The terrorist activity in the area made the extraction itself highly dangerous.

"No risk, no gain, my friend." Tariq grinned as Abram shot him a hard glance.

The risk was high enough to scare the shit out of him if he allowed himself to think about it.

"Are you two finished bonding in there yet?" Paige's voice came through the connecting door. "Or do you need a few more minutes?"

Immediately arousal turned to full, flaming lust. It swept through his body like a tidal wave and sent fingers of electric energy sizzling through his brain.

Seduce his woman? God help him, he would be lucky

if he found the control to undress first. How much easier it would be to push the thobe to her waist, his trousers below his hips, and take her with all the impatience and driving need torturing him.

He'd stayed away from her for three days, he'd fought like hell to find the CIA asset able to locate and set up the extraction team. He had to get her the hell out of Saudi Arabia.

"See if you can find our contact tonight then," he ordered. "I want extraction ASAP, Tariq. If I have to wait much longer, I'm contacting Khalid. Tell our mutual friends who pass along information that in twelve hours I contact the desert lion."

Khalid's nickname among the tribes in the outlying desert areas was cemented. He was known as a savage enemy, a fierce ally.

Tariq nodded sharply, his expression stilling, all frustration, arousal, or any hint of anger smoothing away.

"While you're out, check the tunnel exit as well and ensure no one has found the cavern that leads to it. If Azir and Jafar are still searching for it, then they may get lucky. If they do, then we're all screwed."

Abram watched as the door at the other end of the room swung open to reveal Paige.

Her expression was coolly polite, her emerald gaze straightforward and revealing little of her emotions.

"Do you think you two boys could play together later?" she asked as she propped her hand on her hip and leaned against the doorframe.

Abram's gaze narrowed on her slowly. She knew how such a display of dominance toward him would affect him.

His dick, already iron hard and fully engorged seemed to swell further and harden painfully.

He'd stayed away from her as much as possible. Now, there would be no saving either of them from the hunger raging through him.

"Of course we can, precious," he all but crooned as his gaze drifted over the thobe and he imagined the sweet perfection of her body underneath. "If you're offering to play in other ways, then I am of course available."

Her nostrils flared in irritation. "Well of course you'd be available for your idea of fun," she scoffed. If he wasn't mistaken there may have been a flash of hurt in her eyes.

"Tonight, precious, I am at your disposal however you may wish me." He held his arms out at his side, a part of him cringing that she should be hurt by anything after what she had already suffered. She had suffered because he had been unable to rein in his interest in her enough to at least keep her safe.

Turning, he nodded to Tariq to begin the job he'd given him before moving for the entrance to the other room and the woman that haunted his thoughts and his desires.

As he escorted her back into his suite he was aware of Tariq closing the door between them and allowing them privacy as he prepared to leave.

"Now, what activities would please you within the confines of what I can provide you?"

How he wished they were in the U.S. rather than here. She could dress in the sexy, flirty clothes he had seen her in before and he could take her to her favorite restaurant or perhaps a starlit dinner on one of the exclusive dinner yachts.

He could take her dancing or they could attend a play.

"Within the confines of what you can provide." She shook her head at the addendum. "Which isn't much, is it?"

Her back was to him, hiding her expression, but the pensive regret in her tone was unmistakable.

"It isn't much," he agreed. "But hopefully, this will be over soon. We'll go out then, Paige. I'll take you to a place where everyone will see the beauty that's on my arm."

A few more days at most. As soon as he or Tariq could locate the CIA asset they worked with in the area.

"Tariq told you Chalah was here today?" She turned as she reached the fireplace.

"Yes, he told me," he muttered in disgust. "I'll have to send him to talk to her if she doesn't leave soon. She needs to get the hell out of here while she still can."

"I almost betrayed us all, Abram," she whispered, her expression reflecting the fear he knew was brewing inside her.

"But you didn't," he told her. "And if you had, Paige, no one could blame you. We've all trusted her. Even I never suspected Jafar would go to such lengths to attain whatever it is he's after."

"Did you trust her?" she asked quietly.

Paige watched his expression carefully, a part of her not even certain if she had truly trusted Chalah even before she saw the audio device.

"I trust no one with your safety or with your life, Paige," he told her, his expression thoughtful, intent.

"There have been moments in the past few days that I've even questioned my trust in Tariq."

He moved to her, his much larger body dwarfing her as he stopped in front of her.

Her breath nearly stopped as he reached out, his fingers catching a curl that had fallen over her shoulder.

It was the only way he was touching her, his figure rubbing the soft strands slowly.

"I want you, Paige," he stated softly, sending her blood pressure skyrocketing, pounding off the charts with the somber heat in his voice and in his face.

"You could have fooled me," she whispered. "You haven't even been here, Abram."

She hadn't liked admitting she had been frightened while he had been gone. That a part of her had been certain Azir would come for her while Abram was gone. That he would find a way to hurt her, to perhaps kill her.

She knew if he could do it, he would find great pleasure in it. She had seen it in his face, in his eyes, the day he had backhanded her across the room.

"I've tried to get you out of here first, Paige," He sighed as he laid the strands of hair neatly against her breast before he stroked the backs of his fingers along the curve of her breast.

"But I don't think I can wait much longer to have you. I don't think I can sleep next to you one more night without touching you, without tasting you."

Swallowing tightly she fought to catch her breath.

"You've managed the past three nights." A frown jumped between her brows at the need, the sexual hunger in his voice. "What's changed?"

His lips twitched with an edge of amusement.

"My misbegotten attempt, as I said, to have you comfortable in your forced surroundings."

She shook her head. "I don't believe you, Abram. Do you know what I think?"

His expression slowly tightened into one of dominant male lust.

"What do you think?" he drawled.

"I think you have no intentions of being my lover, Abram. At the most, you intend to do no more than fuck me while we're here. And only then, if you simply can't resist any longer."

And exactly how right was she?

She watched his eyes narrow and glitter knowingly in his dark face. He knew she was right. She knew she was right.

"Don't push this, Paige."

The tone of his voice and the look in his eyes combined with the order sent a shaft of agony tearing through her.

"You've had me sleep between the two of you, naked, like a lover, with no intention of actually fucking me?" Mocking amusement and bitter realization filled her. "Tell me, Abram, did you order Tariq not to fuck me as well?"

His eyes narrowed further. "I do not order Tariq. As my third, that choice remained between the two of you."

Shock had her drawing in her breath sharply. "You would have let him take me without you?" Confusion filled her.

Paige knew enough about the lifestyle Khalid and his friends were a part of, and she assumed Abram shared the same rules. That didn't allow the third, unless it was a permanently agreed-upon relationship, to ever be intimate with the prime lover's woman without his presence.

"That would have been your choice." His expression was savagely tight now.

"My choice?" She shook her head at his comment. "Abram, do you think I don't know the world you live within when you're in Europe or in the U.S.? That I don't know the associates you and Khalid are closest to, and the rules they adhere to in terms of their private sexual tastes?"

His gaze darkened in suspicion. "What would you know about it, Paige?"

"You say that as though it's some deep dark secret that many of your friends and acquaintances share their wives with those who share their tastes." She stared back at him in disgust. "Do you believe, Abram, truly, that no one but those who do it are aware of it? Do you think friends, brothers, and oh yeah—" Her eyes widened in false amazement. "Sisters, are not well aware of it? Do you take me for stupid?"

"I never imagined you were stupid." His voice was rougher now, containing that dark, black velvet roughness that almost mesmerized her senses.

It would have mesmerized her senses if not for the anger burning inside her.

"Then what did you imagine?" she snapped. "What makes you think I'm not smart enough to see what goes on around me?"

"I never imagined such a thing, Paige." Frustration filled his voice as he glared back at her. "I simply do not imagine that it is within my right to limit your contact with a man I have brought to the bed with you."

Not limit her contact? Tariq was *his* third. The very idea of it implied, at the very least, a sense of possession in regards to a lover, if not a woman he had some feelings of depth for.

But evidently, that wasn't the way it was for him.

The pain of that realization, the realization that whatever was happening between them was only physical, that it was without emotion tore through her like a searing flame, burning through her heart.

"Go fuck yourselves!" she hissed back at him as fury whipped through her along with the knowledge that he was showing no possessiveness, no dominance whatsoever in regards to either her body or her heart.

She slapped at his hands as they lifted to her, disgust and ragged emotions slamming a sense of pain through her senses.

"Don't touch me. Don't speak to me and don't either of you think you will ever sleep with me again," she cried out. "There's not a chance in hell I want you now."

She was dying for him. She was aching for him. She wanted to cry out at the knowledge that what she thought had been mutual desire had been something far different. Perhaps so different that it meant he hadn't wanted her at all.

"The hell you don't," he growled.

"You're damned right I don't," she cried out painfully. "Just kiss my ass and get the hell away from me, Abram. Damn you. Damn you!"

She wasn't crying. There were no tears. The pain went far too deep, and hurt far too much for tears, yet. . . .

instead of getting away from her, instead of leaving her in peace, Abram jerked her to him and pinned her in place against his chest.

"Kiss your ass?" He snarled down at her. "I'll do that and more."

10

God, what she did to him. She thought he had no intention of talking to her? That he could sleep with her much longer without losing his mind?

It wasn't fucking her that he had no intention of doing. It was loving her. And he could see in her eyes that she hadn't been merely talking about sex. She had said fuck, she had referred to sex, but she meant so much more.

Her heart was involved and she intended to involve his as well.

Holding her to him he turned his fingers into her hair, pulled her head back, and as he fought the grief he felt at the thought of never loving her, his lips covered hers.

Sweet heat, fiery feminine anger and passion overflowed from her lips. Her fingers curled into fists and pressed into his shoulders, stopping just the second before true rejection. She wasn't saying no, but the threat of it was there.

Give her a chance to consider the true reality of what he might very well intend and she would be screaming her rejection from the rooftops, and he wouldn't be able to blame her. Hell, he would agree with her.

He had no intention of giving her a chance.

As his lips covered hers, his tongue brushed the seam. He considered for less than a second the seduction he had actually considered each night he lay with her, her naked body curled into him.

He decided against it.

Dominance rose inside him. The need, the overwhelming hunger for her sexual submission rushed through him like a tidal wave of epic proportions.

Need beat at his brain. Control disintegrated. Only instinct remained. The instinct of a primal animal, determined to fully possess his woman on every physical level that could possibly exist.

He tugged at the strands of hair he tangled his fingers in. Just enough pressure to drag a moan from her lips and have her arching into his hold.

This was her acceptance of him and her acceptance of what she had to know was coming from him.

He wasn't her lover, and easy had never been a part of him.

Sliding one hand from her back to her buttocks, his fingers curled around her firm, wounded globes as he lifted her off her petite feet, turned, and all but stumbled to the large bed at the far end of the room.

He paused only long enough to strip the hated throb from her body. If he never saw another of those hated garments shrouding the perfection of her body then it would be far too soon.

"Lay down," he growled as he stripped himself. The loose tunic and trousers came off, along with the even looser white underpants and the custom-made hiking boots he had worn.

She didn't move to obey him, rather she stared back at him defiantly, her breasts rising and falling quickly, tight, hard little nipples beckoning him.

"You lay down." Breathless, heat filling her voice along with the defiance. The sound of it had the head of his dick throbbing imperatively.

He almost allowed a smile to tug at his lips.

"Do you think it works that way?" he asked silkily. "Oh Paige, precious, it doesn't work that way." She was pushing at him, defying him and expecting to get away with it.

Turning his fingers in her hair, he pulled her head back and took the taste of her hunger with his lips again.

She tasted innocent. Her lips moved beneath his with just a hint of hesitancy, as though she hadn't kissed in a while. As though she had never been kissed by a man intent on drowning out her deepest hunger.

A hunger he would have, no matter the lengths he had to go to.

Jerking her against him until his cock pressed firmly into the flesh of her belly.

The heat of her body seared the sensitive head of his cock, drawing a pulse of precome from the bloated head.

Sinking his tongue past her lips to possess the sweet nectar of her hunger.

It wasn't submission she gave him. As his tongue pressed against the seam of her lips, they tightened, and pushing forward past their resistance he found her teeth locked tight to him.

Her fists were unclenched, her nails rasping against his shoulders like a little kitten kneading in pleasure.

Removing his hand from her hair he gripped her jaw instead, his thumb and two fingers pressing into the back of her jaw to force her teeth and lips to part.

A ragged little groan left her throat as his tongue forged inside to stroke against hers and to taste her need. It was there, the hunger and heat meeting his and flaming out of control.

Her nails pricked at his flesh as he arched her closer to him. The demand in his cock was beating through his body, thundering through his bloodstream.

Damn her. She nearly had his knees trembling from no more than her kiss. No more than her heated body arching, her stomach stroking against his dick.

Pumping his tongue into her mouth he nearly groaned as she suckled at it, hungry, sweet dreams of her heated mouth that had his cock jerking and throbbing from the engorged crest along the heavy thick shaft.

He wanted her mouth there. He wanted to stare down at her, watch her take him, watch her suck him, watch as her hot little tongue licked around it.

He pulled his head back, the breath rasping from his chest as he watched her eyes slowly flutter open.

Pleasure reflected in the brilliancy of her emerald eyes, the flushed features of her face. Her tongue peeked out to flutter against her lips, the sight of it drawing his balls tight with desire.

"Suck my cock." The demand had her face flushing further and lust deepening in her gaze.

He stroked his hands up her shoulders, pressing against them to ease her to her knees, the demand imperative, the need clawing at his spine.

Not that she did as he expected. She didn't go immediately to her knees. She didn't suck his cock into the fiery furnace of her mouth.

Instead—

She destroyed him.

She tore aside the fragile illusions of cynicism.

She used that ragged wound growing in his soul.

She broke him.

Then lick by sweet lick down his body she began to remake him.

Paige could barely breathe.

Heat raced within her chest furiously, nerves and desire, fear and excitement making her entire body tremble.

As his hands pressed against her shoulders her lips moved to his shoulders, her tongue tasted the salt and male flavor of his flesh.

Her hands moved down his sides as he caressed down her arms, back up, along her back. His head lowered, strong teeth nipping at her ear in retaliation.

Then she retaliated back. Her teeth scraped over his shoulder and she nipped hard, then lowered to the heavy muscle at his chest, then the male point of a nipple.

Abram jerked, groaning in surprise and in pleasure as her hot little tongue raked over his nipple, and sent heat spinning through his senses.

Damn her, she made him want things, made him want things from her that he was certain weren't good for either of their emotional health.

"My emotional health is not inexhaustible," he groaned as her tongue licked and strolled down his chest to the tight, clenched muscles of his stomach.

The closer she got the harder his dick pulsed and swelled. The flesh was tight, so hard it was painful, so damned sensitive he swore he could feel the air around it.

Her nails scraped down his abs to his thighs as she kissed, licked, and nipped her way down until she was only inches from the heavy, engorged head.

And he was sure as hell doing his best to encourage her to lower, faster.

Damn if he wasn't ready to fucking explode from the need tearing through him.

Slender, graceful fingers curved around the side of the shaft, but there wasn't a chance of them fully encircling it. But she was touching it, and those pouty lips were coming closer by the second.

His fingers were buried in her hair again, clenched, and he grimaced as he felt her heated breath against the engorged, throbbing head of his dick.

He watched, his gaze on her flushed features, closed eyes, and her pink little tongue as it suddenly licked over the darkly flushed head.

She licked and tasted, each stroke of her tongue like a lash of painful ecstasy. Once she got her lips around it and sucked him inside, he wouldn't last seconds.

Then her lips were there, slowly, so damned slowly, enveloping the head of his cock and sucking it into the tight, hot depths of her mouth.

He watched. Watched as her lips closed on him, as her tongue began to lick and rub against the underside of his dick as his fingers tugged at her hair, pulling and releasing as she moaned against the overly sensitive crest of his cock.

Holding onto his control was hell, not releasing the heavy tension invading his balls was becoming the most ecstatic torture he had ever known in his life.

Her tongue was lightning and rapture, her fingers silken heat as she began stroking the heavy shaft, her moans vibrating along the nerve-laden crest as he began thrusting slow and easy, fucking those sweet, pretty lips as he'd only fantasized about for many years.

And he wasn't going to survive this much longer. The tight suction of her mouth, her tongue lashing at it.

His hands tightened.

He could feel the perspiration easing down his temple as his control began to fray to the point that he could feel his balls tightening violently.

He was going to come.

Control be damned. He couldn't keep it together here. He wasn't going to last and he wanted to be buried inside her first. He had to be buried inside her before he lost his mind as he had the first time he had her naked body beneath him.

"Enough," he growled.

She didn't stop.

Her lashes lifted. Her eyes watered from taking him deep and she moaned again.

"I'm going to come in that sweet mouth of yours." He breathed out roughly, his voice ragged. "Is that what you want, precious? My come filing your hot little mouth?"

She flushed deeper. She sucked his dick tighter and left him strung out on a rack of impending bliss.

"So pretty, precious," he crooned, watching her swollen lips draw on the heavy width of his dick.

Her mouth capped the swollen crest, worked around it and rubbed the overly sensitive underside with her hot little tongue.

She was destroying him.

He couldn't hold on.

He didn't want to let her go.

He wanted inside her. The full length of his cock sheltered in the sweet heat of her pussy.

His hips shifted, thrust, and moved against the swollen beauty of her lips.

His hands clasped her head and he forced himself to draw back. To drag the painfully swollen length of his cock away from the pleasure of her mouth.

Glistening, moist from her mouth and so damned hard he was dying. Then he lifted her from her knees and laid her back easily on the bed.

Then she shocked him. She had him stilling, his mouth watering, every nerve ending in his body heating in fiery response.

She laid back against the pillows, slender legs parted as her fingers slid into the moist heat of her saturated pussy.

Slender fingertips moved through the wet folds as she stroked and circled the swollen bud of her clit.

Dazed, mesmerized, she stared back at him, stroked her pussy, and whispered a broken moan.

He moved. Quickly, firmly, he gripped her wrist and pulled her fingers from the flesh he was going to own. Every kiss, every touch, every sweet erotic moan.

"It was feeling good," she whispered hoarsely, her

fingers curling against his hand. "Aren't you curious how I please myself? How I fantasize and whisper your name when I come?"

Seeing it would have him coming to the air alone, and that he wasn't doing.

Taking her other wrist he placed both on the pillow above her head with a determined look.

"Leave them there," he warned her. "Don't move them."

Her hot little tongue flicked over her lips as he shoved his knee between her thighs as he moved over her.

He hadn't meant to kiss her lips, he'd intended to go straight to her pussy to lick at the sweet, heated warmth spilling from it.

But those sweet lips beckoned, they drew him.

His tongue pumped into her mouth, stroked and devoured her as he came over her, spreading her thighs to create the sweetest embrace he'd ever known.

Her legs lifted, knees bending as her feet pressed into the mattress, her knees gripping his thighs.

Thick and heavy, his cock slid against the slick wet folds of her pussy. Engorged, aching with a hunger tearing him apart.

His lips slid from hers, ran down the silk of her neck to the rise of firm, sweet breasts and tight hard nipples.

He had to taste her nipples. Candy pink and hard and sweet as hell. He curled his tongue around one and let his hunger have its way.

Paige was drowning. She could feel herself drowning in pleasure so incredible she couldn't find the strength to even attempt to resist even a second of it.

He'd warned her to keep her hands at the pillow, but she had to touch him, she had to hold onto him.

Her head was spinning like a top, pleasure whipping through her system like a fire burning out of control.

Her fingers dug into his hair as his lips drew the sensitized flesh into his mouth.

Sucking, drawing on it, his tongue licking, his teeth scraping. Flares of sensation whipped and raced through her entire body. Arching into it she was desperate to get closer.

She wanted to hold onto him forever. She just wanted to stay here in his arms.

"I waited," she whispered, dazed, so much pleasure. "I waited so long, Abram."

So many years and so many dreams of his touch.

"God, Paige, sweetheart." Lifting his head he stared down at her, his legs pressing hers farther apart as he lifted, his knees digging into the bed, the head of his cock nestling into the satiny soft folds of her pussy.

The clenched entrance flared around the tip of his cock as he pressed forward, his eyes locked with the drowsy heat of hers and he began to work the stiff flesh into the heated grip of her pussy.

Paige was caught by the midnight of his eyes. She was caught by the pleasure-pain piercing and stretching her sex.

Her thighs trembled, her back arching, neck stretched back as her nails dug into his shoulders, her knees lifting, gripping his hips and opening herself to him.

"There, baby," he groaned, his fingers gripping her hips, his gaze still locked with hers.

"Hold onto me, baby," he groaned as she watched his expression tighten, watched his eyes flare.

That heat was burning through her. Like flames licking over her flesh, ripping through her senses. The thick width of his cock pressed in, stretched her and sent desperate aching need shattering through her as she arched, bucking against him, fighting to drive him deeper.

His fingers tightened on her hips, his hips keeping a steady, heated rhythm. He didn't speed up, he didn't go any slower. Keeping his gaze on her, he continued to work deeper into flesh rarely used.

Her head twisted on the pillows, dug into them, and with desperate whimpers she begged for more. She wanted to cry out, she wanted to scream for more, but oh God, she couldn't breathe.

"Please," she gasped, her nails digging into his shoulders, gripping as the muscles of her cunt rippled and sucked in tight hard spasms as the head of his cock lodged inside her. Working against the resistant muscles, the heavy flesh throbbing, burning inside her.

She needed more.

"Abram, please," she moaned. "Oh God! Fuck me. Please, Abram."

His hips jerked, burying him deeper.

Paige lifted her knees, her legs wrapping around his hips as she ground her pussy upward, gasping with pleasure.

"There you go, precious," he groaned. "Fuck that sweet pussy up to me. Give it to me, baby. Work on my cock."

His lips moved to her neck, biting kisses, strokes of his tongue licking over her as he began to move deeper inside her.

Finally.

"Yes," she whispered, her pleasure echoing in the low cry that left her lips. "Deeper, Abram."

She lifted closer, her legs tightening around his hips. "Fuck me deeper."

His hips jerked against her, driving his cock deeper, harder inside her.

She was shaking, shuddering in his grip, but he was shuddering too. She could feel him. His face buried in her neck, his lips moving against the sensitive flesh, his hips moving harder now, pushing his cock deeper inside her.

The pleasure began to whip through her. Sensation upon sensation as she writhed beneath him, her legs tightening around his hips, her arms clasping his neck.

"Take me, Paige." He nipped at her shoulders. "Take all of me, precious."

She didn't have so much as a second's warning. She'd barely drawn in a tremulous breath when his hips bunched, gathering strength, then in one stroke he buried the full length inside her.

The heavy breadth of his cock forced its way inside her. Every hard inch stroking to her furthest depth and deeper. Pleasure and pain became rocketing fire as he began to move. He didn't pause, he didn't give her a chance to catch her breath or to prepare for the sensations tearing across her body, throwing her into a maelstrom of pure bliss. She wanted to scream it was so good, but she couldn't scream. Instinct kept the desperation bottled inside, silent, or nearly silent.

She had to bite her lip. She bit his shoulder.

"Ah fuck!" Her teeth at his shoulder did something. It triggered a reaction. It set loose a primal, sensual creature she could have never expected. A wild, primitive, erotic lover that hijacked her senses.

His hips twisted and surged, shafted inside her and fucked her with driving, forceful strokes. Each rasp of his cock thrusting through her pussy, pushing her to a limit she hadn't known existed. Pushing her toward an ecstasy so fiery she was lost in it, begging for more, dying with each stroke.

Each heavy thrust parting and delving, stretching and burning. She bit into his shoulder harder, fighting the cries welling inside her, fighting to hold back.

"No," she moaned. "No. Please, Abram. Don't . . ." She shook her head. "I want to scream," she whimpered. He growled. His lips covered hers, his tongue delved inside. He trapped the sound. He thrust harder, his cock stroking deeper, fucking her, possessing her, owning her as he never had before.

In that second she felt the sensations rushing, surging. Silent screams were ricocheting through her head and through her soul.

She was coming with a force. She didn't know if she could survive. Exploding around the thick wedge of his cock as it began to throb violently. He groaned into the kiss and began coming inside her. Heated, deep spurts of his semen pulsing, surging inside the spasming flesh of her pussy.

Groaning into the kiss that held back her screams, his arms holding her to him, possessively, desperately.

And for the first time in her life she swore she belonged.

For the first time in his life, he knew what belonging meant.

And it terrified them both.

11

"Move! It's time to go!" Abram hissed at her ear, a sense of danger filling his voice and awakening her with a surge of fear-laced adrenaline.

Paige's eyes came open, staring up in confusion at him, his hand capped over her lips to cover any sound she may have made, borne of fear or surprise.

Staring up at him she saw the icy features of his face, the cold, murderous rage glittering in his black eyes and she knew something, somehow, had just gone to hell.

"Clothes." He lifted his hand and with the other pressed clothing into her hands. "Shoes." They felt like hiking boots and they were shoved into her other hand. "Hurry."

Gripping her wrist as he jerked the blankets back, exposing the warmth of her naked flesh to the chill air outside the covering, he pulled her from the bed.

Coming to her feet she was surprised to find soft, wool trousers, a heavy, short tunic, socks, and definitely hiking boots. She dressed quickly, her gaze trying to pierce the darkness as she caught Abram's shadow moving close to her as he dressed as well.

"Extraction will be in place," Tariq hissed through the darkness. "There are horses waiting in the caverns, but we're going to be cutting it close. Azir is with the Matawa now, and they're itching to get in here."

The Matawa, the feared religious police who enforced the strict Islamic law on all matters from courtship to dress and marital intercourse.

"Why are they here?" Jerking her socks on she tried to keep the fear from her voice as she hurriedly finished dressing.

"For us," Tariq snarled in a sibilant whisper. "Azir called them in. They'll hold you, me, and Abram until he makes the vow to the emissary, and once the emissary is finished they'll secure Abram for punishment of the crimes of sexual deviance and intent to abdicate a vow given to the monarchy, which is the same as treason. Until then, you will be held in the cells below the castle until the vow is given to give you time to contemplate your sins before you're stoned to death." Disgust rang in his voice as she laced the boots then rose to her feet.

"Here." Jacket, gloves, and a hat. "The temperature's dropped significantly. We have to hurry; they'll be here within minutes."

There was a sound of stone scraping against stone, and seconds later Abram gripped her hand and rushed her into a darkness even more overwhelming than that of the bedroom they had been in.

As he and Tariq wrestled whatever door was used

back into place securely, the click of the lock reengaging, they all froze at the sound of heavy pounding at the bedroom door.

"You will open this door. Abram el Hamid Mustafa. Tariq bin Sa'id Mustafa. Paige Eleanora Galbraithe, you are hereby under arrest for the crimes of sexual deviancy and conspiracy to commit treason against the Saudi Arabian empire."

Paige reached out, her fingers clenched on Abram's arm at the sound of the rough, cruel tone and the charges being leveled against them.

The voices turned lower, the words muffled by the wood and stone barriers, only barely reaching her ears as adrenaline began to surge through her.

Why were they just standing there?

Her fingers clenched tighter on his arm, the need to run overwhelming her now. Each of those charges were punishable by stoning for a woman, though only the charge of treason held such a punishment for Abram and Tariq.

She could feel him against her, the tension in his body mounting as he extricated his arm from her grip only to wrap it around her shoulders and pull her to him.

The pounding came again.

"Three." Abram began counting off. "Two." As he spoke he turned her toward the back of whatever cave, cavern, or room they were hidden within.

A second later the loud, raucous sounds of a heavy metal band began to scream through the room.

Paige jumped, only barely managing to hold back a cry of surprise at the shrill music. In the same second, Abram's arms tightened around her and they were rushing headlong into a darkness barely lit by the pen-light Tariq held out before him.

"What the hell happened?" Abram snarled as they began to run through the stone corridor that she was certain had to run on forever.

"I don't know what the hell happened," Tariq hissed back. "I was with our contact arranging extraction when he got the call that the Matawa were moving in on the fortress to arrest the three of us, and that Jafar couldn't be found. Azir contacted them from what our contact, Yassir, learned and he rushed me back to the cave entrance. From what we were being told as we ran for the caverns, Azir called them in and informed them of the charges. He's also having an 'arrest on sight' order placed against Khalid, Paige's mother, and her father if they enter Saudi Arabia. It's a fucking mess, and I still haven't figured out how Azir arranged it."

Azir, Abram's father. He had found another way to betray his son.

"He has minor influence with the Matawa," Abram growled. "He'll be able to keep the order in force only until the authorities in Riyadh hear of it and bring it before the king. But until then, they can do exactly that; kill on sight."

He didn't even sound breathless or tired and Paige knew her legs would have already given out on her.

She tried to draw enough air into her lungs to keep from collapsing, her heart racing hard and fierce as Abram all but carried her at a dead run.

"Did you complete the extraction plan?" Abram's voice was lifeless, all emotion stripped from it now.

"Extraction was all but complete when the call came

in. Yassir managed to call in emergency extraction at that point," Tariq informed him. "We have three hours to reach the pickup point in the mountains. If we're not there, then they leave without us. I talked to the commander of the rangers myself and he intends to make damned certain nothing stands in the way of that information getting into their hands, but he's not willing to watch his men die to get it. Did you get the files?"

Had any of them had time to get anything?

"On my back," Abram bit out. "My pack holds everything we've gathered over the past year. Don't worry; extraction won't leave without us, Tariq. They need this too damned much and they know it."

He had made certain he wouldn't become a casualty to politics or indifference in the plans made to pull him and Tariq, and now Paige as well, out of Saudi Arabia.

"Jafar had Chalah driven to the desert airstrip where a private Learjet made a quick stop and picked her up before heading out again, earlier this evening. That's where we suspect he is, on his way back from the airstrip," Tariq reported, as Paige swore there was no end to the tunnel.

"At least she's out of here," Abram bit out roughly. "Having my friends endangered in this war Azir has been waging against us is going to get him killed."

And she could hear the certainty in Abram's voice that he would be the one to kill his father.

"What I'd like to know is why the hell Jafar was so damned intent on getting her out of here tonight," Tariq questioned, his voice harsh.

"Why hasn't he kept her here, as Azir has been pushing him to do?" Abram asked in return. "God only knows what either of them have planned."

"There are horses waiting in the cavern, and we should arrive at the extraction location just in time if we're damned lucky," Tariq stated as they rounded yet another curve in the tunnel.

"Is there any way they can find the hidden door in Abram's room?" Paige whispered as the fear clenched her stomach and trembled in her voice at the thought of being followed.

"Azir has searched that room and every other room in the castle for the doors to the tunnels he's already closed in. He still hasn't found some of those. Many of the tunnels veer off in several different directions with the ones leading to more strategically located rooms accessed by more than one hidden stone door and tunnel, like a damned underground maze with no map," Abram told her. "This particular corridor empties into an old mine. It's easily millennia old and the exit is no more than a narrow slit in a wall surrounded by fallen boulders. If it were going to be found, Azir would have done so by now."

They hadn't slowed. Both men kept a steady pace that never slackened, one Paige couldn't have had a hope of keeping up with if it weren't for Abram's arm locked around her waist.

Still, she was breathless, tired, and fighting to keep up just enough to keep him from having to slow his pace. She felt helpless, weak, and unable to fight enough to even participate in her own escape.

"Why did Azir turn you into the Matawa?" She

gasped as she struggled to help Abram keep her on her feet. "What was the point?"

"The hell if I know," Abram growled. "It's at least two more weeks before the emissary is due to arrive and Azir has to have me there to give that vow, not under arrest, awaiting death, or dead. It served no purpose."

"He would have held Paige and me until you gave your vow, then saw to our deaths once you gave it," Tariq stated, his voice heated and rough as he led the way through the corridor. "He'll not risk allowing you even a single ally if he can keep you here.

"Paige is an American citizen whose family is more than aware of where she is," Abram growled. "He knows he can't get away with that, just as he knows I would find a way to contact the American consulate, the Saudi royal offices, and any journalist willing to listen."

"And accidents happen in jails all the time, especially the detention cells the Matawa keep. When they did release her, Abram, you know the shape she would be in."

Paige didn't want to imagine the shape she would be in. She'd heard enough about the Saudi prisons from Khalid as he recounted the horrors friends of his had suffered when being held by the Matawa.

"Doesn't sound like my idea of a favored vacation activity," she whispered, her voice trembling as she thought she felt a breeze and detected a touch of fresh air ahead.

"Yeah, well, you need to talk to your travel agent about that, baby," Abram assured her somberly.

"Maybe demand a refund," she whispered.

Yes, that was definitely fresh air.

Thank God. She hadn't known if she could stand it much longer in that enclosed corridor with its dark, dank air and sense of forced enclosure.

The narrow slit of the opening in the cavern wall deposited them first onto a shallow pile of boulders that reached toward the roof of the rock ceiling overhead.

As though they had been tossed randomly at the wall and bounced to the floor around it. Still gripping her wrist, Abram pulled her through the brief stone maze into the main room of the large cave.

The nicker of a horse had her eyes turning to the exit and the group of men and horses awaiting them.

Three of the riders instantly jumped from their mounts, holding their reins loosely as an older rider dismounted and waved them toward the horses.

"My nephew sent the message that Azir's guards and the Matawa are preparing to leave the castle." The rider moved quickly to Abram, handed over a rifle and a handgun holstered on belted leather.

Looping the belt around his neck and under his arm, Abram grabbed the rifle and looped it over the pommel of the saddle before turning and quickly gripping Paige's hips to help her onto the horse standing next to his.

"Do they have a direction they suspect we're riding to?" Abram asked quickly as Paige took the reins he pushed quickly to her.

"To the mountains." The rider spat to the ground after speaking. "Ride hard and beat them there, but they may still get there before extraction."

He was American. The sound of the Texas accent surprised her.

"Good luck," he called out as Abram kicked his heels into the horse's flanks and they galloped from the cavern into the crisp, clear predawn night.

The thunder of horses' hooves echoed around her, drowning out the sound of her heart raving in her chest.

Abram took the lead and Tariq rode at the rear, keeping Paige between them. If it hadn't been for her they wouldn't have to run like this and the Matawa wouldn't be chasing them with such charges.

Of course, if Azir hadn't kidnapped her, none of this would have happened either.

"Yassir is positioning his men to track Azir's head hunters." Tariq called into the communication headset he wore. "He'll let us know if they head our way."

"He'll head our way," Abram assured him. "There are only a few usable locations for extraction and they aren't that far apart."

They could pray and fight to get there first, but other than that it was out of their control, and that terrified her.

The lack of control in both her emotions and responses to Abram when it came to her safety was terrifying. She had been an independent woman with a job, a future, and the ability to make decisions for herself. To risk death over such an idea was a nightmare to her.

Just as the furious race through the night would become, she was certain.

"They're heading this way, Abram," Tariq announced as they neared the base of the mountains that rose before them. "Yassir received confirmation from his spy among Azir's guards. The Matawa commander received a call and they've changed direction."

Abram suddenly veered toward the more shadowed edge of the trail, his curse searing the night.

"They have watches." Tariq snapped. "Possibly snipers."

"Azir doesn't have any snipers and I doubt the Matawa do. But Jafar would have them."

"Would he give the order to fire?" Paige's voice trembled, not as much in fear this time, but in rage.

If she survived this then she would kill Jafar herself.

"I don't know." They were forced to slow the horses to a hard trot rather than a gallop.

"We'll take the next turn to the longer trail up the mountains," Abram told them. "And this, boys and girls, is what sucks about these mountains. We have no trails for the mountain wheels."

"Wouldn't need them if we didn't have to deal with the assholes in *our* family," Tariq grunted.

"Lucked out there, didn't we?" Abram agreed as he turned his horse to another trail.

"I wouldn't call it luck." Paige interjected, a morbid sense of black humor overtaking her. "I think you managed to get on God's bad side that week, boys."

Silence met her observation for a second before Tariq gave a mocking chuckle echoed by Abram.

"We manage to stay on someone's bad side all the time," Abram agreed. "It only began there."

It was a brief sense of lightness in the tension that grew from the battle just to stay alive. They moved farther up the face of the mountain along a curve that placed the jagged, sharp peaks of the huge boulders between them and their previous position.

Abram was trying to block any sight of a sniper's rifle, Paige thought.

"Jafar has joined them," Tariq announced, his voice suddenly heavy. "He's moving along a trail that will catch up with us before the Matawa and Azir's soldiers. He's riding in with a dozen men."

Abram picked up the pace despite the danger to the horses and to them.

"Extraction ETA is coming up," Tariq assured him. "We'll be cutting it close."

"I didn't necessarily want to simply cut it close," Abram growled.

Damn, this was going to hell in a handbasket, he thought, just as Azir had planned. This had been what he was working for all along. Not necessarily Abram's escape, but definitely ensuring that both Tariq and Paige were made aware that Azir held his fate in the palm of his hand.

He would kill himself first, Abram decided. And he would be damned if he left that land for Jafar to take over with his terrorists. He had recourse if he was forced to make that vow. Azir and Jafar would find out just how far he was willing to go to ensure they were destroyed if Paige and Tariq didn't make it out of here alive tonight.

"Yassir has made contact with extraction," Tariq reported. "Their ETA is on time and they're moving into the area. They're coming in opposite the Matawa but Jafar's men will have a view."

"Tell him to proceed, lights black, night sensor engaged," Abram ordered. "We're the smallest team on the mountain and we're starting to get nervous."

Tariq relayed the information as Abram glanced back at Paige, her face so pale it was easily seen in the darkness.

"We'll make it," he promised her, even as he prayed he could keep that promise.

"We're coming up on the clearing," Tariq stated. "Yassir has lost sight of Jafar and his men."

"They're close then, aren't they?" Paige guessed, her gaze tracking the darkness as the first, weak rays of dawn began moving in.

"I have a feeling they've been close from the beginning," Abram stated as he watched the shadows closely.

Dawn wasn't far away. Extraction should arrive within minutes of the gathering legate, revealing the presence.

"Ten minutes," Tariq stated quietly. "We're almost home free."

"Almost only counts in horseshoes and hand grenades. Is that not your American saying?" Jafar stepped from the shadows as Abram brought his horse slowly to a stop.

"Let it go, Jafar," Abram warned him. "Look at it this way, with me gone, you can control the province."

Jafar hooked his fingers in the leather belt he wore over his tunic and watched Abram carefully.

"Ah yes, a perfect plan but for the fact that within two weeks the province reverts back to the regime if you are unable, or unwilling, to accept control of it. And you cannot appoint a successor for at least ten years in the event you have children."

Abram leaned his arms on the pommel of the saddle and regarded his cousin assessingly.

"There is that," he agreed. "But perhaps you could have ensured the vow was made at the very least if you and Azir had not dragged the Matawa into this."

Jafar grimaced. "That was not a decision I made but one Azir jumped into when he learned Pavlos and Marilyn Galbraithe were preparing to travel to the American embassy in Riyadh to protest the kidnapping of their only child, Paige Galbraithe. And I do believe our king himself must have been threatening repercussions against Azir despite the Matawa's protestations of your sexual deviancy."

Abram dismounted slowly, the knowledge that they weren't going to escape unless he managed to diffuse Jafar uppermost in his mind.

He'd wanted to leave Saudi Arabia without shedding blood; he especially hadn't wanted to shed Jafar's blood.

It didn't look like he was going to be able to get out of it.

He looked around at the men materializing behind their leader.

"You've wanted to know if you could beat me for years now, Jafar," he said.

"This I have." Jafar nodded with a pleasant smile. "And always you have denied me this opportunity."

"Let them go." Abram nodded to Paige and Tariq, ignoring their sudden protests. "And I'll give you the opportunity."

"What are you going to do, Abram?" Paige whispered desperately. "You can't do this."

He kept his gaze on Jafar's thoughtful face.

"Where is this a benefit?" Jafar drawled. "Your escape simply for the pleasure of the fight? This will bring me little comfort when the land of my father is taken by the king and we are asked to leave."

Abram nodded slowly. "I see your point. Let's make it worth both our time and blood then. You let Paige and Tariq go either way. If you can beat me until I cannot stand then I'll stay, take the vow, and give you the ten years to ensure your possessions."

Jafar's brows raised in surprise. "And if you can beat me to the point I cannot lift myself?"

"Then you ensure my escape when the extraction team arrives. Even against Azir and the Matawa."

A smile touched Jafar's lips.

"Abram, please," Paige whispered behind him. "Please don't do this."

"Does your woman not have faith in your ability to win?" Jafar laughed.

"I don't have faith in your ability not to cheat!" Paige shot back.

Abram winced at the savagery in her voice as she spoke, and at the insult she delivered to Jafar.

"Strangely, neither do I." Jafar laughed as he stared back at Abram. "Are you willing to risk this?"

12

Abram couldn't say that he had ever felt another person's pain or fear until now. His flesh prickled with a deepening, dark sensation as he felt Paige's grip tighten. Her breathing was louder than before, the anger that had been brewing inside her was building.

If she'd had a gun Abram feared she would have planted a bullet in Jafar's head the moment he revealed himself. Her hatred of him was becoming absolute.

"A trade then?" Jafar chuckled. "Are there any rules?"

"Let's keep it interesting," Abram suggested, almost looking forward to the coming fight. "Fists, elbows, or knees only. Just as we did when we were boys."

They hadn't fought since they'd reached adulthood. The battles that they faced in their lives had made their familial grievances seem petty in comparison.

Jafar stepped forward, his thumbs hooking into the belt loops around his lean hips as Abram shed the coat he wore.

Before leaving the fortress he'd dressed in jeans, a thermal undershirt, denim overshirt, and leather hiking boots. He was not just prepared for the cold desert night, but marginally protected as well.

The clothes were well worn and comfortable, soft and relaxed.

Jafar paused and stared at the clothing almost longingly before giving a little sigh and stretching his shoulders.

"Abram, you are mad," Tariq hissed. "He always beat both our asses when we were boys."

"We are not boys any longer." Abram gave a tight, anticipatory smile as he stepped away from one cousin to face the other man. "And I have a reason to win."

There was no posturing and no preliminaries. They went right at each other, fists flying, snarls erupting from their lips and pure male testosterone fueling each punch.

He had been needing this. A chance to beat some fucking sense back into his cousin since the day he'd realized Jafar was fighting alongside Ayid and Aman.

"Fuck!" he snarled as Jafar managed to deliver an iron-hard fist to his jaw.

"For shame, cousin, such language," Jafar chided him as he jumped back to avoid Abram's answering blow. "I have told you, such disregard of decency will only bring you to a sad end."

"That or my damned family," Abram retorted with a tight grin. "Tell me, Jafar, when did you stop dreaming of freedom and begin to dream of controlling lives instead?"

Jafar paused, his eyes narrowing in affront. His nostrils flared as something akin to an insane rage seemed to glow in the odd, celadon green of his eyes. That rage was the distraction Abram had awaited.

He took the advantage and slammed his fist into Jafar's jaw and followed it with a quick, striking knee blow to the groin.

Jafar's eyes widened in agony as he inhaled roughly. A tight whistling sound spewed from his lungs as Abram caught his shoulders and slammed his knee into his cousin's diaphragm. He followed that quickly with a hard right to his face, slamming a blow into his jaw, and throwing him backward to be caught by one of his men. The older, bearded fighter gave a wicked grin and threw his commander back into the fray.

Abram didn't have the time or ability to draw this little battle out. He could hear the low hum of the helicopter moving in stealth mode, much closer than he had anticipated. Within minutes the extraction team would be in place and ready to collect them.

He couldn't let up. He had managed to gain the advantage, something he had never accomplished as a boy and assumed he would never accomplish as an adult. With fists, feet, and another knee to both the groin and to the stomach, Abram dropped his cousin to the dirt with a savage snarl of triumph.

"I win," he rasped, his voice sounding ragged and torn as he stared down at Jafar. "This time it mattered more than my father's pride."

Jafar stared at him, his breathing harsh and labored, his face bloodied, his odd green gaze strangely amused despite the pain that filled it.

"Be careful, cousin," Jafar warned, his voice low. "To allow a woman to be such a weakness—"

Something flashed in Jafar's eyes, something bitter and filled with wild rage as he cut the words off.

"Be careful, Jafar. Without it, you become the monster you are beginning to face in the mirror each day," Abram said before turning and moving toward where Paige and Tariq waited.

There wasn't a second's warning. Tariq's eyes widened, Paige cried out in fear, and the feel of cold steel against his neck stopped him in his tracks.

Abram froze, regret for his cousin welling in his chest as much as for himself. "You used to be a man of your word, cousin. "And unfortunately, of all things Abram had expected Jafar to remember, it had been the honor of his given word.

"I used to be many things, cousin," Jafar said softly. "Many hard lessons have taught me the error of my ways." The blade scraped against Abram's jugular as he allowed his gaze to meet Paige's.

Terror filled the emerald depths as her tears washed over her cheeks. Tariq stood behind her, forcibly restraining her from crossing the distance.

She would have run to him, he realized in bemusement. Even knowing there was nothing she could do, and that there was a high chance she could have been harmed, still, she would have run to him.

"Jafar, please, don't do this," she cried out in horror. Abram felt the knife begin to bite into his flesh.

"I won't go back," Abram warned him softly, knowing the game his cousin was playing. "I can't go back, Jafar. You know this."

"Return or die," Jafar snarled. "I cannot afford to allow you to leave at this time, Abram. You know this."

"You have no choice. Accept it," Abram answered quietly. "I won't go back, Jafar, and I won't give that vow. You and Azir have lost this game."

"Perhaps I'll put the blade to your lover's throat, Jafar suggested mockingly. "Then would you do as I need you to do?"

Abram almost paused at the way the other man phrased his words.

Almost.

"You would have to kill me first," he warned him. "I won't let you touch her as long as I live."

"Easily done." His arm tensed as the blade pressed harder.

"You owe me, Jafar," Paige screamed out furiously, her voice raw and hoarse as Tariq was forced to hold her back.

She strained against his hold, her expression twisting with rage.

"Damn you, Jafar, you owe me," she screamed again. Abram felt a trickle of blood at his neck and yet he still stood silently, too curious about the path his cousin would take to attempt to break his hold just yet.

Jafar paused.

"You owe me," Paige repeated as the tears rolled down her face. "You still owe me."

And just what the hell would Jafar owe her?

"She is a beautiful woman," Jafar sighed, his hold against the side of Abram's head tightening. "And yes, I owe her much. Without her, perhaps I would be dead."

Surprised, Abram wondered what the hell had been going on over the years that he was unaware of.

"And this is how you repay your debts?" Abram asked him. "With blood?"

Behind him, he felt Jafar breathe in slowly, deeply, as though preparing himself. As his body tightened, Abram tensed as well, covering his own anticipation within Jafar's.

"I'm sorry, cousin," Jafar said. "But I cannot afford your escape or theirs."

As the words left his mouth the viperous red lines of the laser rifles' sights cut through the night, pinpointing Jafar and each of his men as black ropes and army rangers slid soundlessly into position.

They surrounded Jafar's team of men as Abram let his gaze move to Paige once again.

Something in him tightened each time he allowed his eyes to meet the grief in hers and to acknowledge the fear that filled her face as Jafar kept that knife at his throat.

"Release him, Jafar," the commanding voice of the black-masked ranger closest to him ordered.

"I cannot do this." The lazy amusement in Jafar's voice was at odds with the tension in his body.

"Don't make us start picking off your men," he advised when Jafar refused to move. "We will."

"We are called martyrs for a reason." Jafar mocked them though the knife never moved.

It wasn't going to move. What fucking game was his cousin playing? If Jafar was going to cut his throat, then he would have already done so.

Abram found it a little too easy to slam his elbow into his cousin's diaphragm as he caught the wrist holding the knife at the same time.

Thrusting Jafar's arm to the side as he held his wrist, Abram broke away from the hold, twisting the wrist as he moved and taking his cousin to his knees.

Abram released him. He jumped back to safety behind the rangers now circling the team of terrorist soldiers.

"Drop your weapons and we'll leave just as quietly as we arrived," the commander ordered. "Otherwise, we'll kill, if we have to."

The terrorists' weapons were tossed carelessly to the ground as Abram moved quickly to Paige. They were gathered up and confiscated to ensure a safe escape, but Abram had other things to take care of besides watching the soldiers' defeat. He had to get to Paige. He had to ease her fear and her tears before she broke his heart with them. Her arms flew around his neck as she cried out his name. The broken sound of her voice and the trembling of her body had all his protective instincts screaming.

"We have to go," he whispered into her ear as the rangers moved to help Tariq into the harness that would lift him into the hovering helicopter.

Easing from her he took the harness from the waiting ranger and helped her into it before strapping on his own and clipping it to the rope.

Just in time.

As they were lifted into the darkened sky, the lights of the Matawa's vehicles began cutting through the winding vehicle paths that eventually led to their location.

Once the Matawa arrived, there would be no escape without bloodshed.

Within seconds the ropes were pulled into the helicopter, the rangers climbing in and securing their passengers then themselves, before the helicopter shot through the sky.

"Captain Mustafa, we'll be landing at a hidden airbase and loading you on a transport plane straight to D.C." Commander Ramsey jerked the mask from his face as he made the announcement.

David "Race" Ramsey settled back against the frame of the stripped-down Black Hawk helicopter as he stared at them.

"Thanks for arriving on time, Commander Ramsey." Tariq grinned. "It looked as though you might be running late for a minute or two there."

Race gave a small chuckle as his blue eyes twinkled in amusement.

"General Jack Walters will be waiting in D.C. to debrief you, Captain Mustafa, and Ms. Galbraithe." Ramsey grinned at Tariq. "One of you is going to have to advance in rank soon, before things get confusing."

"Yes, sir," Abram responded, only half listening as he felt Paige tense in his hold.

"Captain Mustafa?" she whispered.

"A formality, nothing more," he answered quietly, praying no one would explain before he had the chance to do so himself.

Ramsey's lips quirked, obviously catching the less-than-honest response.

It was another lie told to her. It was one of many, and God knew she didn't deserve the dishonesty.

"Your brother and parents are being notified of your

rescue," Ramsey assured her before nodding to Abram. "It's good to have you back, sir."

"It's good to be back, Commander." Abram nodded. It had been a while since he'd had to consider the rank he'd earned while working undercover in the place he should have been able to call his home.

Abram turned his head and stared for a second at the darkened sun-baked land below them.

There were no regrets.

As he watched the land of his birth recede into the distance he couldn't feel anything for the years he had spent there, except sorrow.

Lessa was buried there, as was the second wife he had barely known, along with their unborn child.

He was leaving behind his youth, but it hadn't served him well while he had it. Just as the land he had been born to had refused to protect him.

"We're going home," Paige whispered against his chest. In her voice he could hear the underlying question.

As her head tipped back to stare at him, he saw the silent question in the emerald depths.

It was a question he wasn't ready to face.

"You have your life back now," he promised her as he deliberately moved her to the seat beside him. While he held her, he couldn't think, he couldn't feel anything past his need for her.

"Yes," she announced softly.

"Your job." He moved in front of her to help remove her harness.

She blinked, her breath hitching as he watched the realization entering her gaze.

She nodded hesitantly. "My job," she agreed, though

that wasn't true, he remembered. She had no job, because of him, Jafar, and Azir. She'd lost that, but maybe she could be rehired or else she could find another, he told himself. Another job, another apartment if she had to, and at the worst, she could find more friends. But she could only die once.

"Please don't." Her fingers lay against his lips as they parted again, her fear of what he might say almost as bad as the fear for her life had been. "If you're going to walk out of my life then just do it, okay? I don't want to know."

Her lips trembled and it broke his heart. But as he nodded slowly and said nothing more, it broke her heart worse. He watched the pain move into her eyes, watched it drain the color from her face. There were simply no promises to give her.

She clasped her hands tightly in her lap and stared dismissively over his shoulder. As though she were done with him.

And God help him, he couldn't blame her.

ARMY TRANSPORT
FLIGHT TO WASHINGTON, D.C.
UNITED STATES OF AMERICA

She was sleeping. Soft lips were parted, innocently belying the dark shadows beneath her eyes and the smudge of tearstains on her soft, pale cheeks.

Tariq simply could not believe his cousin's stupidity. As if he and every man in the army helicopter hadn't seen Abram's gentle though destructive rejection of her.

Sitting in the netted area that posed as the passenger seat, he watched her sleep and wondered what Abram was thinking by walking away from her.

"I have to say, you're a dumber bastard than I thought you were," he commented quietly, his voice just loud enough to assure that Abram heard him.

He glanced at his cousin, catching the look that Abram shot the sleeping beauty as well.

There wasn't a chance in hell that Abram wasn't regretting any thought of walking away from her.

"I have enough ghosts haunting me." Abram sighed. "I can't add to them, Tariq. I don't have the promises she needs."

"She's a woman, not a ghost," Tariq objected with an edge of disgust. "And I didn't hear her asking for any damned thing."

Hell, talking to Abram was like talking to a wall, with the exception that the wall was probably more receptive on occasion.

"Let's keep it that way," Abram suggested, his tone caustic as he leaned closer to be heard over the sounds of the plane's engines.

Tariq sat silently for long moments. He needed to figure this one out, quickly, before his cousin made the dumbest mistake of his life.

"Well, if you're walking away then you can't have a problem with me trying a hand at her heart, right?"

The look Abram turned on him promised violence. "Stay the fuck away from her."

Tariq stared back at him, their gazes locked in a battle of wills that neither were used to.

"Tell me, Abram, do you think every man you give

that order to is going to obey? Do you think Jafar considers this battle done in any way? That it's over?" His brow lifted as he leaned back into the heavy interlocking straps of the cargo seat. He crossed his arms over his chest. "Oh yeah, here's a better one," he suggested. "When you've completely fucked up, figured out where you fucked up, and convinced yourself you can fix it, do you really believe she's going to be sitting home alone, just waiting on you?"

Tariq had no doubt that was exactly what Abram thought. His arrogance could only be bested by Khalid's or Jafar's.

"Stay the hell away from her," Abram repeated. "It's my fault she was placed in danger this time. If it's your fault the next time, then I'll have someone's ass to kick to make me feel better. I can ensure that ass kicking is yours."

If nothing else, his cousin could be predictable when it came to Paige. He was incredibly stubborn sometimes, and Paige was one of the things that he could be incredibly stubborn about, but he was predictable.

Tariq nodded slowly before sliding his gaze to the side to catch Abram's look, heated and filled with longing as he stared at her.

"Don't make the mistake of asking me to be your third again," Tariq warned him, aware of the look of surprise Abram shot him.

"Blackmail?" Abram's brow arched as he turned a glare on him.

"Whatever you want to call it, cousin." Tariq shrugged. "I think I'm rather like Paige. I'm just sick and fucking tired of you teasing the hell out of both of us. And be careful, I might just decide to take that ass whooping to get the girl. It didn't look that damn bad when you were pounding on Jafar."

If Abram's look had been a bullet, it would have pierced his heart, shattered it, then probably found other important parts of his body to deal with.

"I'd make Jafar's ass whipping look like a mother's loving pat," Abram retorted, his tone turning dark, furious. "Don't push me on this, Tariq."

Before Tariq could argue or throw the punch Abram was daring him to throw, his cousin surged to his feet. He moved quickly to the front of the plane where he could sit alone.

And Paige slept on. Maybe.

Tariq's gaze narrowed on her lashes. He could have sworn he'd seen a glimmer of her gaze beneath them. Hell, if he had known she was awake he would have made certain to make it a little more entertaining for her.

There were times the life of a third could be a definite pain in the ass.

Abram stared at the woman that should be his lover, his gaze hooded, hunger pounding at him. The adrenaline produced by the fight with Jafar still thundered inside him, the need still raged and pulsed through his body.

The ending of that fight had left him questioning his cousin in ways he hadn't before. He had never known Jafar to break his word on a deal. What had caused it this time? And why had he been so intent on keeping not just Abram, but also Paige?

The fight had been as much about possession of Paige as it had been about the possession of Mustafa lands,

Abram decided. A possession the Mustafa family would now lose forever. Just as any small amount of control over Paige had been taken as well.

The emissary would arrive any day and find Abram no longer in attendance to take over guardianship of the fortress. An agreement that had existed for more than three hundred years would now come to an end, and for that Abram knew the monarchy would be more than thankful. It was an agreement he knew they had regretted nearly from the inception. From the day they had dealt with the first treacherous Mustafa.

There had been a few over the years who had dreamed of peace rather than war, but they hadn't been in the majority.

He closed his eyes, unable to stare at Paige knowing that when the transport landed he would have to let her go. That or risk his sanity when he had to face the guilt of losing her.

Until Khalid, no son of Mustafa had ever found happiness in love. And Khalid's happiness wasn't yet assured. As long as Azir lived, there could be no assurances, there could be no security. And he was learning Khalid was a far braver man than he.

His brother had found the ability to love, the ability to laugh, and to dream again. Abram hadn't yet found the courage to consider that step. And he learned the night before that being with Paige would take more from him than just his cock.

That was all he had to give. The sex, the heat, the pleasure of two men at once.

It was a pleasure that he hadn't given Paige, though

he meant to. Once again Azir had managed to royally fuck things up for him.

He stared at her again, remembering the pleasure, the sensations searing him from the inside out.

How tight she was, how sweet and hot. The taste of her on his tongue, the delicious spice exploding against his taste buds and intoxicating him. And he remembered the need—the need to watch her face, to hear her screams of pleasure as both he and Tariq possessed her gorgeous body.

How he'd fantasized about it. How he'd longed for it over the years. To take her as the sweet, responsive lover he knew she could be and to give her every possible second of sensual, sexual excitement that he and Tariq were capable of.

A pleasure none of them could know, despite the furious heat of his cock, throbbing, pounding, aching. His balls drew up tight at the base of his cock at just the thought of fucking her again. Of watching Tariq touch her, taste her, watching her face, seeing her pleasure, catching all the nuances of a woman consumed by the ecstasy he was bringing her, as another fucked her.

He'd had her himself. He'd have to make do. He couldn't risk her further. He couldn't risk himself further.

Because losing her would kill him.

13

It felt strange to be home. To walk through the door of her apartment and have the familiar scents wash over her, but to find that aura of peace and security to be strangely absent.

She had been kidnapped from her own home and taken from the country she called home. Unconscious, she had been unable to fight against whatever happened to her. Unable to fight to survive.

The apple-pie scent of the fragrant oils that wafted from the potpourri on her end table teased her sense of smell. The scent of furniture polish, light though it was after nearly a week since her maid service had visited, still added to that sense of cleanliness she had once enjoyed.

The myriad rose, jasmine, and vanilla scents from the unlit candles around the room assured her she was at the one place she had depended upon for safety since moving from her parents' home.

The luggage she had packed the night of her kidnapping sat in the small living area after being found abandoned at the airport. What her kidnappers hadn't foreseen was the identification tags inside each bag.

She would have to deal with unpacking it all now, as well as trying to get her job back and her life in order. And at the moment it all seemed an insurmountable task.

"I do not like this," her father complained, his Greek accent still present even after so many years of living in the U.S.

"Shush," her mother cautioned him.

"I will not shush," her father informed her with a husband's self-righteous anger.

Paige wanted to smile and declare her father paranoid, but she was too frightened that he could be right.

"Pavlos, don't fuss at her now," Marilyn Galbraithe chided him. She shot him a tight expression filled with anger and a need for vengeance.

"When should I fuss at her then, my dear?" he asked. "Perhaps after she is kidnapped again? Or should I wait until I am burying my children and wishing I had done more to protect them?"

He'd given Khalid the same lecture earlier. To give him credit, he had always claimed Khalid as his own despite the agreement that Khalid would be named by his natural father. The agreement also stated that Khalid would receive periodic visits by a member of the Mustafa family who would help him to learn about his father until he turned eighteen. At that time, Khalid had been required to return to the land his father had stained with so much blood.

Not that the "family" member arrived often. Pavlos Galbraithe had always been very generous in his duties as a host and provided a car, a driver, and credit at most restaurants, clubs, and casinos.

For nearly fifteen years it had worked.

"Our daughter and our son will be protected as well as we can provide," Marilyn restated. She had made the same claim earlier. "Until then we can only pray for Azir's early demise."

Both husband and daughter stared at her in shock.

"What, can I not wish the bastard dead and buried?" she questioned harshly, her tone exposing the fear she had been living with for so many years.

"It's just rare for you to voice it, Mother." Paige spoke before her more blunt father could do so.

"Your father is well used to hearing me wish that bastard dead," her mother stated as her face tightened with hatred. "If I could kill him myself then I would do so."

After meeting him, Paige couldn't say she blamed her mother in the least. Still, she wished the opportunity had presented itself while she had been in Saudi Arabia. For Abram, for Khalid, and for her mother, Paige believed she would have killed him just as easily.

"Marilyn, call and make certain Khalid, Marty, Abram, and Tariq made it to Khalid's home for the night. You will not rest until you do so."

Her father shoved his hands into his trouser pockets as her mother nodded quickly and extracted her cell phone from her purse.

Her father continued to watch Paige intently. That look had made her nervous for as long as she could remember. It was a look that assured her that her father was aware of something she may not want him to know about.

Nearing sixty, his gaze still eagle fierce, his body still powerful, and his mind still sharp, he was an imposing businessman, a man none wanted to make an enemy of.

"You've allowed Azir to live all these years," Paige said softly as she met his gaze directly. "Why?"

His head tilted to the side thoughtfully for long moments before he answered. "Because your mother has known enough pain. If she believed for a moment that I had killed him, then she would be certain my soul was damned and we would not meet in Heaven as she has always claimed. Besides, were he to die, I would be the first suspected of it."

Paige glanced across the room as her mother stepped into the bedroom.

"She will take this opportunity to check your drawers, your closets, and so forth to see how you are conducting any intimate life or a lack thereof," he commented.

"Tattling on Mother again, Papa?" she asked with a smile as his weathered face eased into a grin.

"She will say nothing to you, but to me she will complain of grandchildren she does not have and a son-in-law you owe her. Then once again she will make her lists of her friends' sons to introduce you to. And she will stare into the night when she believes I sleep. And she will fear you have lied to us as she lied to her parents when she assured them that Khalid was not a child of her kidnapper's raping of her. And soon she will cry, certain you lied to us and that Azir raped you."

She could hear the question in his voice, the fear.

"Azir hit me," she confided, knowing her father had a second sense when it came to her and Khalid's lies. She wouldn't lie to him about Azir.

"How hard did he hit you?"

She described the abuse, then paused and watched her father's face closely as she continued. "Abram came in and stopped Azir. He had Tariq take me to his suite and I never saw Azir after that."

Thick salt-and-pepper hair was pushed back from his dark face as gray-green eyes held a hint of suspicion.

"I swear, Papa," she promised him. "If Abram wasn't with me, then Tariq was. I was perfectly protected."

Her father nodded slowly, then drew in a deep breath.

"Tariq and Abram often share their lovers as Khalid has," he said somberly. "Did they seduce you, daughter?"

She saw the worry and the concern in his face as her own flushed in embarrassment. Sex was not a subject she discussed so freely, especially not with her papa.

"They didn't," she revealed softly. "But am I so wrong to wish they had?"

She saw the surprise, and also the discomfort in her father's face as he cleared his throat.

"I see." His voice was lowered in case her mother came into the room, she assumed.

"Do you think I'm bad, Papa?" She loved her parents. The last thing she wanted was to embarrass them or give them cause to feel shame because of her desire for Abram.

"Paige, what could make you ever imagine you are bad simply because you are a woman who deserves what her lover desires?" He gave a hard shake of his head and a hesitant smile. "Perhaps that did not come out as I intended, but I would never believe you bad because you are a woman."

"Or because I'm in love with Abram Mustafa?" she asked.

He couldn't hide it, and her father wasn't a man who would lie to her.

The gray green of his eyes flashed with concern. His expression tightened with what she knew was disapproval and fear.

"That is a bit of a surprise," he admitted as he raked his fingers through his hair with a hard sigh. "And does Abram feel the same for you, Paige?"

"No," she admitted painfully. "Abram isn't in love with me, Papa. And he doesn't want to see me again because he's afraid of the danger he will bring into my life. For him, it's over."

"Ah, my little princess," he whispered, his arms opening to her. She had to swallow tightly to hold back her tears.

She rushed to him. She let him pull her into his embrace. His arms surrounded her, cushioning her against his chest as she fought to hold back her tears.

"He is a fool and a coward to walk away from a woman whose heart is as brave and as courageous as yours." He kissed the top of her head gently. "Perhaps, Paige, he no longer knows how to love."

She was saved from replying as her bedroom door opened and her mother stepped into the room.

Paige knew instantly that something was wrong, just as her father did.

"Marilyn." Pavlos moved to her. Paige followed, her heart suddenly jumping in her throat.

Her mother was shaking and pale, her lips bloodless.

"Marilyn?" Pavlos gripped her arms, staring down at her worriedly. "Love, what has happened?"

Marilyn swallowed tightly as she stared up at her husband in fear. "Reaching Khalid was impossible. I finally got Abram to answer his phone." Her voice turned ragged, and a tear eased from her eyes as she inhaled roughly. "Oh God, Pavlos, they hurt Khalid. They shot him and no one knows how bad it is."

It was bad enough. Paige rushed to the hospital with her parents to find Marty, her clothes stained with Khalid's blood, her eyes dark with fear as she sat with her mother, surrounded by men.

One of those men was the director of the FBI and had at one time been Khalid's boss.

With her were both Abram and Tariq. They looked as exhausted as she still felt.

"Marilyn, Pavlos." Zach Jennnings, the FBI director stood to greet her parents.

"Whats going on here, Zach?" Pavlos asked quietly.

"Khalid, Abram, Tariq, Marty, and I were leaving the Justice Department after Abram and Tariq were debriefed. Abram signed the papers disclosing his American citizenship for the past twenty years and his ineligibility and unwillingness to accept the guardianship of the Mustafa lands."

Paige turned and stared at Abram in shock. "What does he mean?" she whispered.

Abram's expression was closed and tight.

"He means Abram turned in the papers his mother filled out before her death and put in safekeeping for him. When he was twelve he lusted after America. He turned those papers in himself and his relatives from Saudi swore to their validity," Tariq answered. "He's been a U.S. citizen since he was twelve, and at eighteen he joined the army. He was secretly trained and sent back to the Mustafa province along with Khalid, to spy on his father and the terrorists moving in."

Abram remained silent, his black gaze holding Paige's as Tariq spoke.

She remembered teasing him years before about needing to marry an American to be able to leave Saudi forever, and his reply had been, "America would never let the son of a terrorist claim citizenship." She repeated his words softly as his gaze flickered with icy anger. "You should have told me that didn't apply to you."

"It would have served my purpose," he said. "Don't you see, Azir will ensure neither Khalid nor I ever enjoy the peace we've searched for."

"Even more than you know." Zach Jennings stepped to them.

"There are reports Azir, Jafar, and a team of Jafar's soldiers have stepped into the country. I'm sorry, Ms. Galbraithe," he said simply. "You're going to have to return to protective custody until they're found."

There was evidently so little that she knew about the man she loved, as well as her brother. While they waited for Khalid to get out of surgery, her father and Zach Jennings answered her questions while her mother interjected with what she knew.

The Mustafa lands were held differently than any

other in the region. Because of a border dispute generations before with Iraq, the Iraqi king at that time negotiated an agreement that as long as the Mustafa family controlled the land, then it would stay within the Saudi border. The Saudi regime couldn't turn the land over to any other family simply because of a claimed relationship to the Mustafa family, nor could the land ever be mined or in any way profit the monarchy unless a Mustafa male guarded it.

It was said the Iraqi king at that time had a son who carried the name of another man. The arranged marriage between his son, a Mustafa, and the daughter of a sheikh who controlled the land for the Saudi regime prompted this particular settlement.

Each generation, at the age of thirty-six the eldest heir would give his vow to the Saudi king and his emissary to protect the land and to ensure its borders remained a part of Saudi Arabia. The heir must vow to conceive sons to protect it and to ensure no one ever used the province to threaten the regime.

Only in the event that the heir had no sons to take the vow, would the land revert entirely to the throne for the king to decide himself which family or tribe would control it.

Abram was the only Mustafa heir to have had no legal heirs born. He could willingly abdicate the guardianship with no repercussions except those his father was now enacting against him and Khalid in revenge for the deaths of Ayid and Amam, the two youngest sons of Azir Mustafa who had died at Abram and Khalid's hands.

"He'll never give up," Paige whispered. She looked

across the room to where Abram and Tariq stood leaning against the wall quietly discussing Khalid's condition.

As though he couldn't stand to be around her, he'd moved from her, putting the entire width of the private hospital waiting room between them.

"Do they know Jafar was behind it for certain?" she asked.

She wanted to find a way to deny it but there was no way to excuse his actions.

Abram's gaze suddenly lasered in on her as though he'd heard the question.

"Paige, darling, Jafar isn't the friend you knew then." Her mother laid her hand comfortingly against Paige's arm.

"How do we know that unless we know for certain he gave the order to kill Khalid, Abram, and Tariq?"

"Khalid, Abram, Tariq, Marty, and you," Zach stated gently. "The information and reports we received state that Jafar is unwilling to leave any chance of an heir being conceived or born that can later risk his, or his family's, control of the land."

Paige lifted her gaze to Abram's once more. God, she needed him. She felt as though she were losing her entire balance, and none of it made any sense.

Jafar owed her more than this. There had been a time when Chalah had been confused, so at odds with her brother and her family that she had nearly made a very unwise decision. At Jafar's request, at his plea actually, Paige had returned to America from Spain, allowed Chalah to live with her, and encouraged the young girl to give college a try rather than returning to the Mustafa province and honoring a marriage contract Azir had arranged for her to a much older sheikh in another part of Saudi Arabia. Fear for her brother had guided her, but Paige had convinced her how much Jafar had been against her marriage to a man so old. He also objected to her marrying so close to the time he had chosen to leave Saudi Arabia himself.

He had sworn he owed her and that she need only ask and he would grant her any request.

And still, he had nearly killed Abram in Saudi Arabia and now? Oh God, now she could lose the only brother she had. The one she could depend upon, who she could trust to hold her secrets. She risked losing him as well as the man she loved.

"Paige will go with her mother and me to the villa in Greece."

Paige was shaking her head as her father spoke. She had no desire to go to Greece or to leave Virginia.

"We need her here, Mr. Galbraithe," Zach advised him. "We need them in the same location to ensure their protection. We'd like to return Paige to her brother's home along with Abram, Marty, Tariq, and Khalid, when he's released."

It was another confinement.

"Why do this?" she whispered. "It's over."

"No, Paige, it isn't." Abram stepped over to her, fury and grief filling his eyes. "It won't be over until one of us dies. I'll be damned if I'll allow him to get away with attempting to kill Khalid because he was unable to force me to his will."

"What if it was not Jafar who gave that order?" Chalah's voice seemed to echo around the room.

Paige swung around to stare at the other girl. Her jaw tightened at the sight of Jafar's sister, here at this time, when Paige was so ambivalent about the last time she had seen her.

Crossing her arms over her breasts, Paige stared at the other girl angrily. "Does anyone have a bug detector? Chalah enjoys allowing her brother to listen in on her conversations. Next it will be your girls' nights out." Her eyes widened in mocking shock. "Where will the perversions end?"

Chalah ran her hands nervously along the sides of the faded, worn jeans she wore.

The frayed hems, holes at the knees, and almost see-through thinness of the material suggested the jeans were simply at the wrong end of worn out, as did the denim jacket she wore over a faded T-shirt.

"I told you I was sorry, Paige," she whispered, her eyes filling with tears and making Paige feel like a bitch.

She was being a bitch, and she hated herself for it.

Pushing her fingers through her hair, Paige ignored both Abram's and her father's attempts to comfort her.

"Jafar called me," Chalah said, her voice low. "He's enraged. He swears on his father's grave that he neither ordered nor instigated this attack on Khalid."

"He called or came to see you?" Abram questioned her coolly.

Turning, Paige watched the confusion that filled Chalah's face. "He called," she whispered. "From the Mustafa province." At that point Zach moved closer to her.

"Ms. Mustafa, your brother is in the States as of today. He arrived in Virginia within hours of Paige, Abram, and Tariq's arrival. And all reports we have confirm he gave the order, over Azir's protestations, to kill Khalid, Abram, Tariq, and Paige. And all things considered, I believe we'll need to ensure your protection as well."

Paige stared back at the FBI director in shock. He couldn't be serious?

But of course he was.

Turning back to Chalah she saw the dazed shock in her eyes, and the betrayal. Jafar hadn't told her where he was, nor had he attempted to protect her. She was an incredible actress. But she really wasn't, Paige thought. Chalah didn't have the patience for such games.

"Jafar wouldn't hurt me," she whispered as she turned to Paige, her eyes large and dark and haunted with fear now.

Oh yes, she knew exactly how that fear felt. She was personal friends with it now. At this rate fear would soon be a part of her personality. She wouldn't know how to live without it.

"Paige." Chalah's lips trembled when no one answered her claim that Jafar would never hurt her. "Tell them. Tell them he wouldn't harm me."

Paige could only shake her head. "He's the same man who put his blade against Abram's neck after he lost the fight to determine if we could leave or be forced to stay," Paige whispered. "I'm so sorry, Chalah. He's capable of anything."

"No." Chalah's denial was weak though.

"He's not the brother you knew and he's not the friend I once claimed, Chalah. So no, I don't believe he would protect you. And if he could use you against Khalid and Abram he would do it in a heartbeat. Think of that. Remember it. Because if you help him again then our blood may well be on your hands." And if Chalah made that mistake, Paige promised herself, she would ensure the other girl paid for it.

No matter the cost to herself.

14

She was back where it all began, but this time, Khalid wasn't going to show up and surprise her. He wasn't going to come pounding on her door at three in the morning just to deliver yet another lecture on the many and varied reasons why it was ill-advised to sleep with his brother. His brother and his brother's cousin.

Those lectures haunted her as she lay in bed. She stared up at the ceiling in the darkened bedroom, her brother's many arguments echoing in her head. She remembered the anger that filled his eyes, his knowledge that no matter how much he lectured, still she ached for Abram. She was fascinated with him. She needed him like she had never needed anything else in her life.

And because of her need for Abram, she had caused Khalid to worry more for her safety than he worried for his own. Had Azir, Mustafa and Jafar not suspected she was Abram's weakness, something he wanted, then neither of them would have been as intent on kidnapping her. And Khalid could have concentrated on his own safety.

Despite Chalah's protestations that Jafar would have never gone to that extreme, Paige couldn't help but remember that knife to Abram's throat, sharp enough, pressing hard enough to actually draw blood. And she couldn't help but believe Chalah's brother would actually kill if tested.

And Jafar was definitely being tested with the date of the emissary's visit coming closer and the paperwork on Abram and Tariq's defection being filled out and prepped to deliver to the U.S. ambassador to Saudi Arabia. And this was the price Abram and Khalid would pay for their determination to break from the Mustafa legacy.

She could lose her brother as well as the man her body burned for, her heart ached for.

Turning, she stared toward the balcony doors and blinked back the tears that threatened to fill her eyes.

She missed him. She was so used to sleeping, cushioned between him and Tariq, that the past three nights she hadn't truly slept at all.

As a weary sigh left her lips her gaze jerked to the bedroom door. It opened slowly, pushing inward a second before Abram stepped into the room. A dark shadow against the moonlit expanse of the window across the room, he moved slowly toward her.

He didn't close the door. There was no need to. Her heart raced at the sight of Tariq moving in behind him, closing and locking the door with a deliberate, audible click.

Her eyes met the dark glitter of Abram's as he paused

at the side of the bed. She slowly sat up, the high mattress placing her head just above his hips.

She swallowed tightly, fighting to breathe at the sight of the heavy bulge beneath the denim. She had to force her gaze to lift, to stare up at him, rather than beg him to fuck her immediately.

"I need you, Paige." He'd only said that to her once before. That bleak, cold winter he and Khalid had arrived from Saudi after the death of his second wife and their unborn child.

"I've always been here for you. I told you that." She'd been eighteen and so infatuated with him that it was all she could do not to tremble in his presence.

He'd been drunk, wracked by grief and he'd come to her even though he'd known he would face Khalid's rage if it was ever found out.

Her gaze flicked to Tariq. Abram hadn't had a third with him then, but he did now.

"No matter what I need?"

Her heart tripped in her chest at the question.

"No matter what you need."

His fingers moved to the metal button of his jeans as he toed the shoes from his feet, his gaze never leaving hers.

"No matter how I need it?"

Her thighs clenched as her gaze moved to Tariq, feeling his eyes watching her, probing the darkness.

"No matter how you need it," she whispered.

As she finished that affirmation Abram and Tariq were undressing. There was nothing hurried or rushed about their movements. They removed their clothes with a sense of anticipation, but patience. A patience that had Paige wondering if she would survive it.

She felt the world narrow to the two men, to the hunger she could feel surround her and the need she glimpsed in Abram's face.

Slowly, she watched as his hand circled the base of his cock, holding it firm and steady as he stepped closer to her, his fingers tangling in her hair.

Staring up at him, she felt the wide crest of his cock at her lips, the heated, throbbing flesh drawing her tongue to taste the heat and hardness. The salty male taste exploded against her senses, intoxicated her.

"That's a good girl," he whispered as his cock head pressed between her lips. "Suck my dick, baby. Show me, Paige. Show me how much you want me."

How much she wanted him? She felt as though she had wanted him all her life, needed him all her life.

Her lips parted, a moan falling from them as his cock slowly sank into her mouth.

It was so erotic. The feel of the strongest and yet the most vulnerable part of him held securely within her mouth as she sucked him inside. Her tongue licked over and around the head as she heard a low, muttered groan rumble in his chest.

"I need to see you, sweetheart. We're going to light a candle." His tone was rough, rasping sexually.

"Just a bit." He assured her as she tensed, her drowsy gaze starring up at him as her pretty lips stretched around his cock. "I just need to see when Tariq touches you, baby."

When Tariq touched her? Paige knew it was coming but she still lost her breath, she still felt adrenaline speed through her, racing out of control.

Sitting on the bed, her legs folded to the side, she found strong, large male hands slowly drawing them out as the two men worked in perfect unison until Abram was kneeling on the bed over her and she was laid back, his cock between her lips as she felt Tariq begin to touch her.

There was no sense of discomfort, no feeling of shame or embarrassment.

She had always known what being with Abram meant, and she had always looked forward to it.

"How very pretty you are," he groaned, his expression tight with lust as she felt Tariq's lips at her hip bone, kissing her gently a second before he licked the area, tasting her as if he hungered for her.

"I've dreamed of this, Paige. Dreamed of watching Tariq touch you, pleasure you." His cock jerked between her lips as he spoke. "Watching him touch you." His words became even rougher, the need in them fueling her own sensual hunger.

"Touch her stomach." He whispered the order to Tariq. "The flesh there is sensitive, and brings her great pleasure." His accent thickened and became deeper.

A second later her lashes fluttered in pleasure. She hadn't realized how sensitive the flesh there really was.

His fingertips stroked over her stomach, calloused and firm. They heated and excited the nerve endings beneath the skin.

"Such satiny flesh," Abram whispered. A second later she felt Tariq's tongue lick, his teeth scrape.

"Tariq has spoken often of this moment," Abram told her. "When the nights were long and dark."

As Abram spoke he slowly pulled back, forcing her to release the feel and the taste of his desire.

He took her hands and pulled them above her head, holding them in place as Tariq's hand eased up her side until it was curving around the firm, aching mound of her breast.

His thumb stroked over her nipple, his calloused pad sending sharp, heated strikes of ecstatic pleasure to her womb, clenching her cunt.

Staring up at Abram she felt her vision dim as Tariq's lips surrounded the fragile bud. His fingers cupped the underside of her breast, lifting her, stroking the nerve endings to fiery responsiveness.

Her body felt as though it were overloading with sensation. Incredible, lush pleasure surged through her in a wash of rich, heated rapture.

As Tariq's lips covered her nipple, Abram released her wrists after pressing them carefully into the mattress.

Forcing herself, she stared up at him, her lips parting to draw in a ragged breath.

"The memory of the taste of your sweet pussy is making me crazy," he growled as he knelt on the bed, one hand stroking his dick as he stared down at her.

His thighs bunched and clenched with each tightening of his fingers at the base. The head glistened with precome as his gaze flickered to where Tariq was slowly driving her sensations with the draw of his mouth around her tender nipple.

His tongue last, his teeth pressed against the nerve-laden tip.

"I want to watch Tariq eat that sweet pussy." He reached out, his fingers stroking down the side of her face.

"Abram." She could barely think. All she could manage was forcing herself to breathe through the pleasure and the thought of Tariq's touch becoming even more intimate.

"I want to watch his tongue part your pretty pussy lips, watch it lick and stroke your slick cunt."

As he spoke, Tariq drew his lips back from her nipple and stared up at her. "Is this what you want, love?" As he spoke, Abram's fingers whispered over her clit.

A low, desperate moan escaped from her at the touch. Her clitoris seemed to swell further. It ached with a pleasure and pain she found agonizing and ecstatic.

"Paige, answer me, love." Tariq leaned closer, his lips lowering to hers as she felt Abram's fingers part the juicy folds between her thighs. "Tell me," he demanded against her lips. "Do you want me to eat your pussy, Paige?"

The sudden, furious thrust of two broad male fingers into the clenched, creaming depth of her cunt had her hips jerking, eyes widening, and a harsh cry tearing from her lips as they met Tariq's in a first, juicy, desperate kiss.

Between her thighs Abram's fingers worked inside her pussy. Stretching the tight depths, fucking past tender, ultrasensitive tissue then arcing his fingers for a too-loving stroke of incredible pleasure at the inner flesh located behind her clit. Tariq's tongue pushed past her lips to find her tongue and tangle with it erotically.

Loyal to the quick, forceful thrusts inside her, Paige fought to keep her senses and lost.

There was too much pleasure, as Tariq's head lifted, his lips moving along her jaw to her neck, her eyes opening to find Abram.

"How sensual you are, little cat," he groaned, his fingers pushing deep again as Tariq's lips moved along her neck to her shoulder. There he nipped at her flesh erotically.

"Answer me, or we stop."

Abram's fingers stalled inside her. Still stretching her as her juices gathered around them, his fingers were a destructive pleasure even as they did no more than possess her.

"Don't stop," she begged desperately, her hips wrestling with his fingers. "Fuck me."

"Answer me," Tariq growled. Both men stared down at her, their expressions assuring her they wouldn't allow her to ignore the question further.

"Is this what you want?" Tariq repeated. "My lips and tongue feeding from your juicy pussy?" He caught her fingers and drew them to his heavy erection. "My dick sinking into it?"

"Yes!" Her fingers curled around his cock, stroked and caressed the satiny silk over pure heated iron as her pussy clenched around Abram's fingers.

"I want you first." Her fingers tightened on his cock. "Let me taste you, Tariq." Her head lifted as he gave a harsh groan.

Moving to his knees he knelt beside her, leaned closer, and pushed his cock into her mouth.

It was incredible. Small delicate fingers gripped and stroked his length as her other hand cupped and caressed his balls.

Tariq felt the roaring flames of pleasure tearing through his system.

Of all the women he had shared with Abram, of all the women they had seduced together, Paige was the one he had dreamed of, the one he had fantasized about the most. And now he knew why. As he watched his cock head sinking past her lips, stretching them, he realized the incredible pleasure was only beginning.

If he didn't move, if he didn't pull free of her, he'd come. He'd fill her hot little mouth with a load of come like nothing he'd spilled in any other female's mouth.

"Enough." He pulled from her, drawing back as Abram pulled his fingers from her.

Moving between her thighs, his hands holding her still as his head lowered to the swollen flesh of her pussy.

Abram watched. Stretching out beside her he caressed her perspiration-slick flesh, held her to him, and watched his cousin part the lush slick folds with his hungry tongue.

Paige strained beneath the feel of Tariq's tongue as it lashed against the folds of her pussy. She wasn't being asked to pleasure them, though she would have, gladly. Instead, they were completely, totally focused on her pleasure.

Abram's hands stroked from her breasts to her lower stomach, his head lowering to allow his lips to caress, his tongue to taste the curve of her breast.

Tariq's hands pushed beneath the curve of her rear, lifting her closer, tilting her hips to allow his tongue to move lower, to flicker against the opening of her vagina, teasing, sensitizing as her hand burrowed into Abram's hair, clenching as Tariq flicked his tongue just inside the flexing, clenched entrance. His moan liberated against her flesh, causing her breath to catch on a broken moan.

Abram's head lifted again, his lips moving to her ear.

"Is he teasing you, love?"

"Oh God, Abram, it's killing me." She tried to thrust against his tongue, to force it deeper inside her. "Let me come," she begged, feeling the desperation she knew they heard in her voice. "Please, Abram, I need . . ." A shocked moan of intense pleasure ripped from her lips as she felt Tariq move his fingers through the cleft of her ass to tease and press firmly at the tiny, hidden entrance located there.

"Abram," she gasped, her gaze meeting his as his head lifted, his eyes black fire as he caught her gaze.

"Relax, love," he crooned gently. Tariq's fingers drew back as his tongue pushed forward. "Just relax for us. We stop whenever you need us to," he promised. "Whatever *you* want, baby."

"More," she moaned brokenly as the feel of Tariq's fingers returned to the clenched opening. Cool, slickened with lubricant, he began pushing his finger inside her as Abram reached down, gripped beneath one knee, and lifted it.

An erotic shiver raced through her body and her lashes fluttered over her dazed eyes.

She felt Tariq's finger sink slowly into the nerve-laden depths of her anus.

Paige's fingers clenched at Abram's shoulders, locking onto him, holding onto his gaze as Tariq's tongue ate at her pussy decadently while his fingers lubricated, stretched, and accustomed her rear entrance to the slowly increasing width of more than one finger.

Abram held her knee back, his gaze never leaving hers, holding her steady, keeping her senses focused when she knew she would have shattered otherwise.

Broken, desperate moans escaped her lips as she fought for release, feeling that edge of oblivion just out of reach as it teased her with the coming ecstasy.

"Abram." She gasped his name as she felt Tariq stretching her further. "Please, please make me come."

Weak, pleading, the hoarseness of her own voice shocked her.

"Are you ready for us then?" A grimace tightened his face. Paige felt her lashes flutter closed again before she forced them open.

Ready for both of them?

She knew what he meant, just as she had always known what was coming once she became his lover.

To accept not just Abram and his possession of her, but Tariq, or whoever his third would be, as well.

"Yes," she whispered desperately as her lips continued to surge against the slow, easy thrust of pleasure/pain pushing into her rear. "Oh God, Abram," she moaned. "Please."

If she didn't come soon she would never survive the sensations increasing inside her.

Pleasure/pain and heated erotic hunger attacked every sensory receptor in her body and in her mind. She couldn't bear to be without touch. If they stopped, if they didn't continue to push her toward that precipice waiting ahead, then she wouldn't survive the desertion.

If she didn't continue the erotic journey to what had to be a coming orgasm, then she would lose her mind in the search for it.

"Come, love," Abram whispered despite her cry of desperation as Tariq's fingers and his torturous tongue deserted her.

As Tariq eased back from her she found herself being lifted, turned, and eased into Abram's arms as he reclined on the bed.

Tariq guided her legs to both sides of Abram's hips as Abram gripped the base of his cock, holding it steady. Paige tipped her head back with a low, desperate moan tearing from her as the wide crest parted the swollen, sensitive lips. She felt him push in to the hilt, filling her, stretching her to the point that pleasure and pain combined to create an inferno of heat and hunger that stole her mind.

As he penetrated fully his hands clamped on her hips, holding her still as she felt Tariq's palm between her shoulder blades pressing her to Abram's chest.

Staring down at Abram in sudden hesitation, she was aware of Tariq pausing behind her.

"Even better." Abram released a hip to lift his hand and tuck her hair behind her shoulder, before he brushed his knuckles against her cheek. "We'll take care of everything, baby. All you have to do is feel good. Just let us love you."

Let him love her.

She had dreamed of that, she had ached for it for so many years.

Paige softened, her body relaxing once again as she let herself be pressed to Abram's chest. Her nipples buried against the heat and hardness of the wide muscles as her hands moved to his shoulders, her fingers gripping them tightly.

Abram's hands moved to the back of her head, fingers threading into the strands as he turned her to him, his lips catching hers in a hard, hungry kiss.

His tongue pressed between her lips as behind her, Tariq moved closer, the slick, thick head of his cock sliding along the crease of her ass to find the sensitive, snug pucker of the entrance.

"Hold onto Abram, love," Tariq whispered behind her, his lips at her shoulder as she felt the steady, heated pressure of his cock beginning to part the tight, flexing little hole.

Abram's kiss deepened, his moan, a dark, male growl as Tariq began to impale the once unbreached entrance into her body.

Sexual arousal was a firestorm of need raging through her body as she cried out into Abram's kiss. It was pleasure and pain rocking her senses as she felt a slow, steady penetration of Tariq's cock entering her rear.

Each inch sinking inside the depths of her ass had her more aware of the thick, heavy intrusion in her pussy and the desperation inside her body for release.

Her vagina milked at the erection filling her as she felt Tariq delivering deeper. Her nails bit at Abram's shoulders, as he released her lips.

Paige gasped, her body jerking, hard shudders racing through her as she felt Tariq press all the way in behind her. She clenched around the dual intrusions, shuddering with pleasure, with agony and ecstasy as they began to move.

She hadn't known that pain could be addictive when mixed with the ecstatic waves of erotic response as they surged through her. She hadn't known that she could completely lose her senses as Tariq lay over her, his broad chest at her shoulders as the two men began to move inside her.

"Abram!" Weak, breathless, she called out his name as she felt her last hold on reality begin to slip away. "Oh God, hold me. Please hold me."

She was going to fly apart at the seams, she could feel it. She was going to lose herself and her mind right along with her senses.

"I have you, love." His voice was a dark, primal growl. "Tariq and I have you."

They were moving, thrusting inside her, filling and stretching her pussy, her ass, possessing both with every tightening stroke as Paige felt her body vibrating, tensing. Pleasure was building inside her, burning, the sensual flames rising higher until she felt the conflagration detonate inside her.

Violent, fiery, her orgasm began tearing through her senses, drawing a shattered, broken cry from her throat.

Her pussy locked down, milking Abram's cock as the muscles surrounding Tariq's began to flex and tighten in response.

As her release shuddered through her body she felt sensations she could never have expected to feel with such depth.

Beneath her, Abram tensed, his hips arcing, pushing inside her as his cock seemed to swell thicker and harder. The heavy flesh jerked, throbbed hard and deep and Tariq's mimicked a second later. As her orgasm reached its fiery height both men gave a hard, muted groan and the feel of their release spurting inside her filled her senses.

She was surrounded by them. She was filled with them, inside and out. Sheltered, held, heated, and consumed. She was exactly where she had longed to be. Completing Abram.

15

Tariq watched the hands of the old-fashioned clock at the side of the bed as they ticked forward. He wondered if he should stay or if he should return to his own bed.

Normally, he would have already made his way to the other room, but normally the circumstances were entirely different.

There were none of Azir's bodyguards standing in the hall to make note of his departure time, nor were they at the castle or in the Mustafa province where Azir or his terrorist cohorts could surprise them and drag Tariq off for a death sentence.

For the crime of sexual indecency. Sexual indecency.

Turning his head he stared at the couple he shared the bed with and wondered if Abram had accepted the fact that he was in love with Paige yet. That he had been in love with her for a while.

Tariq had known, and he suspected that Khalid knew

as well. That was probably part of the reason Khalid had been so diligent in keeping them apart.

Khalid would blow a fuse when he came out of the hospital to learn it was too late to keep his brother and sister apart.

He almost laughed at the concept. Poor Khalid. It would not be easy should he ever have to introduce them as a couple.

"Meet my brother and sister who are, by the way, married."

Ah yes, talk about a conversation starter for any social gathering. That topic would definitely be the one.

"You're still awake." Abram's voice was only barely audible. "You should be sleeping."

It wasn't as though either of them had slept much since their escape from Saudi.

"Restless perhaps," Tariq answered.

Silence met the observation for long moments before Abram said, "That's unusual, for you."

And it was. Normally, Abram was the restless one. He was known to pace, to stare up at the ceiling, or find ways to simply busy himself when he needed to work out a problem. Restless wasn't something Tariq did well. And it wasn't something he enjoyed.

"It sounds to me as though both of you are restless," Paige observed, her voice drowsy as she shifted more comfortably into her position, draped over Abram's chest.

Tariq was almost jealous at the natural, comfortable appearance of the two. They may strike sparks outside the bed in a totally different manner, but there had always been a connection between them.

Abram's hand stroked down her back and up, almost unconsciously, Tariq thought. A need for connection. A need to touch the woman he was silently claiming.

"Should we call Marty and check on Khalid?" Paige asked, her tone quieter, subdued at the thought of her brother.

"If you need to, though Marty is probably resting now," Abram stated. "Trust her to call if there is any problem, love," he stated quietly.

Yes, Tariq thought, there was definitely a reason to feel jealous. He wondered what it would be like to share with someone the everyday decisions life was prone to toss at you.

Sitting up in the bed, one foot resting on the floor, the other propped on the bed, he stared toward the balcony doors with a frown on his face.

Abram was right, restlessness wasn't a part of his psyche, so what the hell was the problem?

"Tariq?" Paige sat up slowly. "What's wrong?"

He moved to shake his head once again, only to have the movement interrupted by the quiet vibration of his phone on the table beside the bed.

His hand jerked out, flipping the phone open as he brought it to his ear.

"Tariq," he answered.

"Is Abram with you?" the male voice questioned.

"He is," Tariq replied.

"We need speakerphone, quickly," Daniel Conover ordered, his tone steel-hard despite the low volume.

Tariq lowered the phone and quickly hit speaker.

"We're here," Tariq stated quietly.

"We have a problem," Daniel said. "We've had two

attempts at the gate in the last ten minutes with no sign
of the attempted intruder. Be certain to stay on guard.
And for God's sake, stay in your rooms. If you have to
leave, contact me first. I have an agent moving on Paige's
room."

"Ms. Galbraithe is here," Tariq informed him coolly,
uncertain of the security agent's right to call her by her
first name alone.

A moment's silence. "Very well. Stay in place, we'll
contact you soon."

As he spoke, both Tariq and Abram were moving
around the room, quickly jerking the heavy curtains
over the windows as Paige stood in the darkness of the
connecting bathroom, dressing hurriedly in the jeans,
T-shirt, underclothes, and boots Abram had advised her
to keep handy, just in case.

"Be certain to stay in contact," Tariq commanded as
he and Abram began dressing as well.

Disconnecting the call, Tariq jerked his well-worn
jeans on, securing them before pushing his feet into the
boots and tying them quickly.

Abram finished seconds before he did and was opening the door to the closet where they had placed their
weapons earlier that day. They had known, or at least
Abram had known, exactly where their nights would be
spent, and he had lain the weapons in just in case.

"Why won't he let you go?" Paige stood at the door
of the bathroom, uncertain in the face of what seemed
to be going on, especially when Abram strode to her and
pressed the Glock into her hand.

"Pride. Anger." Abram's voice was hard, but Paige

had known him for years and she recognized that hint of pain in his tone.

She couldn't imagine her father ever being less than gentle or loving with her, or firm but always kind to Khalid. She couldn't bear it if he were anything less.

"Pride and anger aren't good enough reasons," she said into the dark, keeping her voice low.

"The fucker is insane then." Abram spat the comment out.

For all the softness of his tone, the violence that filled his voice had her flinching. It was the sight of Abram shoving the weapon into the holster beneath his arm that had her mouth drying out in fear. The violence, the gathering rage, it was all reflected in that tight, hard action.

"Abram?" She moved to step from the bathroom when the whole house seemed to shake and an explosion ripped through the night.

Paige stumbled against the door frame as the room seemed to shake and roll beneath her feet. A cry was barely smothered, her heart racing in fear as lights flickered outside and the sound of voices raised in alarm reached from the lower floor.

"It wasn't the house, it was outside." Abram was beside her, his hand grabbing hers as he pulled her toward the door. "It was too damned close though."

"We have to get to Chalah." She gasped as Tariq threw the door open with one hand. He carried the powerful automatic rifle in the other.

She considered it completely unfair that his gun was bigger than hers.

"She's probably the reason they found us so fucking fast," Tariq snarled back at her.

There was nothing of the lovers who had held her so gently, who had touched her so heatedly earlier. These were hardened warriors, and though she appreciated the need, she did not appreciate the delivery of the attitude in her direction.

"Tariq." Abram's voice was warning as they stepped into the darkened hallway.

Tariq turned to the left, ignoring Abram and heading for the staircase that curved down to the main floor. The opposite direction of the room Chalah had been taken to.

Without a word Paige turned to the right, breathing out a sigh of relief as she felt Abram following closely behind her as she moved quickly for Chalah's room.

Tariq cursed furiously behind them.

Reaching the door Abram gave a hard, quick knock before pushing it open.

Darkened, silent, the room appeared deserted as Tariq pushed in ahead of Abram. Paige caught the disgruntled look Tariq shot him.

Another explosion shook the house, this one closer, the flare of light blazing white outside the tall, wide windows. Paige barely managed to hold back her cry, or at least she thought she had. It must have escaped as a small, frightened squeak that seemed to drift through the room.

She could have sworn she heard Tariq curse again. Striding past her he threw open the closet door and a heartbeat later dragged a terrified Chalah from the small, enclosed space.

"Let's go!" Abram ordered as they moved quickly down the hall. "Tariq, has Conover contacted?"

"Nothing," Tariq answered from behind him. "And he should have radioed."

"They managed to get past him and his men once before when Ayid and Aman came after Khalid and Abram," Paige stated. "They could have managed to overtake them again."

They, being Jafar and his men.

Jafar.

Paige glanced back at Chalah's pale, tearstained face. Abram's father, and Chalah's brother. How horrible it must be to face the reality of their hatred.

"Tariq, take Paige and Chalah—"

"Oh hell no," Paige protested. "You're not going anywhere without me."

"No women are giving us orders," Tariq growled as they neared the steps. "Next thing we know, children will be teaching us."

Paige had every intention of telling him exactly what she thought of the comment when they heard the first, sharp report of a weapon.

Tariq and Abram both moved quickly, pushing Paige and Chalah against the wall. The sound of shouted orders from below had Paige's heart racing in terror. She felt a bone-deep knowledge that Abram wouldn't be able to handle hiding for long.

"The safe room," Abram said, turning to Tariq. "There's one on each floor. Activated it sends out an alarm to police, fire, and rescue, independent of the phone lines."

"Why can't you use the phone lines?" Paige whispered.

"I checked them," Tariq stated. "They're out and cell phones are jammed. The safe room sends out a call to law enforcement through cable Internet which is buried underground. If they cut the lines there, it sends out a call then as well."

The phones were out. Paige knew after the last attack Khalid had had a special security system installed that used the backup Internet connection emergency notification.

So why hadn't there been a response yet?

"Abram, it's Daniel Conover." The sound of the security consultant's voice rang up the stairs.

"Conover," Abram called back as he placed his body carefully in front of Paige's.

Tariq had done the same, standing in front of Chalah protectively. "What's going on?"

"Too much, Abram," Daniel called back. "But not enough to give a man a sense of satisfaction."

The safe code came back with an edge of amusement. Abram relaxed marginally.

"I'm coming up, Abram," Daniel announced.

Seconds later he strode to the top of the stairs, dressed in black and looking almost as dangerous as Abram and Tariq. "Police will be here any minute," Daniel stated as he stopped at the top of the stairs, his blue eyes gleaming like hardened gems. "We caught a man armed with a piss-poor shoulder-mounted rocket launcher and a few homemade rockets. We have him in custody but he's not talking. We'll see what the police can do with him in a few minutes."

The sound of sirens wailing in the distance had

Abram turning to glare at the window at the far end of the hall.

The flash of lights, blue and red, flared in the distance as the sirens moved closer.

Fuck.

Abram glared at the window, aware of Paige behind him, her hand moving to grip his bicep as she whispered his name.

"I could have made him talk," he stated quickly. "Azir sent him. I could force it out of him."

"Yeah, well, that shit seems to be against the law here in Virginia," Daniel grunted. "Give me a chance to help them load up our prisoner and then we'll talk."

About what?

Abram didn't voice the thought. As far as he was concerned, there was nothing left to talk about if he was simply going to pack the man his agents had caught off to the local police station. "We can talk come morning," Abram growled as he turned, catching Paige's elbow and turning her back to the bedroom. "I have other things to do tonight."

He was pissed, though he knew it was no one's fault that his need to kick Jafar's ass and shoot his own father was tearing through him.

The rage was building, and it was a rage he knew was only beginning to fester inside him.

"Abram, we'll stop it," Daniel assured him as Abram turned away from him.

"Will we, Daniel?" He grunted. "My brother is in the hospital near death, my lover must live in fear of being killed because she is my weakness, and my cousin, the only one willing to stand at my back has forever gained Azir's hatred. Just as I did so long ago. Perhaps it's time to realize there is nothing we can do in this fight. Had I not insisted on being here, where I was safe to feed my hungers, then neither Tariq nor Paige would be facing the danger that now stalks them."

He didn't give Daniel a chance to answer.

Turning away he headed back to the bedroom, his fingers curved around Paige's upper arm before drawing her into the bedroom.

"Abram, I will see you later in the day," Tariq stated as Abram paused just inside the bedroom.

He turned and stared back at his cousin, then at the young woman watching everything silently, her dark eyes glittering with tears and with pain.

"Leave Chalah alone for the night, Tariq," he told him quietly. "Jafar would have known where we were staying with no help from his sister."

Tariq inclined his head in agreement, but Abram saw something in his gaze, in his expression, that warned him that in this, Tariq would have to cut his own throat before realizing the truth.

Abram closed the door, locked it securely, then turned back to Paige.

Pale, weary, yet with a strength he had always known she possessed. The strength to stare adversity in the face without losing her spirit or her courage.

God, she was the epitome of feminine strength and passion. A woman unlike any he had known before her.

He wanted to protect her. He wanted to place her in his bed and never allow her to leave it. At the same time, he wanted to stand before the world with her and proclaim her as his own. Each time that temptation rose inside him, though, memories of Lessa were there to haunt him.

"I'm sorry." And he was, clear to the bottom of his soul he fully regretted the fact that Paige had been drawn into this hell.

Weary, worried, and frightened, she gave a hard, brief shake of her head.

"There's no reason for you to be sorry, Abram." She sighed. "This has been coming since the day Mother escaped Azir, and we both know it." Had they? Or, had he orchestrated it with his desire for her? With a look, or a word spoken at the wrong time to Azir, or possibly an edge of hunger not as clearly hidden as he had hoped whenever he saw her in public.

He shook his head.

"You know it has," she whispered bitterly. "He couldn't break Mother, and you refused to attempt to break me while we were in Saudi. You knew when we escaped, just as you knew years before he took me that it was coming. Azir wouldn't have had it any other way."

And perhaps she was right.

Moving to her, he could do nothing but wrap his arms around her and hold her tight as he closed his eyes and whispered a prayer that God would keep her safe. That he would protect her, and that somehow, some way, there would be a chance for the happiness he had always dreamed of.

A chance that included holding Paige in his arms forever.

Pressing his fingers beneath her chin he lifted her head, watching as her lashes fluttered and those incredible green eyes stared back at him. Emerald eyes. Cat's eyes. And she was just as fierce, independent, and courageous as any cat he had ever seen.

There was so much he wanted to say. So much inside him. How would he find the courage to tell her how much of him belonged to her?

Feeling her hands, so light, so delicate as they moved to the nape of his neck, he had to grit his teeth against the arousal that suddenly flared to life once again.

He would never get enough of her. It simply wasn't possible.

"I love you, Abram." She said the words he could feel beating in his heart.

"You amaze me, hellcat," he said, feeling an amazement growing inside him. "How can you know how you have always softened the hell I've been forced to navigate as I fought to come to this place in my life? I could never express to you how you have eased the wounds I thought my soul could never heal from."

"And why do I amaze you?" That mysterious little smile played at her lips. "You've always known I love you, Abram, don't pretend you haven't."

Had he? Had it been that knowledge that had eased the nights for him, at first because he had seen the innocence and childish acceptance she gave him just after Lessa's death, and later, after the death of his second wife, there had been so much more.

"Do you know how I've loved you?" The words felt torn from his soul. "Do you know, Paige, how I have sought sight of you each time I've visited Khalid? How I have lived for the visits here?" His hand cupped her cheek. "How I have lived for you?"

He had lived for her for years, and he knew it. There wasn't a part of his soul that wasn't aware of the fact that for so long, she had followed him through each second of his day, each second of the long, dark nights that seemed filled with blood and death.

And now, there was hope. The hope that when the sun rose there could be her laughter, her gentle touch, her loving light that shined for him alone.

"We're going to get through this, Abram," she promised, and for the first time in his life he felt the knowledge that he had no other choice but to survive.

He only had one job to complete before that security would be assured.

The death of Azir Mustafa.

16

The weariness that had dragged at them found Paige sleeping in her lover's arms, exhaustion dragging her deep into that well of slumber that obliterated the senses and dimmed even instinct.

That instinct was too closely honed to ever sleep within Abram though. At least, not at this moment, not this day. And God only knew if he would have another day to ease himself into such peaceful sleep.

His eyes came slowly open.

He didn't blink. He didn't pretend to sleep. He didn't hide the knowledge that he was acutely aware of the company they had acquired.

Dammit, he knew he should have questioned the single terrorist they had captured last night. He should have beaten the truth out of the murderous bastard.

He had to forcibly restrain the urge to tighten his hold on Paige. To take that one last moment to attempt to pull her beneath his flesh, to protect her forever.

There was no chance, no possibility of doing such a
thing though. She was vulnerable, and he had slept too
deeply, his instincts not quite honed enough to have felt
them slipping into the room. He hadn't awakened until
he had felt his cousin glaring down at him with irrita-
ble amusement.

Jafar waved the gun at him, an indication that he
should arise from the bed.

Abram allowed himself to caress the thick, heavy
strands of hair that flowed over his chest as her head lay
on his shoulder. Forcing himself to ease from her, his
gaze tracking the three men that stood next to the bed,
he ensured that the sheet covered her as he pushed it
from his own nudity.

Azir's gaze narrowed on his son's nakedness as a grimace of distaste twisted his features. The other man
that stood with them was stony-faced, his brown eyes
like muddy chips of ice, his scarred, cruel features never
shifting in expression.

The lieutenant Abram had glimpsed over the months
at the Mustafa fortress had never spoken much, never
socialized. He'd always managed to keep himself distant, as many of the terrorists had once done.

Until more of their compatriots had arrived after Ayid
and Aman's deaths. Many of them now moved in groups,
socialized with each other, and had begun slowly drawing the people of the Mustafa province into their grip.

Hell, Abram realized, he was one of the men they
hadn't been able to identify at all. He and Tariq hadn't
even been able to collect his fingerprints as they had for
most of the suspected terrorists.

The other man's gaze was locked squarely on his as

Abram pulled his jeans from the floor and eased them up his legs, feeling the small Beretta handgun he had kept shoved in the pocket at night.

His fingers itched to push into the pocket and jerk it free. But the military-issue P90s Jafar and his lieutenant carried were still aimed squarely at Paige rather than at Abram.

Abram let his gaze slide to his father, Azir. The old man was staring at Paige with such a gleam of crazed hunger that suddenly, Abram understood exactly how Azir could have realized his son's attraction to her.

Azir had developed a fixation on Paige that Abram had missed.

How the hell had he managed to miss it?

As he eased from the bed a small, lonely sigh slipped from her. She shifted beneath the thin sheet as though searching for his warmth.

Trying to keep the movement slow, unthreatening, he pulled the comforter bunched at her knees up to her shoulder.

Azir moved faster than Abram could have expected.

Before he could counter the move, Azir, for all his girth and normal slowness, managed to strike with cobra swiftness and jerk the comforter from his grip.

Abram stared back at him through the dim light of the room, hatred and murderous rage rising inside him.

"Before I die . . ." He kept his voice barely audible, but even he heard the resounding promise in it. "I will kill you with my bare hands. Hear me, old man, because I swear to you before God, you will pay for what you have done in this life long before you meet Allah."

Azir's eyes narrowed, but Abram saw the flicker of fear in the depths for the briefest second.

"Let's move," Jafar ordered him. "We're leaving the house, and you will be going with us. Ensure, Abram, that no one stops us. We have proved to you that we can get past Khalid's defenses, and that we can access your woman. Don't make the mistake of believing you can escape again without consequences."

"That is why you shot Khalid rather than me." He smiled mirthlessly. "How you have changed, Jafar."

Jafar's eyes narrowed. "No Abram, I have changed not at all, I promise you this." Mocking, condescending. Was his cousin actually attempting to convince him that he had never dreamed of the freedoms they had both enjoyed while attending college in the States, or that both of them hadn't, at one time, enjoyed their membership in the Sinclair Club?

"May I dress?" he asked sarcastically.

"By all means." Jafar shrugged. "Dress well, cousin. Your return to the fortress will be noticed, and we would prefer it appears voluntary."

Abram dressed without hurrying, though he didn't move with deliberate slowness either. But he needed the time, he needed a moment to think.

There was a message in Jafar's words, he could feel it. He'd once known this cousin as well as he had known Tariq. At least, he had thought he had.

They had attended American college together, they had shared lovers, gotten drunk as young men, and grew into their maturity as friends.

They had both joined the Sinclair Club at the same

time, joining Tariq in the conspiracy to lie and deceive to cover the funds used for their membership fees.

Was Jafar still a member?

"Stop dawdling." The order came from the lieutenant rather than Jafar.

Abram almost froze for a second, his gaze sliding to the other man. Abram buttoned his shirt mechanically, knowledge rippling through his mind. He began to piece together the answers that had eluded him over the years as he attempted to identify the commander of the terrorists moving into the Mustafa province.

When Jafar had disappeared several years before, supposedly moving into the mountains to aid one of his father's elderly friends, Abram hadn't suspected anything. He had never considered, not even for a moment, that his cousin had been in Iraq working to attack the king to whom he'd once vowed his loyalty.

Abram had believed Jafar was the commander they had been searching for, but that answer hadn't felt right. Ayid and Aman had hated Jafar almost as much as they had hated Khalid and Abram.

This was why it hadn't felt right. Because Jafar wasn't the commander he had searched for. It was this man. The one that stared at him with steady, dead eyes. No emotion. No sense of anything but the evil that filled him.

He turned back to Jafar, the warning in the other man's eyes suddenly shooting through him.

The warning was like a shiver of death racing over him.

He knew his cousin.

He did know him.

And he knew how he worked.

How the fuck had he managed to forget over the years?

He'd messed up, Abram admitted. He'd messed up so damned badly when he had immediately assumed Jafar was exactly what he had claimed to be when he returned, after Ayid's and Aman's deaths.

He should have known better.

"Let's go." Jafar jerked his head toward the door as Abram finished lacing his boots.

"We take the girl." Azir didn't move. "She goes with us."

"No."

Everyone stared back at Abram as the word came from him, the sound of it sharp, filled with determined fury and murderous intent.

"She goes." Azir's smile was cold, calculating. "I will have her as well."

"The hell you will," Abram growled.

"We go now." The other man moved between Azir and the bed, the command in his tone unmistakable now. "The girl is a liability now. We will come back for her if we must." The last sentence was uttered, intended to be audible only to Azir, but Abram had always had damned sharp ears. The instinct honed over the years as he moved secretively through the fortress castle.

"Did they promise you Paige for your cooperation?" Abram asked him then. "Is that why you accepted the deaths of your sons so easily, Azir? Because you believed you would have Marilyn's daughter?"

"She was created for me." Azir breathed out almost reverently. "Born to come to me." He turned back to

Abram. "And you thought you could steal her from me, as they stole her mother from me."

He was even more crazed than Abram had believed.

"We have to go," Jafar hissed. "Dawn is too close and there's no way we'll get past the security agents if we don't move."

"Azir." The lieutenant's voice was filled with dangerous warning. "Now."

"Not without her," Azir refused, his tone grating.

"You'll have to kill us both then. Tonight," Abram warned them all. "If you try to take her, then I won't go two steps from this house with you. I'd rather see her dead than see her suffer beneath your hands."

It would be a horrible choice to make. A choice Abram knew he couldn't make. It wasn't possible.

"We don't have time for this." Jafar's voice was imperative now, as though he were losing patience as well as courage.

Another piece of the puzzle came together. Jafar never lost patience.

It was all a game.

His gaze sliced to his cousin. Jafar was how aiming his rifle more toward Azir and the lieutenant than at Paige. The lieutenant's back was to the bed, and Azir had no weapon at all.

"You lie!" Azir turned to Abram furiously. "You would bleed for her. You would die for her. You would never have the strength to steal her life from her."

"I would kill her before I allowed you to take her," Abram promised him. "Because her death at your hands would be far worse."

Azir's expression twisted furiously. "She would resign herself to her fate."

"As her mother did?" Abram sneered back, setting his hatred and rage free as he fought to keep his voice lowered. "As my mother did? Did you think I would not remember how you killed my mother before my eyes, you old bastard?" he snarled. "That I wouldn't always carry the image of your hands around her neck, squeezing the life from her body?"

Azir blinked back at him as he obviously fought to remember the event.

"We go now," the lieutenant, no, the commander said. "Now, Azir. We can't take the girl with us."

Every man on the property had been hired to give his life to keep Paige from being taken. They would never allow anyone, especially Azir, to escape with her.

"Yes, Azir. Go," Abram hissed back. "Because I will die before she leaves this property. What good will she do you if the king takes the province because I'm too damned dead to give my vow? You won't have a shack to keep her in, let alone a well-secured fortress."

Azir's black eyes glowed in rage. Demented rage.

Abram tensed. If he had once known Jafar, then he knew Azir even better, as well as his insanity. He wasn't going anywhere without Paige. Which meant he wasn't going anywhere but to hell. And Abram swore to himself that he would send Azir to hell.

When Azir moved to grip the sheet and jerk it from her body, Abram moved.

He didn't jump for Azir. He prayed like hell that his cousin would take control of Azir. Abram jumped for the commander even as he realized Paige was awake and moving.

Her screams shattered the night as she began to call for the guards, jumping from the bed, the sheet whipping around her body as she moved with the lithe, quick grace she had always displayed.

And Jafar had control of Azir.

The rifle to his head, his expression cold as Abram took the commander to the floor as he grabbed the gun and flung it across the room.

A fist rammed into his jaw as he moved to jump back to deliver his own punch.

The man had a fist like fucking marble.

Hell, he was an enraged bull.

Lowering his head, the other man rammed into Abram's midsection, throwing him into the wall. Abram wrapped his arms around the terrorist's shoulders, lifted his fists, and buried them in the man's lungs.

It didn't seem to faze him.

A fist cracked into Abram's ribs, drawing a grunt of pain. Abram managed to get an arm lowered between their bodies, pulled back, and delivered a hard blow to the diaphragm.

That at least drew a reaction and a lessening of the pressure that kept Abram locked to the wall and his gun hand from reaching for the weapon whose grip was secured just outside the pocket.

The dimness of the room had kept it hidden, but now, he was free.

Abram wrapped his hand around the weapon, jerking it free. In a heartbeat, he had it leveled against the terrorist's head.

"Lieutenant," he sneered. "Do you want to meet your virgins today?"

Muddy brown eyes narrowed on him.

"Commander?" Abram questioned mockingly. "Or are terrorists using rank this month?"

"We are soldiers of Allah," the commander rasped. "What would a demon such as you know of it?"

"That you're insane," Abram accused him icily. "And this game is over. Have fun when the FBI interrogation team gets hold of you. I'm certain they'll enjoy your and Azir's company for quite a long time before you ever see the inside of a courtroom. If you ever see one."

They would simply disappear, Abram would see to it.

"Paige, open the door," Abram ordered as he heard the sound of shouting, muffled by the door, coming up the stairs.

Paige moved quickly, once again dressed in nothing but a sheet.

Damn, she looked good in it too.

He kept his gaze on the terrorist, though, as the other man tensed.

"No!" Azir screamed in rage as Paige raced past him, too far away for him to reach. "Marilyn."

And all hell broke loose.

Azir jumped for her, and the sound of the weapon Jafar held exploded through the night.

The door crashed open. Security agents rushed into the room and the gun Jafar held was knocked from his grip. His shocked gaze moved to Azir.

Jafar looked as though he himself had been shot.

Agony filled his gaze as Azir stared down at the

gaping wound in his chest. He went to his knees then toppled to the floor.

At the same time, the commander knocked the weapon from Abram's grip, as Abram reacted to defend himself.

He should have saved the effort. As his weapon flew across the room, three agents were on the commander, struggling with him until they had him pinned to the floor.

Abram jumped for Paige, pulling her quickly into his arms and moving her to the other side of the room as the agents restrained and handcuffed the commander.

Jerking him from the floor, his face bloodied now, the once-restrained hatred, contempt, and rage spewing from him, he glared back at Abram.

"It is not over," he snarled. "It will never be over. You will die, and your whore will die."

Abram smiled coldly but before he could speak, Jafar stepped forward slowly. "Before your men ever learn what happened to you, I will have control of them. You died in the failed attempt, along with Azir, to carry out your unsanctioned plan to punish Abram for his desertion of Islam, and to steal the woman he had chosen as his wife."

The commander stared back at him in amazed shock. "You betrayed me, cousin."

Jafar smiled, icy satisfaction filling his gaze. "As you betrayed Islam yourself, cousin." His gaze flicked to Abram. "You do not recognize him, do you Abram?"

Abram gave a quick shake of his head.

"Meet once again, our cousin, Mohammid Mustafa, son of Hamid Mustafa, and his killer. He conspired with your father twenty-five years before to kill my father as well as his own, and to steal from the Mustafa province the wealth the king bestowed on it for the insanity they follow."

Instcad, the king had learned of the murders, rather than the accidents they had been made to appear. That was the reason the province had lost its wealth.

"You went to the king," Abram murmured.

Jafar inclined his head slowly. "And now, I will return as their leader, their commander." His smile was so viciously mocking Abram felt Paige flinch. "Enjoy your happiness, Abram." Jafar finally sighed as he turned to Paige, his expression gentling. "Have I repaid my debt, little one?"

"With interest, Jafar," she whispered.

He turned his head, watching as Mohammid was dragged from the room before turning back to them. "I will once again place myself in your debt then," he sighed. "Watch out for my sister. Do not allow her to ever return to Saudi Arabia, no matter the messages I send." Then his face creased painfully. "Convince her." His gaze turned to Abram. "Convince her of my dedication to the plans Ayid and Aman planted. There are those who spy, who are close to her, and I have not yet identified them. Until I do . . ." His lips tightened.

"Until then, she will believe you are as you seem," Abram promised. "And I swear to you, Jafar, she will be protected to the best of my ability."

Jafar nodded sharply. "There were no others with us tonight," he finally stated coolly. "We came alone, but for the three that distracted your guards. Allow the one you captured to go free, if you don't mind." He gave a mirthless grin. "Had you met with him as he requested, you would have known we were here as well."

"I will know better next time." Abram nodded as Jafar moved for the door.

As his cousin left the room, Abram turned to his lover, to the woman he knew he would have died for. Easily. Nothing would have convinced him to allow Azir to so much as breathe her air.

"It's over," she whispered.

"No, it has only begun." He sighed regretfully as his arms tightened around her. "But the danger to you is over. The danger to us is gone." Then he grimaced. "Khalid."

She bit her lip, then grinned. "He'll be pissed."

"He'll kill me."

"He'll let you live, it just might not be pleasant for a while." She laughed softly.

"And you, my little hellcat, will be worth every bruise." His lips lowered to hers.

He had to taste her.

He had to hold her, convince himself she lived and she was unharmed.

Convince himself she was his.

Just as she always had been.

epilogue

Khalid stared at his sister in confusion, certain he must have taken too many pain pills. Though honestly, he couldn't remember taking a single one despite the doctor's and Marty's insistence that he do so.

Something was wrong though, because it wasn't possible that he had heard her correctly.

"Excuse me, sweets, but I don't think I heard you right," he said with an air of amusement.

It was forced joviality. Something in his gut assured him he hadn't misheard her in the least; she had said exactly what he thought she had, and she had meant every word of it.

Fuck.

This couldn't be happening. It just simply couldn't be real.

He was having a nightmare. That was it, he assured himself. It was a nightmare. It could be nothing else.

His sister glanced behind him, her look directed at

his fiancée who stood behind him. And that look was telling.

He wanted to rub at his chest, but damn if he wanted to make her feel guilty. She wouldn't understand it was his worried heart aching, the heart of a brother who had protected, worried, and looked after her. He still remembered her as the tiny, red-faced, squalling infant who had been laid in his arms when he was no more than ten.

That look, exchanged with Marty, was telling, and it assured him this was in no way a nightmare.

"God," he muttered. "It's my birthday, give me a break."

It was his birthday, and it was his brother Abram's birthday. Abram and Paige had ensured he would never forget this day or its significance.

Paige smiled then.

"You expected it." Leaning forward, her arms folded atop her knees, the waves of fiery hair cascaded around her face and gave her a look of youth and innocence.

She could have been fifteen again.

"You're too young." He sighed. "I see you, Ellie Paige, and I don't see a woman." He was aware of the softness of his voice, the somberness of it. He was aware of the all-consuming regret that his little Ellie Paige, a name he hadn't used in far too many years, had grown up.

Paige Eleanora. Marilyn had given Pavlos the option of naming her, and Pavlos had shared that weighty responsibility with his stepson.

He had imparted something that went far deeper though. An acceptance, a silent, overwhelming verification that Khalid, the child who had heard too much, who had seen too much in international courts concerning the hell his unknown father had put his too-small, too-gentle mother through, was indeed a part of the family, and as loved as that tiny, delicate babe.

And Khalid had chosen Eleanora. Because the name sounded as delicate to him as the babe had seemed.

"What do you see then?" She frowned fiercely. "You're confusing me, Khalid. As usual."

He breathed out heavily. "Because I never told you, did I, that to me, you have never grown past that delicate innocence of fifteen."

"Your birthday," she said softly, and he saw the memory in the soft smile that curved her lips. "You were twenty-five. You had just gotten out of the hospital." Her expressive eyes flashed with remembered pain.

It was a pain Abram knew as well.

Khalid refused to look at his brother, too afraid he would see in Abram's eyes exactly what Khalid feared. That Abram could never let the memory of his first love go enough to give Paige his heart.

"You were there when I awoke," he said softly. "You were like an angel staring down at me."

"I told you you couldn't ever leave me again," she said softly. "Because if you were gone, there would be no one to protect me from all the big bad wolves that were trying to touch me where they shouldn't."

"You terrified me," he admitted with a smile. "You were a baby, and grown men were trying to touch you. You made me want to live again, Paige. You made me have to live again, so nothing or no one in this world could ever harm you like that. You forced me to live, Paige, when all I wanted to do was die from the guilt I felt."

He had no choice but to turn his head and look at his brother then. It was a time of their lives that they had shared. Lessa had been the wife they had shared. She had been Abram's wife, and she had died for their dark hungers.

It wasn't that sense of agony he saw on Abram's face though. There was a gentle smile of remembrance, the pain of the knowledge that she had suffered because of them, but, as he stared into his brother's black eyes, Khalid didn't see the love, the heartrending agony he had seen so many years before.

"We were young men playing secret agents," Abram said softly then. "And Lessa was our ally, our cohort, and our coconspirator. She died for us, and I could never forget her sacrifice, or the fact that I would have died for her. But she was a young man's love. I'm not that young man any longer, brother. I'm an adult, and I know the woman I love."

Abram looked at Paige then, and Khalid saw it.

His throat tightened. His chest seemed to loosen marginally until the only ache he felt was that of the hole that had been left in his chest by the bullet that had nearly killed him.

Azir would have never given up. Eventually, he would have had both Abram and Khalid killed. And he would have killed Paige, after he had raped her, punished her for the sins he perceived her mother committed, and for the unforgivable sin of looking so much like the one woman who had escaped him.

"Khalid, be happy for me," Paige whispered with all

the love he knew she held in her heart, despite the fact
that he had been born of the horror their mother had
suffered.

He had never forgiven himself for it.

Pavlos had forgiven him, and had given him the un-
forgettable gift of bestowing a name on the child created by his love for Marilyn Girard Galbraithe. And
Paige had shown her love by demanding he live, and by
demanding he never forget that he had to protect her.

"Don't hurt her." He cleared his throat as emotion
threatened to overwhelm him. "She's my sister, Abram.
You're my brother, but break her heart, so much as
tweak her feelings and cause a tear to fall, and I promise, we will fight."

At the moment, it would be a fight Abram would win,
he thought with a touch of morose mockery. Hell, he was
as weak as a kitten.

But as he looked up at his fiancée, he felt his cock
begin to harden, felt his blood begin to thunder through
his veins and was amazed once again by his attraction
and his love for her.

Hell, his dick had been hard within hours of consciousness, once he had begun refusing the pain medication
they were trying to pump into him.

He lifted his hand to where hers lay at his shoulder,
gripped it gently, and pulled her fingers to his lips.

How could he ever tell her the difference she made
in his life?

He might not be able to tell her, but he could show
her. Again.

He gave her a wicked smile, reminding her, pressing
home the knowledge that it had only been just last night

that he had convinced her to sit on his hungry mouth and allow him to bring her pleasure with his lips and tongue.

And he would have her again soon.

"Oh my God. I'm leaving. Khalid, that is so gross." Paige was laughing though as she rose. She threw a quick, light hug around his shoulders and kissed his cheek.

As she moved back, Abram stepped to him, his broad hand clasping his shoulder affectionately. "Thank you, brother," he said softly, somberly. "For the greatest gift a brother could give another."

"And that is?" Khalid grunted.

"The gentle innocence, and the safety of the woman who stole my soul."

Abram's grip tightened, then he was leaving the bedroom, his hand laying low at Paige's jean-clad hips as the door closed behind them.

"She's still a baby," he whispered on a sigh.

Marty lowered her head, her lips pressing to his lips. "She's a woman, Khalid."

"She's my sister. A baby," he growled.

"She's a woman, and one day, she may have a baby of her own."

He grimaced. "I'm not going there."

"If they hurry, then their child would be just the right age to play with ours."

And he froze.

Play with theirs?

He swallowed tightly. "You want a baby?"

He felt hot. Cold. His stomach tightened. A surge of adrenaline raced through his system.

"Too late to want, Khalid," she whispered. "We're having a baby."

He remembered. That virus she'd had, the antibiotics, his impatience one night, and her laughing declaration that he could become a daddy.

A daddy.

He broke out in a sweat of terror.

Or was it pure, incredible happiness?

Gripping her hand he drew her around and to him, watching as she looped her arms around his neck, her smile softer than before, her gaze so loving it warmed the very corners of his soul.

He loved.

And he was loved.

Marty had given him the greatest gift of his life when she had loved him. Could he truly begrudge Abram or Paige that same gift they would give to each other?

As he drew Marty to his heart, he knew it simply wasn't possible.

Paige gasped as her jeans cleared her legs, and a second later the buttons of her shirt were torn from their moorings.

Abram seemed to be everywhere at once, his hands and fingers, his lips and tongue working a magic against her flesh that she had no hope of resisting.

He'd torn his own clothes off the minute they'd entered the penthouse apartment it seemed he owned in the heart of the city. Unfurnished but for the bed he'd had delivered that morning.

They had already made use of it once that morning, and now, he was pulling her to it again, his cock thick and hard, imperative, as she felt her own arousal burning out of control, raging just beneath her flesh, demanding his touch.

Her arms wrapped around his shoulders, her nails digging in as his tongue slipped past her lips, tangled with hers, and tasted her, as she tasted him.

His hands were never still. Touching her breasts, brushing against her nipples, smoothing to her back then to her buttocks where he gripped the curves lightly, parted them, and reminded her of the exquisite pleasure of having Tariq behind her, invading her, as Abram fucked her pussy with desperate, ecstatic lunges.

Her vagina clenched tighter, a moan whispering from her lips at the remembered rapture of taking her lover, as well as his cousin.

The naughty, dark hunger was becoming as addictive for her as it was for him. It was becoming a hunger that reared its head and left her soaking her panties with her juices as her pussy heated in need.

As it actually burned with desire every damned time he touched her. She couldn't hold back. Slick, heated, her cunt rippled with the yearning for the erotic touch that only Abram could give her.

"Sweet Paige, what a fool I was," he whispered as his lips moved down her neck, kissing, touching, loving her as she whimpered with the lust she couldn't, wouldn't even attempt to deny.

"Why?" Her neck arched as flares of sensation began to travel from each point that his lips touched, his tongue licked, his strong teeth raked.

With the tips of his fingers he caressed the curve of

her breast, refusing to touch her straining nipple as he continued that slow, oh so slow, downward course.

"For ever denying what you give me with your love." His head lifted, his dark eyes an endless sea of emotion as Paige felt her heart swelling, accepting, and giving in return.

"It wasn't time," she whispered, her hand touching his chest, his heart.

She could feel it racing beneath her palm, feel the adrenaline and the hunger that raged in the fiery stiff width of his cock against her thigh.

"I could have made it time." The regret in his gaze, in the stroke of his fingers against her jaw, in the incredible pleasure of each touch he gave her.

"But would it have been as sweet?" She smiled back at him, knowing in her heart that it was time, and that because they had waited, they would endure. "Would I have been mature enough to understand your love, Abram?" she whispered. "Or your hungers? I had a teenager's confidence, and how thin it was."

His head lowered, his forehead pressing against hers.

"I had a young man's sense of forever," he said regretfully.

"A young man's sense of justice and belief in his ideals," she amended.

His lips touched hers again, brushed, then settled and became harder, dominant, commanding.

She loved him like this. Hungry and imperative, determined to have her as she began to arch against him, feeling the threads of pleasure tightening inside her, around her, rocking through her as he moved between her thighs, pressed his cock against the slick heated moisture spilling from her pussy before pressing inside.

Paige arched and cried out as his head jerked back, pleasure creasing his expression as she felt the slow, shallow thrusts that began to rock inside her, to forge through the tightening muscles, stretching her, sending the pleasure racing through her, the ecstasy building through her.

There had never been anything as incredible as Abram's touch. It was like lightning tearing across her flesh. It was like existing in a place of pure heat, a place where nothing mattered, nothing existed, and there was no pleasure but Abram.

With a last hard thrust of his hips he buried himself inside her to the hilt, a hard groan tearing from his lips as she writhed beneath him and cried out his name in desperation.

Lifting her legs, wrapping them around his hips, she could only hold on for the ride. Each stroke opened and raked against tender flesh and naked nerve endings. Each breath was a moan, a cry. Each touch traveled through her, shredding her control over herself, over her own body, and over her heart.

It all belonged to Abram.

Meeting each stroke, her hips lifting, the flares of pleasure began to collide, to ripple into her womb and tighten her body until she lost her breath, lost her senses.

The orgasm exploded with such incredible force that her nails dug into the flesh of his shoulders, her legs spasming around her hips, her lips parting on a breathless moan.

It seemed to go on and on. To ripple and rake through

her as she felt him surge inside her deep and hard one last time, then the heated spurts of his come filling her.

His arms wrapped around her, pressing beneath her body, his palms covering her shoulders as he whispered her name, his voice guttural, hoarse. Filled with love.

"Love," he whispered at her ear. "My sweetest love. My heart."

Without her, he knew he couldn't survive. She held him. Every part of him. Every beat of his heart, every dream of his soul. Holding her to him, Abram did as he had never done. He did the very thing he had felt such guilt about because he hadn't done it with his first wife, and she had known it.

He gave to Paige that last part of himself.

The part of a male that became more than a lover, more than a heart mate.

He gave her that primitive, possessive core that most men hold back.

He gave her his being and he felt the moment she gave hers to him.

And they became more than just one.

In the midst of a pleasure that could have destroyed them, that could have ripped their lives from them, they had found something they now knew would always save them. Each other.

ALSO BY LORA LEIGH

The Men of Summer series...
HOT SHOT
DIRTY LITTLE LIES
WICKED LIES

The Callahans series...
MIDNIGHT SINS
DEADLY SINS
SECRET SINS
ULTIMATE SINS

The Elite Ops series...
LIVE WIRE
RENEGADE
BLACK JACK
HEAT SEEKER
MAVERICK
WILD CARD

The Navy SEALs trilogy...
KILLER SECRETS
HIDDEN AGENDAS
DANGEROUS GAMES

The Bound Hearts novels...
SECRET PLEASURE
INTENSE PLEASURE
GUILTY PLEASURE
ONLY PLEASURE
WICKED PLEASURE
FORBIDDEN PLEASURE

And her stories featured in the anthologies...
REAL MEN LAST ALL NIGHT
REAL MEN DO IT BETTER
HONK IF YOU LOVE REAL MEN
LEGALLY HOT
MEN OF DANGER
HOT ALPHAS

AVAILABLE FROM ST. MARTIN'S GRIFFIN AND ST. MARTIN'S PAPERBACKS